AND LOVE CAN TURN

Why did these men from her past feel as if they owned her?

Peter was breathing hard. "I want you, Belinda, you invited me up here, what's the matter with you? Come on, it's me, we're grown-ups . . . what's the big deal, for Christ's sake?" He loosened his hold and I slid along the bench, stumbled and fell, holding onto the tabletop, on my knees, my head throbbing, tears suddenly overflowing. "Belinda, don't you understand, it's . . ." And I couldn't hear the rest of it. He stood over me.

"No!" I managed to shout. I felt an adrenaline surge, tried to get up, and he grabbed my arm, jerked me to my feet. The buttons ripped off the front of my dress, sprinkled to the floor like dice.

"It's my turn," he said. *"My turn!"*

GUILTY PARTIES
The New Novel of Suspense by
DANA CLARINS
author of *Woman in the Window*
which the *Los Angeles Times* called
"A first-rate thriller—tight—with tension and twists
to make your heart pound to the last page . . .
Excellent, worth every bug-eyed moment."

Bantam Books by Dana Clarins

GUILTY PARTIES
WOMAN IN THE WINDOW

GUILTY PARTIES

Dana Clarins

BANTAM BOOKS
TORONTO • NEW YORK • LONDON • SYDNEY • AUCKLAND

GUILTY PARTIES
A Bantam Book / June 1985

ISBN 0-553-24978-9

Published simultaneously in the United States and Canada

Bantam Books are published by Bantam Books, Inc. Its trademark, consisting of the words "Bantam Books" and the por-
trayal of a rooster, is Registered in U.S. Patent and Trademark
Office and in other countries. Marca Registrada. Bantam
Books, Inc. 666 Fifth Avenue, New York, New York 10103.

PRINTED IN THE UNITED STATES OF AMERICA

H   0 9 8 7 6 5 4 3 2 1

for Rachel

Prologue

I dreamed that night of the times we were happiest.

A long time ago, the four of us piled into Jack's beat-up old convertible—the sun overhead and the wind in our faces and the radio on loud. Petula Clark going downtown. The Fab Four . . . God, it was a long time ago.

But it was fresh in my dreams.

We were young again and Jack and I had just come back from our honeymoon. Sally and Harry were taking us into the country, antiquing country, to find us the perfect wedding present. The four of us, young and never happier.

Jack and Belinda. Harry and Sally. Some idiot at Harvard, drunk in the Eliot House courtyard, had called us the Fab Four. Very funny at the time.

Jack had always laughed at my fascination with fortune cookies. He always told the waiter to skip the fortune cookies, and I'd have to interrupt and make a big deal out of it. Jack told me I might as well live my life by the horoscopes in *Cosmo*. That struck Sally and me as terribly funny, since *Cosmo*'s horoscope was one of our main sources of inspiration.

Sally was very good at decisions. It was her nature, and when thwarted in the execution of her master plans she was not a good sport. Which, there was no denying, made

1

her such an asset to the girls' field hockey team at Mount Holyoke. Which also made her the best kind of best friend, because she'd die for you or kill for you once she'd stamped you with her approval.

And when she set out to find the perfect wedding present she wasn't about to be thwarted. Period.

She found it all right. That was what my dream was about. We were looking for it again on that weekend excursion to the Pennsylvania Dutch country.

She found it in the dusty back room of a general store that had once been a livery stable. The wheel-of-fortune had been shrouded under horse blankets for a hundred years, maybe more. Perhaps it had belonged to a traveling medicine show, or a circus, or a Gypsy caravan, along about the time of the Civil War. Maybe livery bills had gone unpaid and maybe a taciturn Dutchman had impounded the wheel as security against the day when the debt would finally be erased. And maybe that day never came and generations had passed and finally no one even knew that the wheel with all its fortunes sat hidden in the junk room.

But there was no escaping Sally when her antennae were picking up signals. She found it because she thought the back room "looked spooky." She peeled back the blankets as if they were the decades of the last century . . . and there it was. Wiping away the dust, she opened the little door in the back of the pyramidal wooden stand and peered into the compartment, where, she firmly believed, a boy or midget had crouched in order to control the spin of the wheel when such trickery was required. She was always full of theories in those days and they always made sense if you thought about them long enough.

When she had wiped away enough of the caked dust,

she had taken a look at the fortune that had been waiting through all the years of darkness. A cackling witch in a pointed black hat, holding a magic wand, giving a haggle-toothed grin, and the faded words:

Yours will be a long and happy life.

It was, Sally had declared, an omen.

For all of us.

That was what I dreamed about that long sweltering night before everything began to go wrong.

I

Opening Nights

Chapter One

When I look back on last summer it's odd that the first thing I remember isn't the people who died so horribly or the illusions I'd treasured being irrevocably blown away, not the opening of Harry's *Scoundrels All!*, not even my own one-woman show at Claude Leverett's gallery—no, what I remember is the heat. The ungodly, hellish, unbroken procession of dazzling and exhausting weeks at over ninety degrees when all of us in Manhattan got our wagons in a circle and tried to wait it out. The windows dripped with condensation and air conditioners burned out and Con Ed was on a constant alert, buying extra electricity from any grid that would sell. Your clothing stuck to your damp flesh and you felt dizzy if you tried to exercise. They fried an egg on the dugout roof at Yankee Stadium, and when Baltimore beat the locals a headline in the *Post* read: "O's Scald Yanks 4–3 in 13 at 100°!"

The day Sally called with the bad news was a beaut. Air conditioning gives me colds so I was standing at the open window looking down at the sluggish devils wandering along Prince Street like the lost battalion in a French Foreign Legion movie. I was praying for a breeze, sipping iced tea, and absentmindedly spinning the wheel-of-fortune again and again, hearing the click-click-click. It had been a rough several months—getting my work ready for the show I'd wanted all my life, simultaneously watching our marriage of sixteen years pull apart like an old sofa giving way under one too many fat men. Jack had moved out a month or so before, but in spirit the Jack I'd loved and married and made my life with had been running on a kind of personal empty for a long time. Finally he'd gotten so sick of himself, had thrashed himself so thoroughly, that like Rumpelstilskin he'd disappeared. In this case not through the floor but to a tiny flat high on the Upper East Side, where he, like me, must have cried himself to sleep wondering where in the name of God it had all gone so far wrong.

So, sure, it had been a rough period. Just when my work should have been making me happier than ever, the rest of my life got run over by a truck. It happens every day. To somebody else. Which keeps the shrinks and the singles bars and the dependency clinics and the expensive boutiques thriving, I suppose. The balance of nature, something dies and something else lives.

Which is how my mind was running as I felt a big drop of sweat drip off my nose into my glass. You can only stare at people collapsing from the heat for so long, and I was afraid to look at the results obtained from spinning the wheel. The last time I'd given it a try it had stopped at a laughing devil with a three-pronged spade pushing a sailor under the lapping waves. Which I assumed was the wheel's way of suggesting that ocean travel might be best avoided for the nonce. In any case, I'd had enough of the wheel's opinion for a while.

Turning back to the loft where we'd lived for all of our married life, it struck me as somehow unfamiliar now that I lived there alone. A vast space of brick and wood, painstakingly restored during spasms of home-improvement mania. Plants everywhere, hanging from beams and upright in lots of pots, explosions of airy Boston ferns and lackadaisical date palms and ficus trees and philodendrons and every other growing thing that had enjoyed a vogue during those years. A skylight overhead, a walk-in fireplace in one wall, lots of old wicker furniture dating from the early days of our marriage when we had combed the countryside in a borrowed truck in search of bargains to fill the place we'd bought so cheap with the proceeds of Jack's first novel. Bookcases filled to overflowing, threadbare rugs thrown haphazardly about, several easels of various sizes, trestle tables cluttered with the bits and pieces of my work. And in the corner, that wheel-of-fortune with its faded painted fates, the symbols and figures and characters so quaint and innocent in their antiquity, and, for the most part, optimism.

But even with so many accumulated artifacts of our life together it seemed that Jack had been somehow erased, written out of the loft's history.

It was the proliferation of huge canvases that had erased Jack Stuart.

Some days the guilt consumed me. I missed him at times but I should have missed him more and didn't, simply couldn't. I felt as if I'd let the work run rampant, as if I'd let it drive him out. I knew that it hadn't been that way, but some days just knowing didn't help. It was feeling that mattered and I couldn't ignore the feeling of guilt. My God, what kind of monster would connive to gain the space at the expense of her husband's presence? It was the sort of illogical, nonsensical fear that seems absurd once you get your head on straight. I asked myself: What could have been more natural than to unstack the canvases and get them in view once Jack was gone and I had the loft to myself?

It was the kind of guilt I couldn't confide even to Sally. We'd been telling each other just about everything for twenty years, but this dark little arabesque of shame I kept to myself. I knew I would always feel love and caring for Jack, no matter what, but I was glad he was gone. Cutting through my own sense of failure and the sixteen years of effort was that glittering blade of relief. And it made me feel like hell.

Sally had her rock of a marriage. Sally and Harry. Harry and Sally. How could I tell her what I felt? How could I expect her to understand?

At times the four of us had seemed like a single entity, everyone in sync, four facets of the same multiperson. And it had been the best, the most secure feeling I could ever have imagined.

And now I had not only let Jack go. I hadn't given my all to keep him, to hold us together. Jack said all I'd have had to do was ask. He wanted me to ask. And I said, no, it's best this way, let's do some hard thinking by ourselves, go ahead . . .

I was the one who had smashed the curiously crystalline figure with the four faces. I knew it. I was the guilty one and I was having trouble with it.

But it remained unspoken. There was no way to talk it over with Sally. So I was alone with it and we danced around the edges refusing to face up to it, which was, of course, the only way I could get clear of it.

I stood there in the loft, sweating, while the ice melted in the tea, and I let my eyes rove from one canvas to another, trying to inspect them with a hard critical eye. Yet I couldn't resist them. They cast a spell over me and I couldn't begin to judge them. Again, they were a part of my most private self—I couldn't imagine what condition I'd be in when they went on view—and they fascinated me. I didn't know what the fascination said about me, but I wasn't very comfortable with it. Still, it was there, inescapable.

They were, each and every one, self-portraits. Parts of me, pieces of me. Huge canvases, filling the loft in all its dimensions.

One Belinda Stuart after another.

I might have been getting a little spaced-out just then. I had that momentary vertigo you sometimes feel in the heat.

The ringing telephone rescued me.

Chapter Two

Because I'm a painter, Sally has always thought that asking me to visit a gallery is the surest way of guaranteeing my company. The fact is, I'm not particularly interested in killing time that way. I'm afraid of the sponge effect, I guess, the possibility that I might see something that would stick in my mind and come out again in my own work without my quite realizing it. And, too, it can be so humbling to see really fine work, way beyond my estimate of my own, in some other, unknown painter.

But when Sally asked me to a gallery that day I also knew, since she didn't really give a damn about painting, that there was bound to be something troubling her. I went to the gallery in the East Eighties wondering what the news was going to be, or more exactly, how bad the news was going to be. We were both closing in on forty, and the subject of unidentifiable lumps here and there was becoming more of a fear than it had once been. I suppose that was the news I dreaded most—that Sally was going to tell me she was sick, that there'd been a biopsy, what was coming to be known as the *Terms of Endearment* Effect. Or it might be Harry's X rays or God only knew what. I'd managed to make myself fairly nervous by the time I got out of the cab.

But she was her usual self, waiting for me outside. She had long black hair that hung straight, a very pale complexion with high cheekbones and deeply set dark eyes that as she aged gave her face a slightly skull-like quality when she was tired. She looked tired, or worried, but she smiled and said something that made me laugh and I thought maybe I was wrong, after all. She brushed my cheek with hers and I smelled her Lancôme and we went inside to look at pictures.

As it turned out, it was a brilliant show—Stanley Spencer's earnest, bulbous, mystically benighted figures slogging on through their own wild, tortured imaginations. I lost myself among the paintings, soaking them up the best way, wondering at Spencer's unique vision. I loved his people, obsessed with religion and heaven and sex, alive in an extraordinary way even if they moved in a kind of supernatural fog the rest of us didn't seem to notice.

I lost track of Sally and then I saw her at last and I knew I'd been right the first time.

She'd fetched up against a bay window overlooking the street and somebody's embassy across the way where the flags were hanging limp, at half-mast for some reason. The sun was hot and bright and a fly was banging at the glass trying to get out before he fried in his own juice. The tears running down Sal's cheeks refracted the light like a spill of so many diamonds.

"We've got to get out of here," she said, sniffling and trying to smile. "Harry's in love with another woman."

As we negotiated the narrow curving stairway down to the entry foyer, she said: "Some woman . . . I don't know. Harry." She repeated his name as if it were foreign to her, a word from another language, which, I suppose, was just about how she must have been feeling.

I led the way to a dark, cool, empty, and trendy little café where the lunch crowd was pretty well gone and we could sit inside while looking out at a riot of flowers in the garden. Sally nodded to me when the waiter showed up, sniffled, and I ordered her her usual gin gimlet. Figuring I might need my wits about me, I stuck with iced tea.

She gave me one of her very Sally looks. She somehow managed to blend her own innate arrogance with a helpless, pleading quality: I'd never known the combination in anyone else. And when you coupled it with the stark black-and-white beauty of her features, you had a kind of aristocratic Madonna of the Sorrows that Harry, for one, had found irresistible. Me, too. I wanted to love and protect her, she seemed that vulnerable, but the fact that you knew she might turn on you and give you a flip of haughty airiness gave any relationship with her a tension that bonded you to her like nothing else could have. Her lower lip quivered and at just that moment I'd have done anything to make the hurt go away.

"You must have it wrong," I said. "You've jumped to a silly conclusion based on insufficient evidence—"

"I'm not being silly." The coal-black eyes flared as if a match had been struck. "Have the grace to treat me like an adult."

"Of course, I'm sorry, but we both know Harry. He just doesn't do things like this . . . this falling in love. He loves you. He's always loved you—"

13

"Not exactly, Belinda. Think back—"

"That was in college," I said, feeling my mouth get dry. "He knew me before he met you and when he met you that was it. You know that."

She frowned at me, the narrow lips in a tight little vise. "Come on." The attempt at lightness in her tone fell flat and broke like china. "You met Jack and dropped Harry and when he stopped whimpering and opened his eyes, there I stood with a willing smile and—as I recall—pigtails. It was my regressive pigtail period, wasn't it?" She suddenly grinned, the real Sally again.

I nodded. "It was indeed, and he's never looked at another woman since. And he isn't now, I'd bet on it."

"He's not just looking. He's in love."

"Tell me," I said. "Why do you think so?"

She told me.

And it didn't add up to all that much. A wife's suspicions, a husband of long standing who wasn't paying quite the attention he normally did, who wasn't exactly the same as ever. Flickers of behavior that only a wife would notice. Something going on behind his eyes, a distance in his tone of voice. Harry was so even-tempered, so much a diplomat, so consistent, and now those very qualities which had made him such a good and trustworthy husband were revealing—by their slight rearrangement—his infidelity. Or perhaps it was a contemplated infidelity.

"The thought is not necessarily father to the deed," I said.

She looked up from her gimlet. "Is that actually an aphorism or did you just make it up?"

"I don't know. The point is, it's true. If the thought of illicit sex were the same as the act—well, you figure it out. Remember Jimmy Carter's heart full of lust? Give Harry a break, Sal. He's got a show opening in a week. Wouldn't that alone be enough to throw his behavior off? If tension and nerves can throw me off my menstrual cycle, why can't the same thing throw Harry off his normal game? I mean, you don't even have lipstick on a collar—"

"Well, I thought you'd be a bit more sympathetic, a bit more understanding about what a wife can just *know*— without having to have a courtroom full of evidence . . ."

I was beginning to wish I'd had a drink. Being sober and rational was not necessarily what this discussion called for.

"Look, a little evidence would help a lot. A sighting at Area with a twenty-year-old secretary or a chorus girl— then you might have a problem—"

"That's not my idea of a problem!" She gave me the haughty flip and told the waiter to bring another gimlet. "If he wants to sleep with some little tart on the side, I'm grown-up enough to handle it. I'm not making my point, Belinda. I said he's fallen in love. Not that he's screwing some nonentity. Screwing nonentities calls for a telltale bit of physical evidence. Falling in love messes up a man's head in telling ways, and that's what's happening to Harry. That's why I'm worried—no, I'm not worried. I'm . . . something else. It's not worry. It runs a lot deeper than that." She took a deep sip from her fresh gimlet and looked out at the flowers. She looked wistful now. It was amazing the range of emotions she could put on her face without any noticeable rearrangement of her features. I think it was in her eyes. So dark, so deep, with a faintly mad quality when she wanted it there. She had a tendency to speak without really opening her mouth, through her teeth. Like Gloria Steinem. Like Gloria Steinem she was very bright, but unlike her she had chosen never to make a life for herself beyond being Harry Granger's rich wife. She liked the life. She'd never been one to complain. Maybe that was why I didn't entirely discount her fears about Harry. She didn't cry wolf. It just wasn't like her. So maybe Harry was up to something, after all, though I tried to convince her it wasn't true.

She watched me from behind those deep dark eyes and then impulsively hugged me, as if to say: I can see through you, my dear, but thanks for trying. . . .

Chapter Three

I worked late that night but by five o'clock the next morning I couldn't sleep anymore. The temperature hadn't gotten much below eighty during the night but now there was a breeze and I couldn't bear sleeping through it. I took a shower and stood naked in the middle of the loft with only the beginnings of the morning light from the street. I felt almost human. I wasn't sweating. The oscillating fan on the divider which partitioned off the kitchen area blew at me. I put a Stan Getz tape in the deck and stretched out on an upholstered wicker chaise and watched while the onset of daylight revealed the canvases all around me.

And I saw this Belinda Stuart creature I'd been painting for the past two years.

She was a tall woman with a fair complexion and high, wide cheekbones, a flat forehead: a serious, almost somber face which at thirty-nine retained still a few clues to the pretty little girl she must once have been. Dark blond hair which had once been flaxen, now held by the ancient headband dating from the sixties, hair now tucked behind her ears, hanging straight almost to her shoulders. A straight, conventionally Waspish nose, a long upper lip and a wide mouth, long legs and narrow hips not much wider than they'd been in the old days at Mount Holyoke.

Her appearance was somewhat deceiving since she radiated in the remote features a very now air of self-discipline, self-possession, and lucidity that can so easily strike others as a trifle daunting. She knew that people frequently took a look or two at her and concluded that she was impervious and invulnerable.

Somewhere in her I saw that she was at least as prey to the uncertainties and insecurities of life as anyone else. But not even Jack had ever grasped the truth, Jack who had seen her at the bottomed-out lows and had the best reasons to want to understand. Not even Jack.

Perhaps the eyes were what stood in the way.

There was something in the impulsive, challenging pale green eyes that made you wonder what she must have been like as a girl, twenty years ago, just discovering her own femaleness and its powers. Men who paid attention to such subtleties were bound inevitably to speculate about what toll that challenge must have taken on herself as well as on others, what hearts might lie broken in the wake of those eyes.

Brazen eyes, that's what Sally had called them.

So much for thinking about yourself in the third person. Maybe it wasn't altogether healthy to paint pictures of yourself for two years. Inevitably you wound up thinking about yourself too damn much, and that was something I'd never before been interested in doing. Well, it was too late to bellyache about it now. I'd never been one to look awfully closely at things, at life, at relationships. Sally used to tell me I'd missed a lot.

Late into countless college nights Sally had tried to explain her facts of life to me, but I'd never proven a very apt pupil. She had told me that I'd apparently come equipped with a set of psychological blinders to protect me from the rest of the world and its reactions to me. She always told me I was just Belinda wanting to stay that way, but I was bound to learn that was a hopeless goal, an impossibility. And I hadn't known what to say because I hadn't known what exactly she was talking about. Life had seemed basically simple to me then.

I had possessed an ability to focus my attention on my purposes, determined to attain them. Sally understood about my single-mindedness, whether it came to doing well in my studies or reading all of C. P. Snow or making Jack Stuart a good wife. She understood about the psychological blinders and maybe she had been right.

Maybe without my blinders I'd have been able to see what was coming. Maybe. But then again . . .

Maybe not.

The next time I paid any attention to what time it was, my back was stiff from working and I looked at the big clock on the brick wall and saw that it was four o'clock and the day had been used up. Through the skylight I saw that the sun was gone, replaced by purple clouds. I had once put a great deal of effort into painting clouds. Turner's clouds with the burnished sunlight behind them were breathtaking, but it was Constable's way with clouds that I'd found irresistible. The clouds scudding across Salisbury Plain, Stonehenge looming with a swipe of rainbow faded to gray behind it. Finally I'd had to give up the quest; clouds weren't for me. I never managed one that struck me as the real thing. And these purple ones were plainly impossible. I gave a little prayer for rain.

I wiped the sweat away from my forehead and eyes and took a long look at the painting I'd been working on all day.

Six feet by eight. A woman's ear, an earring made of a single multicolored African bead, hair tucked behind the ear, the delicate bit of temple where the strands of hair magically begin. I couldn't define it but I recognized a pervasive eroticism in the depiction, all psychological rather than anatomical. It was rendered with total attention to realistic detail, as if seen under a gigantic magnifying glass.

It wasn't my ear. It was this other Belinda Stuart's ear. More real than the reality.

It all came down to connections. Carlyle Leverett who owned the gallery had been a classmate of Jack's at Choate. They had known each other at Harvard. And it was natural that Carl, having seen my work and—miraculously—having liked it, brought his boyfriend around to see it. That had been several years ago and the boyfriend was the critic Paul Clavell. When I'd exhibited with a group of other painters at a bar in TriBeCa, Clavell had made a point of writing a piece about the show in *New York*. He had written some nice things about my work and I had thanked Carl. "I only got him there, Mugs," he'd said. "After that the paintings were on their own. Paul's favor was going to the bar and looking, that's all."

Together they had urged me on, bullied me when necessary, pushed me into growth and change and the development of a vision which was, for better or worse, at least my own. There were blind alleys and catastrophes but they kept at me and finally last winter I showed them what I'd been working on.

Clavell sort of reeled back at the size of them. All huge canvases. All bits and pieces of the nude painter, pore-by-pore detail. He immediately began to think like a critic. And he wrote another piece for an art quarterly in which he told of the development of a painter. Me. He wrote that he was struck by the painter's state of mind, the extraordinary ability to center upon herself to the exclusion of all else, the magnification that lent a surreal dimension to each piece.

Leverett began badgering me about the one-woman show. He even had a name for it, he said.

He would call it *Belinda's Belindas*.

When I looked at the canvases, all I could see was an embarrassing, almost pathetic vulnerability, and some days I would have given anything never to have painted them, never to have felt the imperative to paint them. Anything.

Clavell called the collection "alluring. Clinical and poetic, simultaneously. Startlingly, unquenchably erotic."

Clavell spoke of "the utter innocence of existential egocentricity."

Maybe it was true. It was hardly flattering.

But in the end it was pure criticspeak.

The point was, I was still Belinda. As I'd always been.

But that afternoon, after the day's work, with Sally's fears of Harry's loving another woman banging around inside my head, with the unthinkable idea that possibly both our marriages were coming undone lapping at my feet, I remembered Clavell's observations and I must have had an inkling that deep inside my life some kind of over-wound mainspring was beginning to tear loose.

I was still praying for rain when the telephone rang. It was Harry. I'd halfway been expecting the call. It was sure to be about Sally and her accusations of infidelity. We went back such a long way, Harry and I, even longer than Sally and I by a few weeks: he always turned to me when there was any kind of a problem with Sal.

"Well, how are you, Belle?" Harry was the only person who had ever called me Belle.

"Nothing worse than an incipient nervous breakdown over my work, such as it is. Why aren't you deep in rehearsals?"

"Dinner break. There's a dress tonight. I can't eat any dinner, can't hold anything down." He laughed weakly.

"I don't believe that. It's not the Granger Touch. I believe your image—"

"You should know better. Of course, I wouldn't admit it to anyone but you. Look, I want to see you. We've got to talk."

"Mmm. I think I know what's on your mind."

"Really?" He sounded surprised. "You mean you've talked to him?"

"Him?"

"Yes, him. Jack. You remember, surely? Jack Stuart, your husband."

"Don't be snotty."

"Belle, please. I'm not being snotty. I want to talk to you about Jack."

"What in heaven's name for?"

"I'm worried about him. No, more accurately, I'm scared for him. Or about him." He was getting impatient with me. "Anyway, how about tomorrow? Lunch?"

"Can you hold it down?"

"Very funny. I'll know after the dress tonight. Come by the theater at one, okay? Stage door." He laughed nervously. "What did you think I was calling about, anyway?"

"I don't know, Harry. It doesn't matter. I'll see you tomorrow."

"That's a girl. I'll tell you a joke and make you laugh."

Chapter Four

Maybe I should have known Harry's concern had to relate to Jack. They had been inseparable for so long. Together, best friends, they had formed the nucleus of the Ruffians at Harvard. Harry had conceived the idea of the club, had taken it first to Jack. They had so much in common, beneath their surface differences. So much they could never share with the women in their lives.

In Harry's mind, Jack and I had always occupied our own compartments, even if there was a connecting door. Jack had doubtless confided a lot about our breakup to Harry and now Harry was going to try to start building a bridge between us again, proving once more that this marriage could indeed be saved. I wondered if Jack had told him about our last time together. I doubted it . . . but then, they were brother Ruffians and men, and who knew what went through men's minds?

Jack had come by the loft a week or so ago. He managed to keep forgetting to return the key, and in a way I didn't blame him, though the idea that there was another key out there besides Sally's made me nervous. He was living in that little apartment in the East Eighties, yet he retained ties, emotional and material, to the loft. Lots of his possessions remained behind, boxed up, and every so often he'd show up and cart something away.

That night he'd come by ostensibly to change the locks, which were frail and looked easily forcible. But it turned out that he'd forgotten the tools and what he really wanted to do was talk—talk about moving back in for a trial spell and "getting to work on this marriage, kid. We've got too much tied up in it to just let it go poof. Come on, Belinda, sit down, have a drink, let's talk about it. For Chrissake, put down the goddamn brush, relax a minute, and talk to me."

"I didn't ask you to leave," I said. "You thought it was best. Okay. Now I'm not asking you to come back, and this time it's a two-person decision. There's no point in forcing it, no point in just yo-yoing back and forth." I set the brush down, stood back from the table, and mopped away the perspiration with a towel. "You've got to give me just the tiniest break," I said, trying to smile and keep it light. "You know I've got to have these canvases ready for the show. It's important to me, honey, as important as your writing was to you—"

I heard the mistake I'd made but it was too late, I couldn't get the words back. It was hurtful, a barb he hadn't deserved, and he'd never believe I'd meant nothing by it.

"Was! That's just wonderful! I *still* write, if you hadn't noticed. It's just that nobody's willing to publish it . . . which doesn't necessarily mean it's crap!" His face had turned gray and icy. He was losing it and I didn't want to see that happen.

"You know I didn't mean it that way, so why make me the villain? What good does it do? All I'm saying is that I'm under a lot of pressure from now until the show opens—

it's just not a good time to expect me to talk about something so important to both of us."

"God, you ought to hear yourself." He was shaking a finger at me, smiling derisively. "Why don't you just tell the truth? Just say it . . . the only thing you care about are the paintings of your tits and ass—I mean, the ego at work here is breathtaking. To say nothing of all your new friends—that is, men. They're sniffing around you like a bitch in heat—"

"This is an awfully silly, awfully tired speech." I turned my back on him, went back to the worktable, fumbled with junk, and tried to stay calm. Tried not to cry. It wouldn't have been so bad if I didn't still love him, the way you always love somebody like Jack who had once been strong and had begun to crumble while you watched. "The bitch-in-heat is really beneath you, Jack. You know that's not me, you know you're lying. Maybe that's what's wrong with your writing. Maybe you can't deal with the truth. . . ."

It was a nasty sniping contest. I heard myself and despised myself for getting into it, yet I couldn't stop. He was jealous both of my work and of my ability to deal with life alone, and I understood—it was the most natural thing in the world. But somewhere things had gone far enough off the rails that we couldn't get them back on. By this time I didn't even want to. I just wanted us to stop hurting each other.

He fumed, stomped around the loft, took all the requisite shots at the kind of self-centeredness which would produce such paintings, and told me how that lay at the center of our problems. I listened, trying to busy myself cleaning up my work area.

"Hell, you're a child, a spoiled child, you've never given a flying fuck about anyone else." He ran through the meaningless litany, as if all the years of happiness and

pitching in together on everything had never happened.
"You're a snot-nosed little shit . . ."

I couldn't help it: I had to laugh and he laughed too at
the absurdity of the whole scene. He found and uncorked
a very old bottle of Calvados that Carlyle Leverett had
given me as a special present from his own cellar. When I
mentioned it, Jack was off again.

"My sweet Jesus, Belinda, Leverett? I mean really!
Don't you remember? Leverett was the Official Fairy of
Dunster Street! What the hell do you want him sucking
around for? My wife's a fag hag all of a sudden? I mean,
what's going on here?"

It finally came down to sex.

He wanted me, he said he wanted to muss me up, wipe
the Serene Highness bullshit off my face. He grabbed me,
yanked at the tank top and pulled it down, and I thought:
Girl, stay cool, you don't want anything really bad to
happen here.

He carefully touched one nipple while I stood still,
beginning to tremble with either rage or fear, I wasn't sure
which. I locked my eyes on his, willing him not to touch
me. But he squeezed my nipple, his jaw clenching in
anger. He squeezed until I cried out. I looked away but
everywhere I saw my own nakedness, huge, overwhelming, helpless. One canvas after another.

"You want to talk," I said, adrenaline pumping, "about
. . . saving . . . *this*? This *marriage*?"

"I want you," he said. "Right now. On the floor, right
now, right here. Lie down . . ."

I could barely hear him. It was as if he were talking to
himself. There was something wrong with him.

"You'd have to kill me," I said.

"Sometimes, I swear to God, I'd like to."

"You're crazy—"

"Maybe I am, Belinda." He backed away, miraculously draining tension from the scene. His voice changed, his stance changed. He was Jack again. Or close to being Jack. "I don't know. Sometimes I want to be inside you so much I think I could kill you, hell, kill somebody. It builds up inside me. Christ, I don't know . . . I love you, I want you . . . then I don't know, I hate you when you shut me out." He cocked his head, looked at me from the corner of one dark eye, brushed back the long black hair past his ears. "Sometimes I think I might do something really . . . bizarre." He looked around the loft, grinned, licked his dry lips. "What if I took a hammer and knife to your pretty pictures?" He laughed softly.

There was a buzzing behind my eyes, tremors coming from somewhere deep inside me like a psychic earthquake. I didn't feel myself speaking but I heard the words coming from my lips.

"I'd kill you, Jack." I wasn't even aware of how I'd joined the third-rate melodrama. "They'd have to pull me off your corpse if you touched these canvases. . . ."

I watched him turn pale. He finally looked away.

"Whoever writes your stuff," he said, "should be shot."

I sat quietly in one of the big white wicker chairs, listening to the clanking freight elevator descend. I looked at the wheel-of-fortune, afraid to ask it what I should do. Then the heat of the night hit me like a sixteen-ton weight and I realized what we'd just said to each other and I began to cry. I hated myself, not Jack. I felt my composure cracking like an eggshell.

And now Harry was telling me he was worried about dear old Jack.

The truth was, so was I.

Chapter Five

We went back such a long way, the four of us. Our lives had intertwined so elaborately because Harry and I had gotten together first. It was one of those slightly uncomfortable facts that we'd all dealt with and got past, but Sally's bringing it up the day we went to the Stanley Spencer show had taken me by surprise. It wasn't something we'd ever talked about at any length, at least not since undergraduate days at Mount Holyoke. And now Sally said Harry was in love with another woman, and Jack and I had threatened to kill each other, and Harry was worried about Jack. Harry and Jack. Theirs looked like the relationship that would endure. The pals. The Ruffians. . . .

I lay still in the darkness that night, the pillow warm and damp in the heat, the faint breeze of the old fan turning this way and that. But I couldn't get to sleep. My mind was racing, trying to freeze the turmoil and alarm I suddenly felt all around me. Childless, parents long dead, the people and the connections I'd counted on for so many years—those with Sally and Harry and Jack—looked like they were shattering, splintering. Even with Sally I no longer felt as open as I once had. I was afraid to tell her everything for fear of what she would think of me. . . .

At Mount Holyoke I had casually dated a few Harvard men. Then there had been Harry, who looked at life like a master repairman, fixing and tinkering to make it fit his idea of how it should work, never making a loud noise. Harry always said he was a graduate of the Perry Como School of Calm. I had never known anyone who had approached life with such an eye for an angle. He had been terribly grown-up in my eyes and he had been the first man I'd slept with. At a motel not far from Stockbridge. He was very sweet about it. I had been so nervous I couldn't relax for him. He had gently persevered and at last we'd managed it.

Almost immediately I had perversely begun wondering if he were the genuine article. But I had gone on with him, sleeping with him once in a while when he'd engaged a room at the Parker House and I couldn't bear the thought of disappointing him. Why he put up with such a tense, frightened sex partner I never understood, but I was at an age when I was flattered on the one hand and delighted by my sexual power over him on the other.

And then he'd introduced me in passing to his fellow Ruffian, Jack Stuart. Jack had seemed so much richer in character, free of Harry's poses and his search for angles, full of his own meaning compared to Harry, who was fun but a bit of a confidence trickster. Jack *was*. Harry *seemed to be*. I fell in love. Very hard. And it was nothing like being with Harry. I'd never imagined anything like it. I was sure of that.

Only two men in my life and now I was almost forty. Having slept with two men, Ruffians both.

It meant nothing to me that others thought Jack was handsome. He needn't have been. He had presence, charisma, and that was just fine. It meant nothing to me that he played football. He didn't make a big deal out of it. He went to practice, he played on Saturday, and when he carried the ball I hoped those great hulking oafs didn't fall on him and break him. If anything impressed me beyond his own fiery enthusiasm, it was his writing. I loved to read what he wrote. I was delighted in the widespread assumption that he was destined to be the Class Novelist.

After graduation I went to live in New York. Sally went to Europe for a year. Harry and Jack roomed together, also in New York, and I saw them both constantly, as well as Mike Pierce, another Ruffian. Jack's novel was published, film rights were sold, we found the loft, got married, and Sally came back from Europe. She took up the love affair with Harry that had pretty well filled her last two years at college—and we went antiquing and found the wheel-of-fortune. A few weeks later Harry and Sally got married, too, out at her parents' estate at Sag Harbor.

I worked at Pierce and Jacoby, the publishers, Mike's family firm, as a graphic artist in the art department. My painting was something I worked on when I had the time, almost as if I were embarrassed about it. After all, it was Jack who was destined to be the star of the marriage. My role was to bring in a regular check to keep the ship afloat while he labored mightily to bring forth his second novel.

If I had been more familiar with American literary history I'd have been less surprised, I suppose, at the turn Jack's young manhood took. He was one of those bright young fellows, praised much in college, who flared like a comet and then disappeared in the darkness as if he'd never been at all. Two years out of Harvard the blush and the cheering that followed the publication of his first novel faded away. The rest, as they say, was silence. I watched while his hopes came to grief; I was helpless to prevent it from happening.

Call it writer's block or the mysterious loss of the perceptions that had made him such an acute observer of the collegiate comedy which had been the basis of that one novel. Or call it his discovery of the unnerving fact that he had nothing more to say. Whatever he'd had, he'd lost it. He kept writing, but his second and then his third manuscript was rejected by one house after another. And he began to sour.

He took a job at *Time* as a writer/researcher, then went to J. Walter Thompson as a copywriter, and when his attitude cost him that job, he was bailed out by an old Harvardian and given a job at the Greer School across the Hudson in Jersey's green, rolling countryside. I tried to help him see the bright side, but merely became one of the enemy in his eyes. Handsome still in a tight, compact way, he was finally showing some age in the lines etched into his face like a road map of disillusionment with life and himself. Perhaps if he'd been a better writer, more truly deranged rather than just fed up with things, he'd have carried his role in literary history right on through to the bullet that would leave the little gray cells all over the loft wall. Instead, he began commuting to the Greer School, which he viewed as a more symbolic form of suicide but, in his darker moments at least, nonetheless final.

I saw him at forty, facing his own set of unavoidable realities and limitations as best he could, but his pride hadn't gone into hiding along with his writing ability. No, his pride grew in inverse proportion to the esteem in which he and, as it happened, the world at large held his writing. He was too proud to simply adjust, too proud to wait and cultivate the second coming of his talent, too proud to share his vulnerability and fear with me. He remained intelligent and quick-witted, but his festering disappointment and cynicism had destroyed his enthusiasm, disfigured him, and warped me.

As chairman of the English department at Greer he saw his job as a comparatively low-paid dead end, the only dividend being a certain slight prestige among his colleagues. Even they, he was convinced, saw him as a failed novelist, a rookie of the year who was sent down his second season and never came back. Up ahead, beckoning to him with the bony, crooked finger of the Grim Reaper, was a dotage as a particularly disagreeable Mr. Chips.

Infected by the jealousy of his materially successful friends, most frustratingly by that of his oldest pal, Harry, he was haunted by the past, tormented by the memory of the good years we'd all had, when he had been somebody, somebody with a nice clean shot at all the glittering prizes, who'd had them in his sights and let them flutter away and now believed he'd come to nothing—a one-novel writer.

Chapter Six

By the time I got to the theater the next day I'd worried myself sick about whatever condition Jack might be in. I'd called him during the morning just to chat and get a feel for his state of mind, but there'd been no answer. Sally was out as well, so I'd been left to stew in the old familiar juices: the heat was unabated and the sun so bright it turned Times Square into an exhaust-filled, boiling inferno with jackhammers racketing like machine-gun fire no matter where you looked. The bums tottering along in front of the porno movies looked even more disconsolate than usual. Construction dust filled the air. A dump truck was blocking Forty-fifth so I got off at the corner of Broadway and picked my way along the board sidewalk until I got to the stage door. The marquee was up, the logo of

Scoundrels All! looking fresh and hopeful, a lot the way we'd all looked once upon a time. The doorman had my name and pointed me toward the backstage clutter.

I could hear the sound of the rehearsal, a piano and a man and woman singing, stopping and starting. When I asked for Harry Granger they said he was out front. I found him sitting in the back row of the orchestra, his long legs bent up against the chair back in front of him, his chin resting on his knees. The theater was dim, like a foggy cave after the brilliance of the sunshine. A few lights glowed glumly in the lobby behind the orchestra. The director called out something to the actors. A large, bulky man sitting next to the director looked up as I made my way up the aisle, watching me. He looked vaguely familiar, but I was thinking about Harry and Jack and I swept on past, went into the row where Harry stared at the stage. He looked straight ahead, said, "Hi, Belle," and reached out to push the seat down next to him.

"So, you haven't committed suicide," I said.

"Not quite. There's still hope." He frowned and rubbed his eyes. He was a tall lanky man with sand hair, a slightly beaky nose, and pale blue eyes, as if his genes had set out to make him a redhead and not quite finished the job. An intense and interesting-looking man. He was wearing a fresh gray sweatshirt and chino pants. The gold of his wedding ring and a ten-thousand-dollar Piaget wristwatch caught my eye as he clasped his hands on his knees. Sally believed in giving world-class presents.

"How did it go last night?"

He deepened his frown. "It's not there yet, you know? We've got all the pieces but we're tinkering with the structure today." He shrugged. "We're kidding ourselves, probably. Anything we do now probably won't make a damn bit of difference, but at least we're staying busy instead of running around looking for bathrooms to throw up in." He looked over at me. "You must be getting a little tense yourself." He leaned over impulsively and pecked my forehead. "We're both gonna be big hits. Bank on it."

"I'm a little tense, to put it mildly. Doing the same thing, tinkering, trying to stay busy."

"I hated to take you away from your work," he said, stifling a nervous yawn, "and I didn't mean to worry you but I really had a scare the other night. With old Jack. I debated telling you or not, then I figured, who the hell else could I tell? Thing is, I got a look at this place he's living . . . We're talking spooky, Belle. Jack's not in such good shape, I'm afraid. Christ, I gotta stand up or I'll be paralyzed. Walk around the house, okay?"

He seemed unable to tear himself away from the building in which the fate of the show would be decided so soon. We stood in the back of the house, I asked him to spill it, and he nodded. He kept walking, working his way up and up the stairs. He handed me an apple from a brown sack. I shook my head, he shrugged and began munching.

"Thing is, I had dinner with Jack. Stopped by to pick him up, first time he's let me see his place. Christ, Belle, I didn't know what the hell to say . . ." He shook his head and ran his fingers through the long sandy hair. The apple was very crisp and each bite sounded like a gunshot.

"Well, do say something, Harry. The suspense is getting a little thick up here." We'd climbed the last flight of stairs to the second balcony and the stage seemed very small and far away and not very important. He plopped down in a seat and hung his legs over the top of those in front of him.

"He loves you, of course. As expected. But he's in pretty rocky shape. Misses you, says he doesn't know how to live without you." He looked at me expectantly, chewing.

33

"I'd say old Jack is more resilient than you Ruffians seem to think."

"I'm not so sure, Belle. Seriously. You get older, you lose some of the bounce. No one knows better than old jocks like Jack. Time is tougher for them to handle. Takes more away from them, and Jack's lost quite a lot, hasn't he?"

"I'm sorry I'm not more sympathetic," I said. "But I have my own experiences with Jack to go by."

"Oh, sure, I know it hasn't been a picnic lately—"

"'Picnic' is a bit of an understatement. In any case, he's not at death's door—he just needs some time to pull his socks up . . ."

"Funny you should say that."

"What?"

"Death's door."

"I don't understand, Harry—"

"Well, seeing that apartment of his—you haven't seen it?"

"I'm not on Jack's guest list at the moment."

"Well, if you make the list, skip the viewing. I saw the place and I got to thinking about death. The apartment is a shrine, Belle. Really. A shrine."

Down on the stage the couple had begun singing again, but I couldn't make out the words. They began to tap-dance very slowly, almost in a trance. "What are you talking about? A shrine to what?"

"You. Obviously. A shrine to DiMaggio wouldn't have been worth dragging you up here, right? No, he's got endless, countless pictures of you, he must have looted all the scrapbooks, all the desk drawers full of forgotten snapshots. I'm telling you, Belle, the whole damn thing—all the past—is stuck up on the walls of this grungy little apartment. It's spooky as hell. Like you're already dead."

He dropped the apple core into his sack, cracked his knuckles for punctuation, and my mind took one of those swerves, heard Jack telling me he'd sometimes like to kill me. "I don't mean to worry you—"

I laughed. "Hard to tell, my dear—you could just stop—"

"Ah, well, I'm not quite done. Just for a note of the surreal, mind you, there's that goddamn shotgun his dad gave him leaning against the wall over in the corner. I saw that thing and all I could think of was blood dripping down a wall. I don't know who he's gonna kill with it—Mike Pierce, maybe, he says he saw you two having a drink somewhere a couple of weeks ago. He delivered himself of the opinion that you and Mike are sleeping together and he didn't seem too happy at the thought."

"Good Lord!"

"I take it you're not sleeping with Mike?"

"Are you asking for Jack?"

"Who else?"

"Don't be insufferable, Harry. You're treading very close—"

"Sorry if I hit a nerve."

"Dammit! Of course I'm not sleeping with Mike! How could I be, I'm busy sleeping with the New York Jets, according to Jack."

Harry laughed and defused my irritation. "Well, I'll tell him not to shoot Mike, then. The thing is . . ." He paused and stood up, jammed his hands down into his pockets.

"Go on, Harry."

"Well, if it's not Mike he shoots, what if it's you? For wanting him to get out and for allowing other men into your life. I don't know, call me a dickhead, but I've been thinking about it—"

"Harry, for God's sake!"

35

"Or," he pressed on insistently, "more likely he'll use the damn thing on himself for not being able to control his own life and make it turn out the way he wanted. It's funny, the way people foreshadow things. We all used to wonder who would be the first Ruffian to go, and how would we deal with that. Well, ever since I saw that apartment I've had the feeling that whoever it is, Jack's going to be responsible."

We were going downstairs and my legs were weak and I was damned if I'd let Harry see how upset I was. How the devil could he say these things to me, anyway? I might have jumped from the balcony in sheer fright.

"And what precisely do you suggest we do about this situation?" I tried to keep my voice from shaking.

"Think about it, I suppose. Once I get this show open, I'll try to take him in hand. In the meantime, be careful, he's not all that stable." He looked at me. "You're pale. Look, I probably overstated all this—it's just an impression I got. But I had to tell you."

"Have you mentioned it to Sal?"

"No, actually. Things have been a little harried at home." He chuckled weakly. "Show opening. My having done something, God knows what, to get on Sal's wrong side—well, there I'm afraid I'm *under*stating. She's pissed about something, one of her paranoid states. I'm not making light—I'm worried. Between her and Jack, it is not the best week of my life." We reached the downstairs lobby. The sun glared from the street. "And then, Peter's coming from London. Staying with us." He sighed.

"Peter?"

"Venables, Belle. Peter Venables. You must remember Peter. A Ruffian returning for the show. He's coming from London, you know." He looked at me quizzically.

"It'll come back to me, I'm sure."

"Well, when you see him, don't give him that dumb, empty look. He was one of us and you know him perfectly well."

"I remember the name," I said lamely. I did, too, and a faint, shapeless image was forming in the middle distance.

He held the door to the street open for me. The heat slammed us like an explosion in a Con Ed main. "Listen, if you can find out what's got Sal acting so . . . well, so fed up with me—would you let me know?" He gave me a beseeching look and grinned. "Everything happens at once, right?"

I put on may dark glasses.

"Thanks for coming. And be careful, Belle. Not to worry, just be careful. We'll get Jack straightened out. See you for opening night, sugar."

We'd forgotten to have lunch. Just as well, actually.

Chapter Seven

Not to worry, just be careful . . .

It seemed that everything he'd said had been carefully designed to make me worry. The idea of the shrine Jack had constructed worried me more than I could possibly have told Harry. It made Harry think of death. Everything he'd said at the theater was dancing around inside my head like a tribe of dervishes. The shotgun . . . the first Ruffian to die . . . I tried to work but I wasn't accomplishing much of anything. All I could think of was Jack alone in the apartment with all the old snapshots and the shotgun.

Contemplating murder? Suicide?

I didn't want to believe it. Harry was letting his imagination work overtime. After all, he was involved in getting his show up, hardly in the calmest state of mind himself. So why should I let his opinions bend me out of shape?

Obviously because he and Jack were so close.

But Jack and I were close, too, and I couldn't believe things were so bad.

Still, by evening of that steamy, humid day, I'd had it with trying to paint. I haphazardly cleaned up my tools and the workplace and went to soak in a cold tub. Naturally the telephone rang and I pulled the bathroom extension across the tile. It was Harry again. He was calling from the theater. I could hear the murmur of the preview crowd behind him.

"Listen," he said, "I let you down today."

"You can say that again." I sighed.

"I completely forgot to tell you a joke. Which I had specifically promised. What can I say, Belle? Too much on my mind—"

"Harry . . . It's okay. I'll live."

"But I'm a man of my word—"

"I know, I know—"

"I can't tell it to you now but I've got one for you. The one about the armless bell-ringer. You remember to ask me, promise?"

"Don't you think you'd better attend to your show?"

"In a minute. Listen, you know what I told you about old Jack today?"

"Seems to have stuck in my mind." Here it came, the disclaimer, the I-was-exaggerating routine, pay-no-attention-to-what-I-said. "Well, the more I think about it, the more concerned I become. Not just about the shrine, the shotgun, this kind of dark mood he projects. There was something else. Has Jack told you he's writing again?"

"Not a word," I said.

"Well, he is. I saw the manuscript on his desk. I sort of casually picked up the first page while we talked—I didn't think I was prying—and he came at me like a madman, told me to leave his things alone, it was none of my business, why was I coming into his place and spying on him . . . Belle, it was like I was suddenly dealing with another man altogether, not the old Ruffian we know and love." He laughed bleakly. "I don't know what it is he's writing . . . I just hope to God it's not the world's longest suicide note."

"I really think you're overreacting, Harry—"

"You haven't seen his place, toots, so let me be the judge of what is and isn't realistic. All I'm suggesting is that you might give him a buzz, just shoot the bull, try to get a feeling—"

"I don't feel like calling him," I said. "I'm sorry—"

"Okay, okay. Maybe he'll call you—anyway, listen close, see if you can pick up anything. Look I'd better get into the house and see if I like this thing any better tonight—by the way, have you talked to Sal? Any word on what her current problem with me is?"

"None. I haven't talked with her."

"Well, Peter came in this afternoon and I suppose they're renewing old acquaintance and whatnot. Keep your fingers crossed—maybe it'll take the heat off me." He laughed again, tiredly. "I'm no damn good for anything until this show is up and the verdict is in. Take care, Belle, and let me know if you come up with anything on Jack."

* * *

Harry and Jack and Sally were driving me crazy.

I felt as if I had lost the normal ability to know at least vaguely what might be coming next. Nothing seemed to be what I expected. I was experiencing a kind of psychological vertigo, and the constant need to fiddle with the paintings and the incessant heat weren't helping. The sense of disorientation sapped me, working with the heat and the nervous tension building inside me.

I was getting fed up with all the inner drivel I couldn't seem to shake loose from the next day: finally I slammed down the brushes, mopped my forehead with a paint rag that was scratchy and stiff, and took off my jeans and T-shirt. I lay down on the floor in a pool of sunshine and did fifty leglifts to work off the frustration and energy. Then I took my four thousandth cold shower of the summer.

Letting the fan dry me off, I realized I couldn't stop worrying about Sally. It was unlike her to fail to call me, but there hadn't been a word since the gallery day. I didn't want to be guilty of intruding, but I'd held off long enough. If she was having a tough time, I might be able to help. So I figure the hell with ladylike discretion and called her.

But it wasn't Sally who answered. It was Peter Venables.

"Belinda!" he said as soon as I'd asked for Sally. "It's so good to hear your voice. It's Peter Venables. My God, you sound just the same . . . and I've got you first on my list to call." I must have said something because he went on: "Are you all right? You sound nervy all of a sudden—"

"No, no, I'm all right, Peter. Just surprised. How are you?" I was calling him up out of my memory but it had been a long time ago and I didn't have the best recollective powers anyway. Tall, thinnish, rather fine features. Yes, Sal had always said she found him handsome. Sort of actorish. Yes, that was Peter Venables.

"Great, just great. Dying to see you, Belinda. It's been so long. Harry says you're still a knockout—"

"Brace yourself for the ravages of eighteen years, Peter."

"Nonsense, Harry's a man of his word. I just got in yesterday from London. Sal and I went out on the town last night—no, that sounds too strenuous. But we did have dinner while I started catching up on everybody." He'd picked up a slight British accent that was quite charming.

"We must get together soon," I said, trying to come close to his enthusiasm and falling way too short. "But I really need to talk to Sally right now—"

"Well, that's a problem. She seems to have gone out already—no forwarding address." He chuckled.

"Do you know when she might be back?"

"I haven't a clue. They keep pretty weird hours around here—listen, I don't mean to pry, Belinda, but you do sound worried. Is everything all right?"

"I . . . well, I've been a little concerned about Sal lately. Just a mood she's been in. I'm sure you've cheered her up immeasurably. And I'll brain you if you mention my asking—"

"I wouldn't think of it," Venables said. "But as long as you brought it up, I might as well tell you, I was going to mention something along those lines to you. I'm rather worried about both of them. It's a bit tense around here and I'm at a loss."

"Oh, no . . ."

"Listen, meet me for a drink this afternoon. We can compare notes, if you feel like it. And I can feast my eyes on you once again. You up for it?"

I sighed. "Sure, Peter, why not?"

"Jolly good! Hollyhocks at six?"

"Where's that?"

After a moment's pause he said: "I thought you might remember the place. It used to be quite popular in the old days." He gave me an address on East Fifty-sixth. "It'll be good to see you, Belinda."

I hoped I was remembering the right guy.

Chapter Eight

When I got to Hollyhocks I was sure I'd never been there before, whatever Venables might have thought. The crowns of the trees hung listlessly. The cabdriver's radio had said it was ninety-six degrees in Central Park. A dog looked up from a fire hydrant and decided I wasn't worth barking at, not in this heat. Ducking under the marquee, I descended a few steps and went through a polished brass door. At first the darkness and the cooled air both managed to be impenetrable. I stood blinking as the long bar took shape, the tables with white napkins, shining stemware, the long mirror in which I finally saw myself. Immediately I liked the place, all of its shining surfaces and lots of years built carefully, layer on layer, until character had been given form.

Peter Venables was waiting for me at a small table in a corner with his back to the wall so he could see the room. He waved. He was wearing a pink shirt and chinos and sneakers and a very old sailcloth jacket, and when he stood up, I was struck for a moment by how much he resembled Harry in the dim light. Tall, the same square shoulders, a trick of inclining the head. Closer, of course, he was dark, almost swarthy, and his eyes were large and dark and liquid. He shot me a darting smile and kissed my cheek.

"Belinda," he said softly. I smelled his cologne. Nice.

"This is a great place," I said, sitting down. "One of those New Yorky bars everyone is always talking about—"

"Do you remember it?" He looked at my blank expression, then laughed ruefully when I shook my head. "It's funny. I was so sure it would all come back to you. You've been here at least once, Belinda, because I was with you—"

"You're kidding! It must have been ages ago."

He got the waiter's attention and I practically begged for a gin-and-tonic. I was trying to summon up memories of Peter Venables but it wasn't going to work. I recognized the face but there weren't any little anecdotes that went with it.

"Seems like yesterday to me," he said. "It was spring break, the day Sally's parents had that incredible party at Sag Harbor. We were all supposed to meet here and a limo was coming to pick us up—her dad laid on the whole thing for us. You and I got here first, and when I realized that, I was suddenly scared to death, absolutely tongue-tied. I suppose we were twenty-one. And I'd never been alone with you before, you know—responsible for holding up my end of the conversation. God, it was so different from being in a group with everybody talking. Anyway, it was a disaster, you must have been bored half to death—"

"Peter," I interrupted, "let me ask you something—why were you scared of being alone with me? Give me a candid answer."

He stroked his chin and thought. "You had a kind of mystique, I guess—"

"But why? I wasn't so bright, I certainly wasn't an intimidating wit. I wasn't a snotty bitch, was I?"

He shook his head. "No, you're on the wrong track. It was . . ." He took a deep breath. "Okay, it was entirely physical. The way you looked. Beautiful."

"Oh, God! The delusions of extreme youth!"

"It was the look . . . I wondered if you'd look the same way now." He leaned back, smiling at me as if he knew something I didn't know and could never find out. Suddenly I wished I hadn't let the conversation take this turn, hadn't paid any attention to the accusations Jack had thrown at me the other night. Watching that funny smile as Peter Venables watched me, I wished I hadn't come to Hollyhocks at all. "You don't. The years have made some changes—"

"Just as well. Don't be disappointed."

"Oh, no, Belinda. You misunderstand. Your beauty has deepened, taken on definition. It's like one of my investments, with interest accumulating over twenty years." He lit a cigarette while I hoped I wasn't blushing and wished I were back at the loft working. Where I should have been. "You were lovely and sexy and unattainable then," he said. "The years seem to have made you less remote, more confident with yourself . . . and that makes you more human, somehow. Everything that's changed has changed for the better." He smiled at me again, through the smoke, almost as if it were the smoke of a postcoital cigarette. "You asked," he said. "You wanted to know."

"So I did," I whispered, mostly to myself. "I just wish it made more sense. None of what you're talking about ever crossed my mind. It's funny to think that you were looking at me in this strange way and I was so unaware. I was shy of boys, really. I used to make Sally give me topics of conversation a guy might find interesting. I thought we were all just kids . . ."

"Oh, we were in a way, but not entirely. I remember when you gave Harry the gate and he was pretty bitter about it. That was the night Harry told me that if he couldn't have you, he was sure as hell going to have Sally. The thing was, Harry had never known anyone with that kind of money and he just couldn't get over it . . . and, by God, he was good as his word. He married her and now he's a big producer and he's made a great deal of money on his own." Peter tapped his glass with a forefinger and the waiter scurried away for two more gin-and-tonics. "Life worked out so well for Sally and Harry, and where's the happy ending? She cries all the time and Harry just gets up and leaves the house." He ran his fingers along the line of his jaw, long, thin fingers. I suddenly remembered those fingers on a piano's keys, so long ago, somewhere I'd forgotten.

"Is it really that bad?" I said. "I didn't have a clue—" The vertigo was sending me spinning. Sally had never said a word until the other day. Yet, we'd told each other *everything*. What was going on? Who could I go to and ask?

"Well, she's had to be tolerant of all his girls on the side—"

"What? *Harry?* No, you must be mistaken."

"Oh, Belinda, grow up." The smile reappeared. It was hard imagining he'd ever been shy and tongue-tied, watching me and wanting me and being afraid. "These things happen, they're commonplace—"

"Not with us! Not with Harry and Sally and Jack and me."

"Sally's like a lot of women—she can make an accommodation on the issue of fucking a few girls for fun so long as the girls don't become just one girl, so long as the fucking doesn't become an emotional attachment." He shrugged, watching me. What he said sounded like what Sally had said that day. *Treat me like an adult . . .* "So, I don't know what's gotten into Sal all of a sudden. Up until now she must have thought the marriage was worth Harry's little amusements—but now she's not so sure, I guess." He leaned back, sipped his drink, watching me over the rim. "You wouldn't know what's going on, would you?"

"No dammit! Why can't he just behave himself? She's such a good wife. And Harry, he's the best, a really good soul." His gaze made me feel simple-minded, hopelessly naive, but he'd been away for eighteen years, he didn't know the way we'd been. "He and Jack have been inseparable over the years." Something inside me registered the weight of what Venables had told me and my arms felt heavy and my stomach wasn't quite right.

"You want to know what's the trouble with Harry? It's his age, but not just his age—it isn't that he's feeling old. He's still feeling young, but he doesn't know how long it will last and he's scared time is running out. He's still looking for the Holy Grail and its name isn't Sally, I'm afraid—"

"Drop this," I said. "Please."

"Let's eat, Belinda. You look weak from hunger."

I went rather numbly, felt his hand on my arm. I should have made an excuse, gone home, but I wasn't thinking. Well, I was thinking. But I was thinking about all the wrong things, all the things that had seemed so safe but were suddenly blowing up in our faces.

* * *

He knew a little Italian place not far away and we strolled through the lengthening shadows. Over dinner I watched his confidence—about what, I wasn't absolutely sure—grow, his nervousness fade. I felt myself undergoing precisely the opposite reaction, but he was interesting on the subject of life in England and the Persian Gulf and the Arab emirates and other places I knew nothing about. He'd obviously made a great deal of money and seen more of the world than I ever expected to. As well, he'd raised a daughter by himself, though he made no mention of her mother. Over coffee I lapsed into what he apparently thought was an unhappy silence.

"What's the problem, Belinda? Have I been babbling on and leaving you out of the evening?"

"Not at all. I've been fascinated. Such a life you've led. No . . . it's just that I got to thinking about Sal and Harry again, about his infidelities. That really bothers me. And the way you reacted. It seems so cynical . . ."

"I think I'm just being realistic. I'm not here to judge others, you know. Tough enough being me. I'm sure Sal has accustomed herself to it—"

"I hate that," I said. "She shouldn't have to—"

"There are lots of things in life we shouldn't have to do." He smiled languidly, bemused at my attitude. "You doubtless shouldn't have to put up with the end of your marriage . . ." He shrugged.

"Sal told you?"

"Of course. However, bad luck for you is good luck for someone else. That's the way life works, in my experience, anyway. Indisputable truths and so on." He gave me an angled glance, pursed his lips as if contemplating a method of approach. "Do you feel up to the truth about old Harry, then?"

"I don't know what's true and what's just a comfortable illusion," I said softly.

"Well, you're not going to like it, I'm afraid. Perhaps I should just keep my mouth shut—"

I shook my head, tried to laugh. "Should have thought about that several hours ago."

"I think Harry's problem goes all the way back to Ruffian days. He never got over losing you to Jack—no, come on, sit down, relax." He put his hand over mine, held me in my place. "I'm not kidding, Belinda, so please don't make faces. Hear me out." I sat, waited, wanting to pitch my coffee cup past the flowers into the mirror. "I think once upon a time Harry wanted to marry you more than he has ever wanted another thing. Then one day he looked up from his latest deal and realized you were gone. Jack had made off with you. Now, my own theory is that Harry has been looking about for another *you* ever since. It's one of life's little jokes, isn't it? Sally's still your best friend, she married Harry—he couldn't get his hands on another you so he married the exact physical opposite . . . and your chum! Don't you love the symmetry of it? I mean, it has an appeal, if you look at it dispassionately." He gave me another slow, dark handsome smile, this one tinged with a world-weariness. "My guess is, Harry's finally found himself another Belinda and Sally's figured it out, some of it anyway, and doesn't know what to do about it.

"I hope it's all as farfetched as it sounds to me." I was trying not to tell him how unpleasant he sounded.

"Oh, I'm afraid it's not farfetched at all." He turned the sliver of lemon peel from the espresso between his fingers, as if it might have some mysterious value. "It's all based on what a woman looks like. In this case you. If a man settles on such a creature, as I believe Harry did, then he'll put up with any difficulties, overcome any obstacle, until he finds another one. Rare, I suppose, but when such a man settles on such a creature—well, that's that. Do you mind if I smoke a very small cigar?" I shook my head. "Those men are the ones who never give up, actually." He exhaled and looked at me through the cloud. Shrugged. "That's just the way some men are."

"Men are mysteries to me," I said at last. "Granting for a moment that you're right about Harry—it's crazy. A face, a body, it's just a shell, the dust jacket. I can see a man setting his sights on a dancer, an heiress, someone who'd make a great mother. But a woman's nose? Her hair? The shape of her breasts? Crazy."

"No. It's just not logical. Women have very logical minds, rather pedestrian, it seems to me. Men are more prone to flights of fancy, clouds of romance. So you object to the illogicality of it and I can only tell you there's a hell of a lot out there that has nothing to do with logic."

When we left the restaurant and were forging through the heat of the night, Venables took my hand, lifted it to his lips. "You really are an innocent, Belinda. Trusting. You know what I think?"

"I'm rather afraid to ask."

"I think you're much the same as you were. When I knew you before." He flagged a cab. "Anyway, let me see you home. It's still early and tomorrow's a schoolday." He grinned innocently and winked and I couldn't rid myself of the feeling that I'd never met him before tonight.

I don't know why I asked him up for a nightcap.

Maybe I was lonely, shaken by the news of Harry and Sally, confused and unwilling to sink back into the loneliness of the loft with all the damned canvases. So I asked him up.

While I was in the kitchen making an iced tea for myself and another gin-and-tonic for him, he prowled the edges of the room looking at the paintings. He gave a long whistle.

"Belinda! Sal said your work was like nothing I'd ever seen before but . . . this—my God, these are just incredible! Whatever gave you the idea?"

"Maybe it's just latent narcissism." I said. I really didn't want to go into it with him.

"Lucky for us," he said. He was staring at the painting of my breast. I came in and handed him the drink. "But if you're so shy," he said, "how can you stand having people see these?"

I shook my head. "It's another Belinda. Not me. At least I'm counting on feeling that way once they're on exhibit—I've got my fingers crossed."

I turned to lead the way over to the couch, when he touched my arm. A pressure, not a tight grip, and I knew what was coming. I turned, preparing to gently deflect his advances.

But he was pointing to the corner. The wheel-of-fortune. "And what's this? I've never seen one of these up close, either. It's my lucky night."

"Wedding gift from Sal and Harry. Back in the year one." Once again my assumptions had proven misguided. What the hell was wrong with me? We walked over to the wheel and he gave it a whirl, click, click, click . . .

"Well, let's see. Maybe I should give it a serious turn. All right? Is that a good idea?" He slid one arm loosely around my shoulders. His forehead was glistening in the dim lamplight. The heat wouldn't let up.

"It's up to you—"

"I'll take it seriously only if I approve of what it tells me."

"A good policy," I said.

He squeezed me. He spun it firmly and it seemed to spin forever. I felt somewhat light-headed watching, a bit dizzy. It slowed and finally clicked its last.

He leaned down, read the fortune.

"'The future belongs to the bold,'" he said. He looked up at me, smiling. "What do you think about that, Belinda? Where do you stand on boldness?"

"I really don't know. But I am tireder than I thought, Peter. Let's call it a night. The heat's really getting to me—"

"Me, too." He put his drink down on my worktable.

"It's been a nice evening, Peter. We must—"

He did it very deliberately. He tilted my chin and kissed me. He kissed me for too long a time and I tried to disengage myself easily and he wouldn't let me go and I knew that everything was suddenly all wrong. He pushed me back against the worktable, pressing himself against me. He was hard against my belly and he was forcing my mouth open and I tried to yank away but I wasn't strong enough. My legs felt weak and my head was spinning. He finally moved his lips to my ear and whispered something and I gasped please, don't do this, please, stop, Peter, you don't want to do this, it's not right . . . He was breathing hard and rhythmically pushing against me, working himself up. "I want you, Belinda, you invited me up here, what's the matter with you? Come on, it's me, we're grown-ups . . . what's the big deal, for Christ's sake?" His arms held me like a vise and when I tried to say something my mouth was dry, my lips stuck together. He loosened his hold, moving his hands around to my breasts and I slid along the bench, stumbled and fell, holding on to the tabletop, on my knees, my head throbbing, tears suddenly overflowing. "Belinda, don't you understand, it's . . ."

And I couldn't hear the rest of it. He stood over me. "On the bed," he said, his voice low and insistent, a kind of growl, soft, menacing.

"No, goddammit!" I managed to shout. I felt an adrenaline surge, tried to get up, and he grabbed my arm, jerked me to my feet and the buttons ripped off the front of my dress, sprinkled to the floor like dice.

"It's my turn," he said. *"My turn!"*

"You bastard! Your turn to what? What do you think this is?" I wiped my eyes, backed away. "Why are you doing this? No, I don't even want to know—just get the hell out! Get out of here!"

I don't know what I expected. But my heart was slamming in my chest, I felt buttons underfoot, and my nose was running. I tried to pull the front of my dress together. My stomach was churning. I willed myself not to vomit. He stood staring at me, straightening his clothing, then seemed to cock his head, reached out to me again. With what little strength I had I hit him across the face with the palm of my hand. He stopped, looked at me as if he'd just noticed the situation turning dark and foul, and pulled back his hand to hit back.

"Don't," I said.

And his hand stopped at the top of its arc and hung there, like something dead and strung up. All I could think of was Jack, his anger, his scowl, his bitterness. And the hand dropped. He stared at me, biting his lip. There was a cut at the corner of his mouth, a thread of blood, just like in the movies.

"Just don't do anything," I said. "Just leave. Don't speak to me. Don't say a word. Just get out and leave me alone and none of this goes any further."

"You really are a bitch, aren't you? Ice cold . . . always were, still are. Just a bitch." He brushed past me. He stopped at the doorway to the elevator. He stood looking at the canvases, nodding to himself as if agreeing with something I couldn't hear. "Well, Belinda, if you want it rough, rough it shall be. Not only am I bold, I also persevere. We'll have another little talk . . . perhaps you'll come to see it my way. Do you think so, Belinda? Does that strike you as possible? It *is* my turn. Surely you realize that. In any case, I've enjoyed this little discussion. I think we've made great strides. Good night, Belinda." He laughed, stepped into the elevator, and I heard him laughing in the street below. "Good night, Belinda . . ."

Chapter Nine

I suppose I've led a sheltered life and what happened that night with Peter Venables was no big deal. I kept telling myself that for a couple of days but I couldn't get the ugliness of the moment out of my mind—the gradual way the evening had changed, the sudden explosion of violence, the buttons bouncing on the floor, the blood on his mouth, the way I willed him to lower the hand he'd raised to strike me. . . .

It hadn't been just a deflected pass, an amorous impulse that had ended sheepishly. It had ended with that dance along the edge of the abyss, and I could still hear his laughter in the elevator, his insinuating remarks hanging like a noxious gas in the loft after he was gone. Jack would have said Peter needed a new dialogue writer, too, but I guess that was the way people talked when emotions sent them crashing on the rocks.

For two days I tried to figure out what I should do. I felt as if I had been betrayed by Peter Venables. As if he had violated an agreement of our youth, when we had first moved in the same orbit. He remembered me as a friend and now he had chosen not to treat me as a friend. And what of his old comradeship with Jack? The bond of the Ruffians? What prompted him to come on with me, still the wife of his old pal?

What had happened to the trust that everything else grew from?

Was Harry really a man who had his girlfriends in a row, for his own amusement, apart from the life and the Harry I knew? And did Sally accept the situation, acknowledge it? Could Venables possibly have been riding anything but his own erotic fantasy when he said that Harry had been looking all these years for another *me*?

I couldn't sort out what Venables had said, what might be true from what his own mind had summoned up like bad dreams.

How many of us were guilty of betraying the past? I suppose that was the question I needed answered.

I was alone with all this. The only people who might have known the sense of hurt and loss I felt were precisely the ones I couldn't talk to—the people who had dwelt there in the long ago with me. We were all the people of the past. But maybe I was the only one who had clung to it, its shining innocence. Maybe I was the only one who had thought it was the paradigm.

Sally.

She was the one I wanted to turn to. I wanted to let my thoughts overflow and hear her set me straight.

But she was part of it.

That was the way I saw it.

She was part of the betrayal.

I don't know. Maybe I was going a little nuts.

The night before *Scoundrels All!* opened I had one of those dreams that wakes you up feeling frantic and sick, covered in sweat, head aching. I went back to sleep finally and when I woke up in the sticky gray morning I had no memory of the dream.

I made coffee and a piece of toast and sat staring out into the heat, which seemed to have grown thicker and thicker as the days passed. The man on the radio said the humidity was in the high nineties and it looked like we were in for a storm later. That was the best news I'd had in I don't know how long.

Then I heard a backfire in the street below and it all came back to me and I got suddenly short of breath and went to the window feeling like I ought to cry out for help.

There had been no people in my dream.

Just the shotgun from Jack's apartment.

I saw the black holes of the barrels, slowly swinging toward me like the guns of Navarone, and I saw somebody's hands steadying it, fingers tightening on the triggers.

Then the explosion came in my face.

But I wasn't dead. Or I didn't feel anything. Because the next view I had was of a wall covered with blood and tissue and the blood was running in pink streaks and the stuff splattered on the patterned paper was falling away in chunks.

Sally arrived in the afternoon, a nervous wreck because of the opening only a few hours away, but smiling and in a much better mood than I'd expected. Her troubles of a few days before seemed to have evaporated. Of course, I now realized that we hadn't been quite as close as I'd always thought. Maybe it was all an act. Maybe she was being brave. Maybe she'd found out that her fears about Harry were empty. Maybe, as Peter had said, she was accustomed to Harry's affairs and had decided she didn't care about this one, either. When I saw her, my oldest, best friend, it struck me that I hadn't a clue as to which of the possibilities applied.

She came off the elevator carrying in her arms, like a gigantic infant, a cascade of yellow roses wrapped in tissue, tied loosely with a thick yellow ribbon, a floppy bow. She marched on into the kitchen and began searching for vases.

"What in the world—" I said.

"You've got paint all over your face, dear. Two vases aren't going to be enough." She was wearing a pale blue linen dress, sleeveless, with white piping. She was too pale herself for the outfit but with the jet-black hair and the sharp angles of her face she looked great.

I found her a third vase. "What is this?"

"For you. They were propped on that pathetic little wooden chair down in the lobby. Just sitting there. I asked a man carrying a box bigger than East Rutherford into the warehouse if he'd seen them delivered. He told me he couldn't see where he was going, let alone check out deliverymen. Here's a card."

I tore open the envelope.

Apologies are in order. I'll make them in person.

The fan on the counter passed its waves across my face like the flutter of invisible wings, and I felt a shiver ripple along my spine. Sally was watching me, hands on hips, feet apart, waiting impatiently. "So what does it say?"

I handed it to her and she cocked her head inquisitively. The light at the windows was reflecting the deep purple of the afternoon sky. The first raindrops were tapping on the skylight. I couldn't tell her about Venables. I'd told him I wouldn't and he was their houseguest on top of that and the show was opening and who needed any more problems?

And Sal and I didn't tell each other everything, anyway. Not anymore.

"May I ask what that is supposed to mean?"

I made a face. "It's nothing. A guy . . . a guy I barely know made a mistake the other night . . ." I shrugged.

"Ah, the adventures of the newly single!" She picked up two of the vases and smiled at me quizzically. "Well, I won't pry. But let it be recorded that I am utterly fascinated."

"It's not very fascinating. Let that be recorded."

I followed her into the work area. The thunder's first crack went off like a cannon and I flinched. Like a child frightened by loud noises and the gathering darkness.

"I'm betting on Jack. Or—hmmm—could it be Mike?"

"What? What are you talking about?"

"Belinda, are you all right?"

"Yes, of course, I'm fine."

"The flowers. I was talking about the flowers—I'll bet they're from Jack, who misbehaved and is sorry . . . or from Mike. I mean, you have been seeing Mike—"

"Please, Sal. Mike is an old friend. You know that— we've had dinner a couple of times and Mike is the spitting image of Bertie Wooster and he's a dear. But he never, never would make a mistake about me. Okay? I rest my case."

Sally was leaning against the wheel-of-fortune, staring out into the rain, nodding. I mopped sweat from my face and dropped the towel on the table.

"All right, all right. It's your secret." She pressed a forefinger to her lips, looking at me from the corners of her eyes.

* * *

Sally was jittery as all get-out, which was why she'd come by the loft in the first place. The anonymous flowers—at least anonymous as far as she was concerned—had merely deflected her from her own state, and even then only momentarily. I was glad when she dropped the inquiry. I sank back and listened to the rain drumming insistently on the skylight. It was bouncing on the glass.

In a few hours Harry Granger would be back on Broadway with the first show he'd produced since *Gargoyles* three years before. Opening night, a six-thirty curtain so the critics could make their deadlines, a party and the wait for the first television reviews and the *Times* to hit the streets. So Sally was about ready to start banging off the walls and I understood. Aside from everything else, Harry had a million dollars of his own money riding on the show. I watched Sally gulp thirstily at the gin-and-tonic she'd made herself.

"You know Harry," she said. "He keeps that calm pose and he never sweats and he's always amused but he was wound up pretty tight today. I could tell. He says he's at the theater and I suppose that's just possible. If not he's off somewhere . . . working off the tension." Suddenly her mood and tone altered. Bitterness had crept in unannounced. "You know, for so long he seemed such an innocent. They all did, really, all the Ruffians. Remember that day at the Waldorf when he was being too ingenuous even for him . . . Muffin! My God, I couldn't believe it. Muffin!"

We'd all been having a drink in Peacock Alley and Harry had mentioned a friend of his having a girlfriend on the side. "A bit of muffin," Harry had said, winking. Sally had screamed in helpless frustration: "For God's sake, Harry, grow up! It's *crumpet*, a bit of crumpet on the side, not *muffin*! Get it right, will you?" Harry had blushed and looked around and—quite sincerely—apologized while Sally, Jack, and I had gotten quietly hysterical.

Now she was moving from one of my canvases to another, as if she'd never seen them before, inspecting them closely, clinking the ice in her glass. "Men," she said, "are going to love these. I feel like blushing and they're not even of me! Men . . . Jack, Harry, Mike, they're all just little boys in long pants. Too sensitive when it comes to their own egos, too vulnerable, too selfish, too cruel, too prone to the easy and thoughtless betrayal . . . out of touch with reality, all coiled up in their little games. Belinda Stuart, where could my drink have gone?" She went to the kitchen and built another, kept on talking while I watched her from the white wicker armchair. Lightning clawed overhead, the clap of thunder bounced off the buildings in Prince Street.

"A necessary evil is man," she announced, returning. "Now, take Harry, he just can't help taking advantage of people. You, on the other hand, can't take advantage of anyone—you just trust people. You're laboring under the common misapprehension that men are *people*. Not so! They are *creatures*. As in 'from the Black Lagoon.' You'd trust him, the Black Lagoonite, you'd trust anyone. . . . You just can't believe the worst of people. And that will be your downfall."

She came back across the loft and stared at the wheel-of-fortune as if it were an old and trusted friend. I wondered: she hadn't mentioned her houseguest, Peter Venables—should I tell her the Venables story? But, no, that wouldn't have been right. Besides there was no point in fueling this new man phobia.

"You trust Jack, for instance," she said. "Love is something a woman can't always help, but trusting is just stupid. You're always ready to defend old Jack—"

"Hardly," I interrupted. "It seems that I'm always the one picking on him—"

"—and Jack is as indefensible as any of them. Did I tell you I called trustworthy old Jack today? I didn't want him to think he'd been sent to Coventry just because of your split, so I called him to make sure he was coming to the show and the party tonight. Big mistake! He asked me if you were coming, then he wanted to know if Mike was coming—I said for heaven's sake, of course Mike's coming. He's one of *us*! Well, you wouldn't believe the fit that Jack threw. He got going on you and Mike, how he couldn't believe I'd be a party to such a thing, how you and he are still married and you're running around with Mike . . . He said he couldn't trust himself in the same room with the two of you! Can you believe it? Whatever happened to wit and style and sophistication?"

"He won't be coming tonight, then?"

"I rather doubt it."

"God, that's a relief." I sighed. "But Mike is hardly worth all this fuss. Talk about an innocent bystander, it's poor Mike."

"I must say," Sally mused, "Jack does worry me every so often. He's just going to have to pull up his socks and act like a man. You really have bewitched the poor devil. And after almost twenty years, it's something of a miracle, if you ask me."

The afternoon wore on. The loft darkened. Lightning continued to crackle over the city like electrical stems, jagged, plunging down into the heart of Manhattan. The rain came down like dishwater emptying out of a sink. Sally had another drink and sucked on the bright green wedge of lime. The yellow roses glowed as if they were lit from within. I listened to Sally talk about men, the show, Harry and Jack, a background drone I wasn't paying all that much attention to.

"Male bonding! What a drag, when are we going to stop hearing about male bonding? The Ruffians. The problem with men is, they make their macho little pacts and they never grow up. They just hang together, pals forever, and the world becomes a huge locker room where they can snap towels at each other and giggle over some bimbo with big ones for all eternity—" She stopped and smiled crookedly at me. "Okay, I'm terrible. But, oh how I've suffered!" She jumped up and swaggered to the wheel-of-fortune, where she stood studying the paintwork. "I mean, look at Harry's goddamn show!" She whirled back to face me. Her exclamations and nerves were beginning to give me a headache. "Nothing but Ruffian bullshit, old Harvard days, chums! I mean, there's a million bucks riding on a bunch of men who won't grow up, trying to relive their youth on a Broadway stage!" She sank her fingers into the straight black hair, raked it back from the sides of her face. "No wonder I'm going crazy! Male bonding is creeping across my tiny self like a fungus!"

One moment she was laughing and then the thunder hammered at the skylight again and her face began to come apart and redefine itself as if she were about to burst into tears.

"Are you all right, Sal?" I went to her, wanting to help.

She turned quickly away, back to the wheel-of-fortune. "Let's see what the gods hold for tonight, a hit or a miss." She sniffled, spun the wheel, planted her feet apart as if challenging the future. It finally clicked to a halt.

Sal read it slowly. "'You will have everything you have hoped for.'"

She looked at me, trying to smile.

"Oh, hell," she said, "everything is such a fucking mess, honey." She began to cry with her head on my shoulder. I put my arm around her, felt the shuddering as Sally clung to me. I cooed to her. Everything would be all right. But as I stroked her shiny black hair, the paintings in the shadows caught my eye and I wasn't sure.

Chapter Ten

Mike Pierce was a perfect gentleman. Always had been, always would be. It was his fate. He was tall and thin with long, straight blond hair, eyes round as cueballs and bluer than an Eskimo's thumb in hitchhiking time. His wire-rimmed glasses were round too. He wore his innocence like a snappy bow tie, which he also favored. A perfect gentleman, maybe that was his trouble. He was a Ruffian, too, of course. Now that he was chairman and chief executive officer of Pierce and Jacoby, Publishers, I still thought of him as a silly, charming, endearing brother substitute. Which made Jack's jealousy all the crazier.

Jack and Mike. How in the world had it worked out that I was coming between them? That was the way my mind was working as the limo crept slowly along Forty-fifth, struggling westward from Times Square in the thick rain, wipers beating, air conditioning blowing a gale, umbrellas glistening wetly like black pieces on a soggy checkerboard. The heat beyond the thick dark windows was relentless. There was just enough breeze to swish the rain beneath umbrellas. The lights of Broadway gleamed back from the puddles. Earthmovers seemed to sink in pools of dirty water like beasts not holding their own in the evolutionary struggle.

Mike turned to me and patted my arm. "I said, you're very silent tonight. Anything wrong?"

"Nerves," I said. "Sorry if I'm somewhere else—"

"Nerves. Opening night? Jack?"

"Both of the above."

"Look, Belinda, don't give this Jack thing a second thought. His state of mind is like tennis elbow. A good long rest and it's gone."

"Tennis elbow? Losing me, our marriage, is like tennis elbow?"

"In principle. Not in degree, of course." He grinned. "Besides, maybe it'll get patched up."

"Pierce," I said. "Sally says he's upset. Really upset—"

"Sal's been known to exaggerate. Harry says she's going through one of her difficult spells—"

"Well, maybe she's got her reasons. I'm not so sure Harry's the one to analyze Sal's behavior. He just may need an analyst of his own."

"No kidding?" He turned his big round blue eyes on me and looked as if he might ring for Jeeves at any moment. "You don't say . . . well, well. I do believe I've touched a nerve."

"Just pay attention to what Sal said. If you see Jack, you'd better duck. A word to the wise."

"While not actually foolhardy, I am tremendously brave. However, I will also keep an eye peeled. All will be well, my girl." He blinked and I shook my head and pecked his cheek.

* * *

At six o'clock the crowd clogged the street in front of the theater, the lucky ones squeezed beneath the marquee with its *Scoundrels All!* logo in Harvard crimson. Everyone was dressed up and soaked through with perspiration and sprays of rain. Everyone seemed to be shouting to be heard, faces were red, laughter too loud. Bright, artificial smiles looked like the direct result of root-canal work. Hope was everywhere. The sight made me wonder if my own opening would be so frantic, so harried, so riddled with fear and tension.

I held on to Mike's arm, smiled faintly at familiar faces, and nodded at snatches of conversation I couldn't quite make out. The whole scene was a kind of orgy of self-consciousness, people with a good deal to lose but trying not to show it, pretending that nothing hung in the balance. Another opening, another show.

Harry's head was visible above the crowd, inclined to the comments of two men I recognized by sight, one a legendary womanizer and show-business angel, the other a famous agent who knew everyone and never missed anything. At a party once years before I'd seen him take a package of chewing gum from the beringed hand of a very young woman with turquoise and purple hair and Jack had whispered to me: "See that? That's how they do it. Cocaine wrapped in five little sticks, like gum." He'd been terribly amused when at first I couldn't believe it.

A large, bulky man in a very crumpled linen jacket with a floppy silk handkerchief dribbling from the pocket looked benignly out across the crowd from Harry's side. He alone seemed serene and somewhat amused by the proceedings, as if his cumbersome size kept him from becoming too frantic. I'd seen him before, I was sure of it, but where? I was watching him without really being aware of it when he caught my eye, seemed to be staring at me, expressionless. Then, as if he'd made a connection that was just eluding me, he slowly grinned and I looked away. Should I have known him? He wasn't the type you'd forget.

Mike was waving at people, chattering away. The show's director stood more or less alone, a tiny bearded man, looking like a child's toy wound right to the breaking point. He glanced at his watch, then disappeared through the stage door. Slowly the crowd began to push through the doors, through the lobby, down the red-carpeted aisles toward their seats. The black uniformed ushers whisked up and down, checking tickets, handing out programs.

My stomach was knotted, my throat dry, and I wondered how Sally was holding up. I couldn't see her in the crowd. Mike Nichols was a few rows ahead of us, standing, still wearing a rain-spotted, belted trench coat, his face amazingly boyish beneath the blondish hair. There was Tony LoBianco, dark and handsome, radiating energy and intensity, as if he were about to spring at someone or something. Doc Simon, shy and tall and scholarly, was talking to a man who looked like a banker, which figured, since the playwright had finally, officially, made all the money in the known universe.

Scanning the faces, I knew I was actually looking for the two I hoped most weren't there. Jack. And Peter Venables. The thought of both men was pushing my stomach off center. Praying I wouldn't turn and come face to face with them, praying for the easy way out. I kept thinking of Jack slamming the phone down and cutting Sally off . . . and Peter's beautiful yellow roses and the note that filled me with dread. *Apologies are in order. I'll make them in person.*

Finally, thank God, the houselights dimmed and I hadn't seen either of them.

Within seconds I felt as if the curtain had gone up on a kind of personal psychodrama, as if I'd stumbled straight off the edge of the real world and was free-falling through time.

Chapter Eleven

For some reason that summer nobody had quite bothered to prepare me for the show I saw. Maybe it was because I had been so wrapped up in my own work, maybe because I hadn't been listening when they tried. Whatever the reason, I wasn't in the least prepared once the actors and actresses had taken the stage, and it was hard to shake free of the disorientation.

With music and dancing and a witty book, *Scoundrels All!* was *our* story, the story of the Ruffians and Sally and me, and it came at me in a series of waves, reviving memories I'd never known were buried in my subconscious, memories of people and events I hadn't been aware of at the time. It was like seeing one of Alex Katz's paintings in a Fifty-seventh Street gallery, a scene of his sharp-featured people at a cocktail party, pretty women with flat, predatory looks, well-dressed men with cuffs showing just the right amount as they climbed one social or business ladder after another . . . like seeing the paintings and slowly realizing that you were there, you'd been one of the people at the party. It was both unnerving and seductive and I felt myself almost guiltily being excited by what I saw, as if it were my own private secret.

I'd been so wrapped up in my own concerns in those days that I'd hardly noticed the world around me. Classes, clothes, time spent with Sally, driving her little red convertible along narrow leaf-blown roads, working in the studio at all hours, painting and losing track of time, then meeting Harry Granger . . . and later Jack Stuart.

Now, astonished, I watched all our lives cavorting across the stage, laughter rippling and applause exploding from the audience. Reality had been softened and given pastel hues as it was filtered through the lens of nostalgia. Like a faint recollection that had almost slipped through the cracks of memory, my past was coming back to life, and we were all up there on the stage. Whatever names they were called, they were us. Jack, the athlete with the handsome face, tossing a football in the air, singing a song about the big game Saturday with Yale . . . Mike wearing white duck slacks and a straw boater at a jaunty angle, dancing an engaging soft-shoe . . . Harry politicking his friends about his idea for a club, an oath of loyalty, and a commitment for a lifetime, all so innocent and idealistic . . . and there were the girls, a blond and a brunette arriving on the stage in a snazzy red convertible.

I was having some difficulty keeping the lines between fact and fiction from blurring. Which was the real Belinda? The one on stage or the nearly middle-aged one watching? Did I really say that? Is that the way I behaved, the way I appeared to others—the self-centered ultra-Wasp who seemed to pluck for herself first one man and then the other?

The love stories wound sinuously, sometimes comically, through the saga of the founding of the club and the conflicts among the members and the crisis of the football game . . . Harry falling in love with the blond, then losing her to Jack, then Harry taking sudden notice of the brunette.

But it was all in a kind of fairyland where the hurts never lasted and everybody finally loved everyone else and everything was all right. . . . Jack was singing alone in a spotlight, wearing a corny letter sweater with the flickering illusion of a pep-rally bonfire through a scrim behind him. Not much like Harvard, really, it might have been an artifact like the Thurber and Nugent play, *The Male Animal*, it all seemed so quaint and long ago. Jack was singing about the blond girl he'd fallen for and how he was going to have to take her away from his best pal Harry and would it wreck their friendship and how could one Scoundrel do such a thing to another?

And, like a sentimental fool, I thanked God for the darkness of the theater. My cheeks were wet with tears.

The show was ending.

They were all onstage for the finale, singing "The Scoundrels' Song," the show's rousing, uplifing theme, now reprised wistfully as the actors seemed to age in a trick of the light, as if in a living preview of things to come, their voices raised in a kind of hope mingled with the beginnings of trepidation. They were setting off into the mysteries of real life thinking they knew it all and were prepared for what lay waiting for them up ahead. They were dancing gently, another old soft-shoe, arms linked, stars in their eyes, their voices growing ever more distant as the lights went down. And then, like phantoms, they were gone.

For maybe ten seconds the theater was utterly still.

And then the applause began, the audience began to stand.

I sat there, my vision blurred. The time warp was affecting me. I felt even more vulnerable than I had in the past few weeks. So much had happened to destroy all the memories and faith and assumed certainties during the last skein of days. The show had plunged me so deeply into the past and that receding dream life and the bittersweet sorrow at the loss of promise and the wrecking of the illusions that had once fueled us all . . .

And yet somewhere I still felt the hope, and that was what was making me cry.

Mike reached down, touched my arm, and I stood up, smiling, applauding.

I felt a tapping on my shoulder, looked around.

Jack was grinning at me. He winked conspiratorially, the old Jack, at the curious and magical use to which our lives had been put. I winked back.

When I turned around again, as the applause was finally dying and the curtain calls had all been taken, he was gone.

Chapter Twelve

I've never been much good at parties. That night was no different. And aside from dreading the noise and the crowd spirit such gatherings generate, I was still fixated on the idea that I simply had to avoid Jack and Peter Venables. I should have gone home, but retreat of that kind, cowardly and precious, was out of the question,

given the occasion. And I had to admit I wanted to see
Sally and give Harry a hug for old times' sake. If only the
show had not—so unexpectedly—torn me up so completely, so emotionally . . .

So I smiled and nodded and managed to drift unobtrusively away from a knot of guests surrounding one of
the performers, wedging myself between an antique ar-
moire with carvings of the North Wind blowing a gale and
a tall date palm shimmering in the gentle breeze from the
terrace. The French windows overlooking the common
garden of the town houses were thrown wide and I felt
little hints of cooling drafts, an occasional fine mist. I
nursed the glass of champagne and hoped no one would
strike up a conversation. I couldn't shake the spell of the
show. I felt as if I still stood with my nose pressed to the
glass, peering through a window into the past. The party
pulsed onward without my participation, like something
from *All About Eve*. I felt like a stranger, existing more in
the long-ago world of the play than a grown-up woman
who belonged at the revels.

Harry and Sally Granger lived in a remarkably lavish
brownstone on the north side of Forty-seventh between
Second and Third, that tiny enclave known to true New
Yorkers as Turtle Bay. Katharine Hepburn had bought her
house as a young actress; Ruth Gordon, Garson Kanin,
Stephen Sondheim . . . all had been neighbors of the
Grangers. The house had belonged to Sally's parents for
many years, she had grown up there, and it was subsequently bestowed on Harry and her when Mom and Dad
retired to their home at Sag Harbor and a villa in the hills
overlooking the Mediterranean. Watching the rain fall on
the lush, dark garden, I remembered how Sal always con-
tended that her father insisted on dwellings overlooking
something "because he's so appallingly abbreviated him-

self." The old gentleman had never exceeded five-feet-three, but all the money had somehow made him seem taller.

The set designer couldn't have done anything more perfect, more glittering for the opening-night party. Staircases curved gracefully to a long balcony where a small combo played Gershwin and Vernon Duke and Sondheim—and, sporadically, the score from *Scoundrels All!* The chandeliers hung like gigantic tiaras on ropes of diamonds. Candles glowed everywhere, mesmerizing, casting a roseate glow. There was caviar, cold poached salmon in a green sauce, sliced roast beef and chicken, cold pasta alla putanesca, the platters arranged on vast buffets, with sleek waiters and waitresses moving among the guests, deftly avoiding the sudden sweeping gestures of excitement, hauling silver trays the size of hubcaps. I had to smile at the spectacle. Beside me, through the doors to the awninged terrace, the rain bounced like a billion triphammers and hung in gauzy sheets above the quiet fountain in the garden, on the flagstones, beneath the heavy drooping trees.

The rooms were full of a strange mixture of friends, people I'd seen mainly on television and in the newspapers, some not quite identifiable faces from long ago that sent distant bells pealing, and strangers. The actors and actresses from the show mingled happily, soaking up praise. The backers were drinking determinedly, speaking softly, shrugging, waiting tensely for the first television critics to pass judgment.

Harvard friends of Harry's, gathered painstakingly together for the occasion, tried to act as if they'd all seen each other yesterday, and some of them probably had, in Wall Street and in Park Avenue law offices. Across the long room I noticed the Harvard professor who had been something of a gray eminence in the days when Harry was rounding up the Ruffians and giving them their identity. But I had forgotten his name, of course. Then I saw that he was talking to the large, heavyset man in the linen jacket whom I'd caught staring at me in the street outside the theater. Once again, as if there was something magnetizing us, I saw him turn slowly to look at me over the crowd between. Again he smiled at me, then turned back to the professor.

Who was he? I bit a thumbnail and something came back to me. He'd been at the theater the day I went to see Harry. He'd watched me walking up the aisle . . . Why did he keep smiling at me, as if he knew something I didn't? Was he supercilious or one of the friendlies? Or was I suspicious of anyone and everyone in the wake of Jack wanting to kill me and Harry betraying Sally and Peter Venables betraying me and Jack . . . and then those damn yellow roses? But, no, those must be Venables' peace offering. Or had Sally been right? Maybe they were Jack's apology. And where had he gone after the show? Why hadn't he spoken to me before if he'd spent the evening sitting behind me—behind *us*, Mike and me, which was maybe the answer to that particular question.

God, I was fed up with all the irritating, abrasive little questions! I exchanged my empty glass for a full one as a silver tray floated past.

On the terrace, beneath the awning, the heat engulfed me, but I welcomed the scent of the flowers in the heavy planters and the wet earth and the sound of the steady rain. It rattled on the awning, dripped from the fringe. And I heard a voice behind me.

"Well, Belinda, you look beautiful and sad all by yourself out here." His voice was soft and deep, somehow reassuring, but I didn't know who he was. "But I could be wrong about the sad part." The big rumpled man in the linen jacket. He still wore the bemused smile. And his eyes caught mine again, didn't skitter away like other people's.

"I'm sure you could," I said, "but probably not this time." I frowned at his widening smile. "But I didn't need you to tell me."

"Well, try to find it in your heart to forgive me." He leaned against the railing with his back to the rain. "I'm a professional observer, a constant fault and . . . well, I'd hate to get off on the wrong foot with you after all these years."

"Look, you seem to know me and I guess I'm just not making the right connections. I don't mean to be rude . . ." I shook my head, gave a little beseeching look. His hair was receding, it was brushed back in wings over his ears, curled over his collar. His foulard tie had managed to skew off to one side. His French-blue shirt had a collar point that had struck off on its own. Something was bulging in one of his jacket pockets. All the other men wore formal first-night clothes.

"Maybe it'll come to you. Someone from the past."

"Don't be a jerk, okay?"

He laughed at me. "Welles," he said. "Hacker Welles."

I felt myself blushing with embarrassment. "Hacker! Oh, my God, what a fool—you wrote the show! Oh, Hack, really—"

"It's good to see you, Belinda."

"Oh, I feel like such an idiot! Please forgive me, but it has been an awfully long time, hasn't it? If you knew me, you'd know that while I habitually can't place the face and

73

I can never, ever remember the name . . . I'm babbling. Shut up, Belinda!"

"Listen, I was the least memorable of the Ruffians. And I've been on the West Coast for a long time. And I've changed. Used to be a lot more hair and rather less of me. Not much for a girl like you to remember."

"Well . . . Hacker Welles." I kept thinking about his blue eyes, how watchful they were. His face was broad, candid, open. He seemed so supremely at ease, observing me from behind the barricade of his writing. "I feel funny, as if you've spent a lot of time looking inside me, seeing how the machinery works . . ."

He laughed again at that.

"It's the play, of course, seeing how you portrayed me—"

"I don't really know much about you. Your type, maybe, but not you. Of all the characters, you were the hardest to write. So I was stuck with the way I perceived you way back then. And you were pretty elusive, Belinda."

"Elusive? Hardly."

"Even now, I can't tell if you're honest and ingenuous, or if you're playing some kind of game with me. That's what I had to deal with when I was writing the blond—but listen, I don't mean to get into all this. I saw you the other day at the theater and then tonight. I hate these nervous-breakdown parties but I hoped I might see you here. So what's going on with you and Jack? Harry says there are some problems—"

"As usual, Harry's right, but I really don't want to talk about that. What did you mean, 'elusive'?"

"I used to watch you. I took a long time to make up my mind about you. I guess maybe I never did." He grinned as if we were sharing a secret of the past together. "For three years, while you were hardly aware I even existed, I watched you and your boyfriends, my two buddies. Were you just a gorgeous airhead Wasp who never gave away any feelings—"

"Good God!"

"Or did that kind of sad expression and that level stare, that sort of somber face, hide something wonderful and sensitive . . . which might lead to your appreciating one such as me? Well, boyish fantasies being what they are . . ." He shrugged, eyes twinkling. As if the thought were so amusing and irrelevant now that we were adults that it was laughable.

"Are you sure we're talking about me?"

"I never did get up the nerve to find out what you were really like. I heard about you from Harry and then Jack, and then, just like the play, we all sort of danced off into real life, where I suppose most of us got our asses handed to us."

I felt myself relaxing for the first time in days, weeks. He was so burly, slouching, rumpled, and the talk flowed so easily for both of us. I kept prodding him with questions and listened while he told me about the writing of the play and how Harry had urged him to develop it as a musical, take a shot at writing some lyrics. I listened as he told me how he'd set about working his way through the forests of memory in search of a story, something that would make a plot. "That's the problem with adapting something from life. The stories never hang together. Anyway, I did the best I could." He shrugged as if he weren't at all sure he gave a damn what anyone else thought. "Now that you've heard all my excuses, give me your reaction to the show—the unvarnished truth, so long as you adhere to Joseph Conrad's dictum."

"Which is?"

"He was eager to entertain all criticism so long as it was unqualified praise. What did you think, Belinda?"

I waited a long time, looking at the rain, the slick flowers in their pots. "It made me sad. That's why I was out here by myself when you found me."

He nodded. "Yeah. Well, it makes me sad, too, I guess."

I plunged onward. "And it made me nervous, seeing our past reinterpreted that way. I don't suppose people actually look at their lives quite that analytically."

"But you didn't take offense?"

"Oh, no . . ." I felt myself blushing again. "I thought it was wonderful."

"You didn't think you were portrayed too coldly?"

"I hadn't thought . . . No, I must not have. She was a bit of a bitch, I suppose. Maybe that's what made me nervous."

"Think how I got to feeling, having to spend a year going back, living those days all over again." He was looking into my eyes as if they were the vaults of those days, where the secrets were locked away. "There we were in the sixties, up to our necks in our own privileged innocence, somehow managing to ignore Vietnam and assassinations and civil rights. Where were we, our little group, when everybody else was off marching and demonstrating and burning draft cards and bras? You know what I did? I made my own protest. I burned my library card. And I lived it all again and I kept asking myself, why were we so bloody insulated? Did we simply not want to be serious people? Were we just too wrapped up in ourselves?"

"And what did you decide?"

76

"I never really did. But somehow we all managed to trivialize one of the great and tragic eras of our history. We were masters of self-indulgence. We were all, in our own ways, unindicted co-conspirators. An idea whose time had not quite come but was lurking just ahead, around the next bend. We were all guilty parties, Belinda, we just never got caught."

I was surprised by the sorrow in his blue eyes, which had been so light and impish and confident only moments before.

"Or did we?" I asked.

Eventually, after another glass of champagne, he thanked me for the use of my life in his play. "I'm going to miss you, Belinda." He shook my hand.

He drifted away and later I saw him with a pretty girl from the show who came and took him away from some group, claiming him with an air of propriety. I wondered what the girl was to him, was he sleeping with her? She looked to be twenty-one or twenty-two.

Alone again, not wanting to go back inside to join the party, I tried to put him out of my mind. Odd, I hadn't remembered him at once, but the fact was—like Peter Venables—he seemed a virtually new and unknown person to me. How had I ever gotten so disconnected from people I'd once known?

There had been something about Hacker Welles tonight. Maybe his air of unconcern, his confidence at such a tense moment waiting for the reviews—something about him both attracted me and vaguely frightened me. He acted as if he had once seen something so bad that it had bleached away fear of anything like an opening night.

And he had been watching me. Long ago as well as now. Thinking about me, every day for a long time. He'd miss me, he said. I was mindlessly pleased by that, but there was also something out of kilter, too, if I could just pin it down.

Did he still find me an airhead?

Did he know I painted?

But then, I wouldn't be seeing him again, so why should I care what he thought of me?

The fact was, however, that I did.

Chapter Thirteen

The music cascaded like tinsel from the balcony, sprinkling the irresistible high spirits that come to life when things seem to have gone so well. But there was also the continuing cutting edge of forced hilarity, people dancing in the shadow of the sword. In this case, the critics. All we could do was wait.

I was staring across the room at the remarkably vibrant blond girl with Hacker Welles. She had been me in the show. What had Welles called her in the play? Jill? Yes, Jill. The girl was, of course, an actress, not a college girl wrapped up in her own tiny, out-of-proportion world as I had been. I marveled at how much further along life's road this young actress had come that I at the same age. I almost introduced myself to her when I glimpsed her standing alone for a moment. Hello, I'm the original of the character you played tonight. . . . No, it was hopeless, I'd sound like a moron. I just couldn't get into the idea and the spirit of the party.

"Belinda, correct me if I'm wrong, but I don't believe we've met since Harry and Sally's wedding. Sag Harbor, all those yellow-and-white-striped tents, a windy day . . . I'm Tony Chalmers." He was short and round, but his hair, going a bit gray, was still worn in a frizzy halo—an Afro, people had called it then, back in the archaeological era known as the sixties. He'd been a tutor or a young instructor and Harry had latched on to him, made him a pal, declared him faculty adviser to the Ruffians and an honorary member.

"I believe you're right," I said, remembering how he'd always been a calming, thoughtful presence when the Ruffians had thrown a party in Harry and Jack's room on the top floor of Eliot House, overlooking Memorial Drive. "It's been far too long—"

"Well, college connections sometimes fade pretty quickly. Though not Harry's, God knows. He got me back into the old Ruffian lore." Chalmers puffed at a short, chipped black briar. "Asked me—told me, is more like it—to give Welles a hand, memory work. It was an interesting experience, sifting through the sands of time, trying to fit the bits back together. How did you like Hacker's handiwork?"

I told him I'd loved it, adding that it had made me feel my age, and a little sad.

He nodded. "Bound to have that effect, I suppose." He sucked on the pipe, tamped a finger into the bowl. "Nostalgia. It's funny, when Harry brought up the idea of a show based on the Ruffians, I had my doubts. I always had a funny feeling about the club . . ."

"Really? It seemed so innocent."

He squinted at me as if wondering how much he dared confide in me. Men at their little secrets, making rules for their little games.

"No, no, I guess there wasn't anything out of line." He puffed again. He'd taken on some professorial habits which made him seem older, but he couldn't have been fifty yet. "Sometimes, though, men and boys, they can get too close, share too many confidences and trust each other too much . . . sounds contradictory, I know, that's what a club like Harry's is supposed to do. But when you have a bunch of guys so close, you're also running a real risk—there might be a misunderstanding, a difference of opinion—and pow! You've got a problem. These were bright, volatile guys. I was always afraid the top might just come blowing off one day . . ." He bobbed his head, scowled, shrugged, and burst into a wide grin. "But, lo, I need not have worried. Nothing violent, nothing nasty, and it's a sweet, happy little show . . . sigh of relief, standing bravos."

As I listened to him run through some Ruffian reminiscences, I remembered what Jack had once told me about Chalmers. "He's the only man in the world," Jack had said, "who knows more about the Ruffians than we do ourselves. He knows more, you see, because we all went to him with problems we couldn't take to each other. A professional people collector, old Tony."

Finally the professor ran down, drifted away in a cloud of pungent smoke, leaving me alone. Thank God, he hadn't asked me about Jack. Perhaps he already knew how things had turned out.

Suddenly I wanted more than anything else to be alone. I found a bottle of champagne, half-full, grabbed it, and went off down the hall toward the study. The door was ajar, and I closed it behind me. A breeze moved the draperies, the rain drummed outside. In a corner a small television glowed with a baseball game, the sound turned down. The furniture was heavy leather, a large desk, stacks of bound playscripts, a couple of framed theatrical posters on the wall, a green-shaded student's lamp.

I sank like a stone onto the island of a couch, resting my chin on my arm across the back, watching the ballplayers in white dashing against the dark green of real grass in some ballpark somewhere. It was all so clear-cut. You hit the ball, you ran, you were safe or out, you scored or you didn't, you won or you lost. Jack had once told me that baseball was the only game in which you scored when the ball was somewhere else. Jack loved baseball and hated tennis. "What kind of game is that?" he would say contemptuously. "You get penalized if you hit the ball too far—ridiculous!"

I was crying again, watching as the batter swung and drove the ball high into the night sky, up past the light standards, then the tiny comet of white, plummeting downward, the crowd on its feet, mouths open, all in silence, the outfielder leaping at the fence as the comet disappeared beyond his reach . . .

Tears on my cheeks, like a befuddled child, I watched the mute crowd screaming. With no sound, they might have been painted by Munch, an army of pain and despair beating their palms, crying out in the night, mouths caverns of agony. . . . I knew it was a ballgame, I could see it, but the lurking afterimage was one of agony, as if the awful reality clung like a beast to the back of illusion.

The door opened and there was Sally through the blur of tear-stuck lashes. She took a tissue from a box in the desk and handed it to me. "Come on, dry off. No reason to cry, you don't have a penny in this show." I giggled helplessly, felt the tears gush again, like a nosebleed that wouldn't quite give up. Sally knelt on the couch beside me, softly patting my shoulder. "It's okay, it's all going to be all right . . . now, what's the matter, tell Sal . . ."

"It didn't turn out right," I whispered, "that's all. Not the way it was supposed to. Jack's a mess and Harry has a girlfriend and we don't have the kids we thought we'd have . . . and what the hell ever happened to the little red car?" I sniffed and rubbed my nose. "I *loved* that car—oh, the hell with it!"

"Are you just the slightest bit sloshed, my dear?"

"I'd better be. Otherwise I'm having a nervous breakdown."

"You? Not exactly nervous-breakdown material!"

"The point is, it's not like the play, Sal. We didn't all just kiss and make up and dance off into the wings singing a pretty song. That's the way it was *supposed* to be, but the reality is all shot to hell!" I swallowed hard, turned to look into Sally's dark eyes, into the face I knew as well as my own. "It's the Hope Gap, don't you see? The gap between all our hopes and the realities . . . none of the other gaps matter, the gender gap and the missile gap, forget 'em, it's the Hope Gap that gets us where we live. . . . Ah, Sally, what does it all mean?"

"I'm the wrong person to ask," Sally said. "I've always thought that as long as I could turn to my Belinda I could be sure it all made sense. You were the one on top of things, with your fortune cookies and the big wheel that told the future." After a while she said: "And anyway, how do you know it's not all going to turn out all right? It's not over yet. We're still in the middle of the game. Harry always says that things turn out just fine for the Ruffians— and we're sort of the ladies' chapter." She lit a cigarette. Her hand was shaking and she steadied it on her knee.

"Speaking of Ruffians, I see that Hacker Welles was making his presence felt on the terrace."

"Oh, God, I felt like a fool. I didn't remember him, he had to tell me who he was—"

"And? That used up ten seconds—"

"And he was very nice. We talked about the show."

"He's been in LA for years, worked on TV shows, worked on some movies. Godawful marriage to some TV star, I forget who. She was running around on the side, then dumped him for a guy with a production company, Harry told me—I've probably got it all wrong."

"Well, I'll never see him again, anyway."

Sally went on, smiling faintly. "I always found Hacker absolutely impenetrable. Opaque. Oh, brainy and so on, always watching and breathing through his mouth—"

"I'm glad I don't remember that!"

"Adenoids. Must've had 'em fixed. But he was always holding himself back, above the battle. Made me wonder who the hell he thought he was, anyway. But Harry says the son of a bitch can write—that's a quote—and I guess he can. I mean, it was a good show, wasn't it?"

"Oh, Sally, I'm so happy for you and Harry—it was a lot better than just good. Welles is a really fine writer, I think."

"Funny, you're already in his corner."

She was smiling at me again and I said: "What does that mean? Funny how?"

"Oh, Harry and I were talking about him the other day—one of our few conversations lately, actually—and Harry just said sort of casually that good old Hack always had the world's biggest crush on Belinda! Well, it was news to me . . . and it turns out you didn't even know who he was! But the fact is, he followed you onto the terrace and he looked like he was on the trail—"

"Even if he did have a crush on me, that was almost twenty years ago, Sal." I was becoming more than a little sick of this theme.

"So? Maybe he's getting around to making his move twenty years later. He's a deep one, our Hacker!"

Harry found us still sitting together in the study. He was grinning, spirits holding up under pressure. "What gives? The two prettiest girls at the party hiding from the Ruffians? Can't have that."

"Belinda was feeling a little down about Jack—"

"Oh, Belle," he said, putting his huge hands on my shoulders, squeezing. "Don't you worry about Jack. He's a Ruffian, we stick together when the going gets tough. Support system." He gave me a little shake and everything was supposed to be fine. "Listen, it's time for the TV reviews. Come on out, I've got video recorders going so we won't miss any."

"We can watch them in here," Sally said.

Harry gave her a questioning look, said, "Okay, I'll stay with you two." He poured us all fresh champagne and turned up the sound.

The critic on Channel Two was smiling.

"Pack up all your cares and woe," he said, "here we go, back to Harvard in the sixties, and it's a trip to never-never-land, I promise you. Through the looking glass to a place I for one have never been—this isn't the sixties *I* lived through, folks—but let me be the first to tell you, you're gonna love it! A new show opened tonight, it's called *Scoundrels All!* and it's bound to be good for what ails you. It's an old-fashioned kind of comedy reminiscent of George Axelrod, with some lovely, tuneful, occasionally bittersweet songs thrown in, all about a group of chums who form a club—doesn't sound like much, but it's about innocence and friendship and falling in love and solving your problems and getting ready to face real life later, because real life never intrudes on this fairy tale. These characters are as out of step with their time in history as possible, as remote from us as Bertie and Jeeves, and now on a hot summer night twenty years later they couldn't be more welcome. *Scoundrels All!* was written by Hacker Welles, directed by Lou Silvano, and produced by Harry Granger, starring a gaggle of wonderfully talented, attractive young actors and actresses—it has the look of a winner all over it. Why? Dare I say it? Because Escape has become fashionable again and who needs Relevance? What is relevant here is that we can all take a look at youth and innocence and remember for once the way it might have been in a world without the realities that weighed so heavily on us all."

We were staring dumbly at one another, smiles spreading slowly, when the study door burst open. A man wearing a top hat at a very jaunty angle came in. "Harry, it's unanimous! This thing's gonna run forever!" He then let out an altogether shattering war whoop and in the distance the band began to play the music from the show.

Harry put his arms around us, pulled us close to him. I heard him say: "Remember this moment, ladies. We may never be so happy again."

He hugged us for a long time, as if he didn't want to let go.

Chapter Fourteen

The reviews ended the suspense, turned the party loose, raised the decibel level, and erased the smudges of fear. Sometime after we left the study Harry told me that what I needed was a dance and led me to the huge circular foyer below the balcony where the lights were low and the music loud. He threw himself into his own eccentric dance and I laughed as he clapped his hands and shouted out quotes from the reviews, punctuating them with heel-stomping of the flamenco style. He was so happy, so relieved, and I forgave him all his sins, wondering if Sally did, wondering if there was a woman he loved and where she was tonight while he celebrated with his wife.

While I danced a slow one with Mike, I watched Sally dancing with Harry, her face sober while he laughed and hugged her. Impulsively he kissed her and she flung her arms around him, almost desperately, holding on for dear life. I felt a flood of warmth toward them, felt like congratulating them on having gotten to where they were on this night of nights.

Mike was nuzzling my ear, telling me that he really was rather charlied, what with all the champers, his Bertie Wooster face with its steamed-over spectacles so dear. I told him he was just about the cutest thing around and he went smiling to search Blandings Castle for more bubbly. I stayed in the shadows, praying that I could make my getaway before either Jack or Peter showed up. I couldn't imagine where they were but that was irrelevant. I spotted Hacker Welles in a group with the blond actress and he saw me, caught me before I could look away. Watching each other had become a self-conscious joke. He drifted my way.

"Belinda," he said, finishing off a celery stick. "So good to see you again,"

"The reviews were wonderful. Why aren't you making a fool of yourself?"

"Oh, I am, in my own quiet way."

"You are?"

"Oh, sure. Keep it all inside, though. But, believe me, I'm making a tremendous fool of myself."

"Tell me, how did you ever get to be such a great fool?"

"Gosh, Belinda. Early to bed, early to rise, I guess."

I felt my laughter explode unexpectedly, champagne splashing over my hand.

"You're making quite a mess of yourself there."

"So, that was the third time I've caught you watching me tonight. I'd say you're still watching me from afar, like the old days you remember so well."

"Impossible! You really think so?"

"Definitely. Still trying to make up your mind about me. You're very slow."

"Oh, all right, so I've been watching you. And I am still trying to make up my mind. I need a long time."

"So it would seem."

I coerced him into dancing with me.

He held me firmly and moved no more than was absolutely necessary. He seemed not to be giving any of it a thought. I told him I was a painter, that I was having a show. He whispered in my ear that being able to daub paint on a canvas didn't prove that I wasn't an airhead. I gently kicked his shin. He told me that voilence is always the last resort of the intellectually bankrupt. I kicked his other shin. He said he was reconsidering. I found myself wondering if just possibly I could break through his shell of amused self-protection. What had that wife of his done to him? *Early to bed, early to rise.* He was funny. I had to give him that.

We were suddenly distracted by a commotion in the front hallway. Raised voices. Exclamations of welcome. Harry and Mike appeared from the hallway, beaming, flanking a latecomer.

"Well, I'll be damned," Hacker said. "Another Ruffian—you remember Peter . . .

"I suppose," I said.

Hacker laughed. "What a memory! Peter Venables. He and I had a real bond back then. We both thought you were this unattainable knockout and we were both too scared of you to—"

He saw me frowning.

"Come on," he said, pulling me along, bearing down on the man I'd hoped I'd never have to see again. "And if you don't remember him, don't tell him. He'd be crushed. Tender blossom, Peter Venables. . . ."

The fun I'd been having with Hacker Welles faded as the tendrils of the past squirmed out of the darkness. Talking to him had made me forget the show, Jack, Venables, Sally's unhappiness, the works. Now, watching him go to greet Venables, grab him in a mighty bear hug, something bothered me and I felt petty. It was the Ruffians. It was the fact that Hacker had left me to go engulf Peter Venables. It was petty, but the flicker of resentment was real. I had to admit it. Hacker didn't know how Venables had behaved with me the other night. I couldn't blame Hacker. But somewhere inside me, I did. I couldn't be sure his knowing would have made any difference in his feelings toward another Ruffian. And I hated that.

"Boys will be boys," Sally said, standing beside me. "Peter Venables. He was such a sweet boy and so handsome." I flinched inwardly, wished I could tell her the truth. "Do you remember him? No, of course not. Memory like a sieve. But he has been a breath of fresh air to have staying here. Come on, let's go be sociable."

And we were included in the group, Venables kissing Sally's cheek, then hesitating when he turned to me. "Well, my, my . . . Belinda."

"Hello, Peter." It was a struggle not to shrink away from him. He looked so sweet, so innocent, more boyish even than Mike.

"You're a sight for sore eyes," he said.

"So much for a Harvard education," Mike said. "I don't believe I've ever actually heard anyone say that before."

"Well, it's true," Venables said. He took my hand and smiled, as if to remind me of what had happened, winked. I ignored him, pulled unobtrusively away. I listened to the chatter, watching Welles, then Sally, then Venables, wishing to God I had never been told how Hacker and Venables had mooned over their idea of me eighteen years ago.

I was yawning, trying to eat, watching the steady rain, trying not to think about Venables, when he found me. His smile was quick, darting, gone almost before it was there, like a nervous tic.

"Seems like kismet," he said, "here we are again. An omen. I've been thinking how much I enjoyed our evening—"

"Then you're one sick and sorry bastard," I said.

He smiled again. "Why carry a grudge? Life's way too short. I want to see you again, Belinda. I *will* see you. I've been so patient. And I meant no harm—"

"You really are crazy," I said. "You actually frighten me."

"Fear and excitement go together."

"Good-bye," I said, but he took my arm. It no doubt appeared casual, but it hurt.

"If you don't mind my saying so," he went on calmly, with the certainty and reason of the true obsessive, "I never thought you and Jack—much as I love the guy— were absolutely meant for each other. Just an opinion, mind."

I bristled like a cat being rubbed the wrong way. "Since I hardly know you, I don't quite see how you could have formed any opinion at all. Opinions are remarkably cheap, in any case."

"You are such a bitch," he said. So quiet. "You're remote. I *do* like that."

"Listen Peter, I'm really very tired. I'm tired of you and I'm tired of playing your very childish game. It's time to go home."

He looked at me appraisingly. I felt naked. He leaned forward and began talking to me again. I blotted out the words.

I don't know how long Jack had been at the party. I don't know how long he'd been watching me. Long enough, as it turned out.

The conversation with Venables had topped off the evening, dropping me directly down Alice's rabbit hole. I felt weary in every bone, just wanted to get back to the loft and be alone with my paintings.

I was looking for Mike over Venables' shoulder when I heard voices raised, not in the happy manner of those greeting Venables but in anger and frustration. Something was bubbling over and I thought at once of Tony Chalmers' fear that someday the top would come off the Ruffians. A man's voice, obstreperous, drunk, was coming from the front hallway and the band was playing a Gershwin tune. The man was laughing, then shouting at some unfortunate to get the hell out of the way, then demanding at the top of his lungs, "Unhand me, you cur!"

I knew the voice and the mood all too well.

It was Jack and I was shrinking away from the fact, trying to make myself small. First Venables, now Jack in one of his states.

He came in yelling at somebody, heads turning his way, the music lilting onward. "He loves, and she loves . . . birds love, and bees love, and whispering trees love, and that's what we should do . . ."

He came on, bearing down on us. Venables stood stock-still, not quite comprehending what was going on with Jack.

Jack, face flushed and sweating, pushed him with his chest, tottering himself, and putting his hand on Venables' shoulder to steady himself.

Venables was laughing in a comradely way. "You seem to have tied one on, old boy!" He turned to the waiter. "More champagne for Jack Stuart!"

Jack kept crowding him backward toward the buffet. He was ignoring me for the moment. I heard Peter's laughter die an unpleasant death. "Come on, Jack, enough's enough. Relax."

The band played and the singer sang.

I was trapped in a bizarre self-propelled bad dream from which I couldn't wake. Dancers were stopping to look at Jack shoving Peter. His chiseled face was red and distorted with drink and anger, his eyes were dulled with the pain eating at him from within, and he shoved harder, Peter bumping heavily into the table. Glasses shattered. Peter tried to slide away and somehow avoid the inevitable.

It was hopeless.

Jack feinted with a left and sucker-punched him with a right, shouting all the time, "She's still my wife, you bastard! My wife, my wife!"

Peter took the blow, stood there holding his hand to his face, swabbing blood from his nose. A pink bubble clung to one nostril.

Suddenly he burst into laughter at the absurdity of it, held out an open hand to fend off his attacker.

The laughter fueled Jack. He came at him again, swinging wildly as the onlookers gaped. And from nowhere Hacker's arms encircled Jack from behind, yanked him backward. Jack slipped, they both tumbled to the marble foyer floor. Mike was immediately bending over to help them up. Jack bellowed, "Get away, let me at that prick . . . stay outta this, Hack . . . shit, help me up . . ."

I watched them haul Jack to his feet, watched them take him down the hallway, saw the collapse of his face as he passed me, as if the keystone had been removed. I heard a voice at my side.

"Some things never change. We're still fighting over you, Belinda."

It was Peter Venables. He was dabbing at the blood with a white handkerchief. Smiling at me.

Chapter Fifteen

It really couldn't have been worse.

The band had fizzled to a stop, musicians peering over the balcony railing relishing the idiocies of the rich. Everyone stood goggle-eyed and then exploded into bright, frantic conversation, as if they could by the sheer volume of their words bury the unsightly event. It didn't work. No, I thought as I followed the combatants and their seconds down the hallway, it couldn't have been worse.

Peter Venables came out of the study and found me waiting. The blood had been washed away. I stared at him.

"Got what was coming to me, is that what you're thinking? Well, maybe . . . but Jack was being thick as two planks, surely. Drunk is drunk, I don't hold it against him, but still . . . Look, Belinda, I'm drenched with blood and I think there may be something amiss with my nose. Harry said he'd like to talk with you and Jack. And Hacker and Mike say they'll drag me off for a rubdown and a nightcap—"

"Why tell me about it? Just go. Just get away from me—"

"That's my Belinda. I wonder, though. I don't like leaving you with Jack, the mood he's in—"

"I can handle Jack! What is it with you? Just get out of my life—for God's sake!"

"Come on," he laughed, "ease up. And go easy on Jack—"

"Peter, why not just give me a break? You and the other Ruffians can stick up for each other all you want, but I don't have to, not after the way you and Jack have distinguished yourselves tonight. Just watch my lips . . . leave me alone! Don't you hear me?"

Welles and Mike came out of the study and claimed Venables. Mike kissed my cheek. "Harry says he wants to talk to you. I'll wait—"

"No, really," I said, "it's all right. You guys go ahead. I'll be fine. Please, go ahead. I've got to see Jack."

"Come on, laddie," Welles said, tugging Mike away.

The three of them headed off down the hallway. Sally was saying good night in the foyer, guests were filing out. I felt as if I'd been at the party for a week. Venables and his refusal to simply leave me alone scared me. Jack almost seemed a welcome refuge. I felt as if I'd finally fallen off the merry-go-round.

Jack sat at the end of the couch, hunched forward, his elbows on his knees, his head hung down, supported in his palms. A mug of coffee steamed on the end table. His head bobbed periodically. He might have been crying, I couldn't tell. I sat staring into space. Sally smoked vigorously, diamonds shining like little campfires in a dark night. Harry lit a cigar, got up from behind the desk to look at the rain spattering the terrace. He pulled at the black bow tie, let it tumble loose, and turned back to face us.

"Come on, Jack, it's not as bad as all that. You might have done your number too late, when the audience had left."

Jack looked up and took a deep breath. "Faultless timing. Always count on Jack." He drank some coffee, held it in his mouth, chewing it. The redness had gone from his face, which looked defeated now, pallid with a blue tinge.

"Stop feeling sorry for yourself," I said.

Sally spoke up: "Don't rub it in. He knows—"

"Don't tell me what to do, Sal."

"Oops, sorry. You know what I mean, though—"

"No, Sal, she's right," Jack said. "I should be apologizing. Hell, I *am* apologizing. To all of you." He looked sheepishly in my direction. "You must wonder how many apologies I have in me. Well, lots. I seem to need 'em."

He had always been able to turn me around effortlessly, at least until lately. Until I'd finally had enough. Now I was backsliding. His hands were shaking and I took them in mine, held them tight. "So you had too much to drink . . ."

He squeezed my fingers, looked at me like a pet expecting to be socked with a rolled-up newspaper. "It was the show. Harry, this goddamn show really lit up my scoreboard. I was in shock when I left the theater. The past just sort of steamrollered me. The center wouldn't hold, as Mr. Yeats would say. Mine sure as hell didn't, anyway." He shrugged. "I just couldn't bear all those metaphors onstage and all the faces of my fellow Ruffians in the audience. I mean, why am I the only screw-up? So I went to Joe Allen's and sat at the bar sopping up Bushmill's and wondering if I just might not be better off dead—no, I'm not being melodramatic. I'm serious. What have I got to look forward to? Stupid Greer School, screwed up everything with Belinda . . ." He bit his lip, clamped his jaw shut. His voice was breaking. He was fighting for control. And all I could think of was that old shotgun in his apartment. . . .

Harry cleared his throat, made a dismissive sweep with his cigar. "That's just the Bushmill's talking. Look, everybody, it's been a wonderful night. We've all bought a tiny piece of immortality. We got to see a bit of our lives preserved under glass—not many people do. None of us is immune to the emotional effect of this show . . . we're all bound to be shaken up by it. Hell, it's like your first love, right? You never quite get over your first love, do you? Tonight it was like running into her again, only she's unchanged, still young and beautiful . . . and we've put on a few years. So, we get that bittersweet jolt . . . a tear or two. And the need for a couple of extra drinks."

Sally lit another cigarette impatiently, dropped the lighter on the desk. It clattered in the stillness.

"Belinda was my first love," Jack said to no one. Just talking in the night.

"Oh, God! Let's drop first loves!" Sally looked from face to face, then laughed nervously. "We're all wrecked. Let's call it a night."

"Not yet, my dearest," Harry said through a haze of smoke. "It's a great night and we're not going to end on a sour note. We four go back a long way, we've been through thick and thin together. Agree?"

"Sure, sure," Sally snapped.

"Well, it *matters*, wife o' mine. We're a part of each other's past and present. Intertwined. Like fingers laced together. We're not going to let tonight end badly. Listen to me—never forget how much we've all loved each other. And for how long."

Jack looked up from the carpet, into my eyes.

"Now," Harry said, everything about him changing, the moment past, "now, let's watch all these wonderful reviews again!"

Drained, we watched him slip the cassette into the machine and push the buttons.

Sure enough, the Ruffians were a hit.

Jack insisted on taking me back to the loft.

"It's the least I can do. And I'll behave. I promise." He was fearfully sober, the way shock and shame blast away at booze. It was one o'clock and we waited for a taxi, tires hissing on the wet pavement. It was still raining lightly and the heat was undiminished.

"I've got to get myself under control," he said. "I know that. But it would be easier with your help, kid. That's all I'm saying."

It wasn't a conversation I wanted to have. It was too laden with all the traps a mariage holds, at least a marriage in very bad trouble.

He settled himself in the far corner of the back of the taxi. Rain streaked the windows, the wipers beating. The cabdriver was playing his radio, singing along under his breath. . . ."

"Harry was right. I still love you, kid." My eyes were closed. I heard Jack's voice, which had lost its pleading quality and was almost toneless. It seemed far away. He might have been on Neptune. "He was right about loving each other. It's been such a long time. I know you love me . . . you must. You'll always love me."

I didn't open my eyes. I didn't want to look at my husband. I wanted to stay disengaged. I didn't love anybody.

We went up in the clanking elevator, wordless. My head was beginning to ache. Jack wiped rain and sweat from his face. I hadn't wanted him to come upstairs but there was no fight left in me. I flicked the light switch, turned on the fan, threw the windows all the way open.

In the bathroom I patted my face dry on a thick towel and took four aspirin. When I came out he was standing by the wheel-of-fortune, watching it spin. "I miss this thing," he said. "It always seemed to give me good news."

The yellow roses on the worktable had opened like perfect paper flowers. The card lay beside them.

"I want to go to sleep, Jack."

"Who sent these?"

"I don't know. It doesn't matter."

His eyes narrowed. "What do you mean? There's a card right here—"

"Would you just leave it? Please? I don't know who sent them!"

He picked up the card and read it. "What the hell is this? Who? Come on, *who*?"

"Jack! Please!"

"For Christ's sake, what's the point in lying to me? You must know who they're from—"

"Please, no scene. Just go, Jack."

"What do you think I am, Belinda? An idiot? I know you're fucking Mike! I know it . . . and I saw Welles and that goddamn Venables drooling all over you tonight. I wasn't arriving when I hit Venables, I was leaving, I saw you dancing with Hack, he wanted you then and there and you were egging him on—"

"That's it," I cried, voice shaking. "Out! Just get out." I was beginning to sound like a broken record and my head was spinning.

"The hell I will! These guys act like you're in heat . . ." He was coming toward me, his eyes blank and empty, as if he might never have seen me before. He was backing me up, finally grabbed me. "You want a man—"

"I just want to be left alone, please."

I tried to twist away but he was too strong.

"No, Jack."

"Yes, Belinda." He loosened his grip. He seemed to press an interior switch and his anger was gone. He looked at me, kissed my forehead gently, like a lover. "Don't say no tonight, honey," he whispered. "I know you, Belinda—"

"Why are you doing this to me, Jack? You say you love me—"

"Because I've got to break through, I've got to reach you—because I truly need you, Belinda, I need you to hold me. I'm so damn scared of everything . . ."

I lay down on the bed. He was right. He knew me, he could read my eyes. I felt him covering me, felt him yanking my dress up around my waist, felt his fingers raking across my belly and hooking into my panties, pulling them down. I couldn't fight, I didn't want to. His hands felt good, familiar. He knew me, everything about me, and I had hurt him enough, I'd driven him away in the first place and he was my old Jack for God's sake. . . .

He was hard, fumbling with his pants, spreading my legs with his knees, holding me open. It was Jack. It wouldn't hurt me . . . and I felt so much for him, it was all so complex. A kind of loving. A kind of sorrow.

Soon I was soaked with his sweat and he was inside me and he was whispering in my ear, "For old times' sake, my love."

I woke in murky grayness of early morning.

The rain had finally stopped drumming on the skylight.

Something was hurting me. I moved slowly, groggy. I was alone. The sheets were damp, rumpled.

And everywhere, all around me, were yellow roses, shredded, crumpled, smashed flat.

The hurt I felt was a thorn digging into my thigh. the scratch was red with a thin line of dried blood.

It came back to me slowly.

Jack lying still beside me, his breath whistling. Then he had gotten up, stood looking down at me. He had whispered my name, bent down to kiss me softly.

Halfway across the room, his anger and frustration had flared again, he had come back to the bed and I'd felt the roses pelting me. One after another, petals and stems ripped to bits, landing on my bare flesh.

Then he had gone and I had curled into a ball, hugging my pillow, and dived into the pool of exhaustion.

II

Belinda's *Belindas*

Chapter Sixteen

The next morning was not exactly a treat.

I was somewhat hung-over, still awash in the emotional whiplash of *Scoundrels All!* and the lovemaking with Jack that had brought back to me all his vulnerability and gentleness and sadness. I made coffee and showered and cleaned up the rose-littered bed and then sat down on it, legs crossed, feeling like the fetal position was only seconds away.

What a night! It played back in my mind like a tape gone amok, images crowding one another and overlapping in illogical ways. Kicking Hacker Welles's shins and enjoying his deadpan humor, blood dripping from Peter Venables' nose, the home run lifting into the glow of the light standards while the tears spouted and I couldn't stop them, Harry with his arms around Sally and me as the reviews seemed to validate our whole lives in a peculiar way, Jack with his head in his hands in the study . . . Jack holding me while we made love.

I hadn't made love in six months. More than six months. Jack and I had been to bed at New Year's. And not since. I hadn't really missed the physical act all that much. I hadn't even missed the human warmth. I had instead wrapped myself in myself and gotten on with my life. Now having sex with Jack seemed a slightly unusual event, not unpleasant, but emotional more than sexual. And more than that, it seemed ephemeral. Almost as if it hadn't happened at all. I was afraid that that wasn't what Jack was thinking this morning. . . .

You know the way dreams come filtering back to you during the course of the following day, bits and pieces like a landscape illuminated by lightning flashes. The whole image doesn't come all at once, but you can put it together like a puzzle. As I sat there on the bed thinking about Jack and sex and the mess of the previous evening, images flickered at me. At first I thought it was a dream forcing its way back to the surface. It was insistent, like a voice calling in the night, calling for help . . . and then it was there, behind my closed eyes, and it hadn't been a dream. It had really happened.

Jack had left me, I was breathing hard not knowing what to think as the torn rose petals drifted down on me, and I heard the clanking of the elevator as he descended. There was a faint rumble of thunder and the rain had steadied again. I wanted to go to the bathroom and clean up.

So I got up, my head spinning, and something drew me to the window to look down into the street, to watch Jack take his leave. I leaned on the sill and saw him come out into the street. He stood still for a moment, took a deep breath as he glanced up and down Prince Street, then slowly struck off for the corner. The street was empty, which was why I happened to notice someone step out from a darkened doorway opposite the loft. A tall man who wore a dark raincoat. As he passed beneath a streetlamp I saw the glitter of a white shirt and a black tie. A tuxedo. I recognized the figure, the walk, and I thought for a moment it was Harry. He was following Jack. But why in the world would Harry have been waiting in the shadows to follow Jack away from my home?

It made no sense and I strained to see and then I saw that it wasn't Harry at all.

It was Peter Venables.

He had waited while we made love and now he was following Jack.

It struck me as enormously sinister. But then, it had been a long night and when I woke I'd forgotten all about it.

At least for a while.

Between the opening of *Scoundrels All!* and the opening of my own show at the Leverett Gallery, the heat of the summer grew even fiercer, if that was possible. For a couple of days I felt a big physical letdown and I doubtless thought about things too much.

I stayed in the loft, didn't speak with anyone, felt the fan blowing across me and tried to stay calm. I drank iced tea and ate fruit and cold chicken. I painted. The feel of the brushes in my hand, the observable result, gave me the confidence to let my mind roam across other things, the things I couldn't control.

I ran through all the familiar thoughts about Jack: I couldn't help it, not after all those years. And I worried about his state of mind and that old shotgun. But my guard was up: I couldn't let him drag me down into his despair, just when my life was taking off.

I wondered what was going on at the Grangers'. Not just between Harry and Sally and the mysterious, unidentified third party—Harry's girlfriend. No, I really wondered what the presence of Peter Venables in their home was doing to them. Was Sally still looking on him as the sweet boy she remembered? What did they think caused Jack to attack him at the party? And why did I find myself unable to go to Sally with the story of Venables' behavior toward me?

There were times I wished I'd never seen *Scoundrels All!* I wished I could be impervious to the past and its irrefutable connection to the present. What we had been haunted what we had become, and I resented the play's intrusion and exploitation. But there it was, there was no escaping it. We were all caught in the same trap and I wondered if any one of us would get out unscathed. Given his essential nature, maybe only Welles—our creator, our puppetmaster—would survive to tell the tale.

It all came back to men.

It was the men who had come like shadows from the past to surround me, chattering like tribesmen whose language I didn't understand. Men closing in on me, telling me things I didn't want to hear, things I didn't want to believe.

Men who remembered a Belinda I had never known existed. . . .

I left my telephone-answering machine on.

Hacker Welles called. "Belinda, Welles here. Wanted to tell you how much I enjoyed talking to you. Being around you may be a little dangerous, but then, I'm incredibly brave. Am I repeating myself? I think it means I'm getting old. I want to see you again before I'm too old to enjoy it."

He called again the next day. "Belinda, Welles here. Did you ever hear of Sumner Welles, big guy back in the FDR years? Well, we're not related. But you've heard of Orson Welles, I'll bet. Aha, I knew it. Well, we're not related either. Look, you know my thoughts about your being a beautiful airhead? Okay, I admit it—I was only half-right."

I was sitting on the high stool beside my worktable, listening to a replay of Welles's last message and grinning, when Carlyle Leverett arrived.

He came loping off the elevator, storklike, wearing the same kind of light blue wash-and-wear suit he'd worn at Harvard. He had a great bald dome surrounded by fluffy Art Garfunkel hair and a large nose, a large mouth, large protruding ears, very large horn-rimmed glasses straddling a bump in the nose, and the largest bow tie imaginable. He had the largest known Adam's apple in a long neck and he looked like he was being strangled by a butterfly. He flapped in like the great auk, planted a kiss on my forehead, looked at the final painting I'd done for the show—Belinda's mouth, the tongue licking the corner of the mouth, and a drop of brandy escaping the tongue and gliding down the chin.

He stroked his own chin. "That's the dirtiest picture I've ever seen." He hugged me again. "I've never been so hot in all my life," he said. "Why don't you put an air conditioner in here? Is there more iced tea? How are you feeling?"

He went to play in the kitchen, getting tea, and I told him I was scared to death.

"You? Don't be ridiculous. Nerves of steel, ice water in your veins—that's you. Scared of what?"

"The opening, people seeing my work, the critics killing me . . . What if it's a disaster? What if they laugh their heads off?"

"Then, my dear, we have a *cause célèbre*. In the first place, *people* are going to love your work. It's so illustrative, so decorative, so sexy—the poster market is going to be immense. The critics will break down into their own various camps—hell, I could write most of the reviews myself this evening. Some will like it, some will hate it. The point is, it's good-looking stuff, Paul will write very favorably about it—he'll have a reservation or two to keep his integrity intact, but it'll be a good notice. My gallery is not exactly chopped liver. You're not some friendless waif from Dubuque braving the critical jungle alone and unarmed." He stopped to drink his tea and loosen his tie. "Listen, this is all obvious. Why do you need me to tell you? Silly woman!"

He put his briefcase down and opened it, took out a proof copy of *The New Yorker*. "The poster is going to make you, my child. We're offering it at fifteen bucks and this is the ad we've put in the magazine."

I nodded. "I know, I know," I said softly, hoping he was right about the poster. Belinda's chin—I always thought of the model as a third party, not me—rested on her bare knee, her arm clasping the knee, though all you could see of the arm was the upper part wrapped in an Egyptian silver snake. There was just the faintest possible swell of breast below the snake. Some poster, Sally had said. She wouldn't let Harry see it because he wasn't old enough, she told me.

We were sitting quietly in the heat when he mentioned the reviews of *Scoundrels All!* It occurred to me that while he was an old Harvardian and friend of Jack's, I hadn't seen him at the opening.

"No, I stayed away from that particular ritual of self-fulfilling nostalgia. Good reviews, I suppose it'll run forever. Ah, well, good luck to them." He grimaced.

"What's the matter?"

"Oh, just some unhappy memories of those happy-go-lucky, fun-loving Ruffians. Nobody ever gets over the past. I guess that must be the point of the show—college and whatnot. It stunts you, as far as I'm concerned, and you have to struggle to outgrow it. The Ruffians fight to stay where they were—makes no sense to me. I find myself approaching middle age and every once in a while somebody I know drops dead and I hear about it over cold sesame noodles and I'm not hungry anymore . . . the past flies up and slaps me in the face and I want to get the hell back to the present where I belong. The Ruffians, now, they're different. All these guys are brought back together by this show and they start flexing their tired old muscles, thinking about being kids again . . . and something in me wants to throw up. No offense, Belinda, I know how deep your connection is."

"Me? What about you? You were friends with all those guys."

He nodded. "That's the problem, I suppose. Taken as individuals, not such bad eggs. Mike, he's a decent guy. Jack, well, he's a jock with a pretty dark side, but he has his points. But let me warn you, at this late date, as a group they can be a beastly lot. They don't even really know it. When dear old Harry, everybody's best friend, got wind of my homosexuality at Harvard—not the loud, icky kind, as you know—he made sure the word got around mighty fast and the Ruffians took it upon themselves to remove me from their lives . . . I mean, we were *friends*— . . . and suddenly Paul and I, by being close as we were, we weren't fit company. I know, this all comes as news to you." His Adam's apple bobbed, he grinned crookedly. "But we're all grown up now and bygones are bygones and so on. What does it all mean? Don't ask me. Everything's always changing, anyway."

"But they really were so rotten to you?"

"It was long ago and far away and there's not really any point in dwelling on past agonies. But the fact is, sure, they were rotten." He laughed as if it were someone else's history. "I always thought they should have called themselves the Villains. That's what they were."

Chapter Seventeen

I decided at last that I had to talk to Sally.

I had to tell her the truth of what had happened with Peter Venables—not just the evening I had spent with him and the way he had persisted at the party, but also the mysterious appearance in the middle of that rainy night when I'd seen him watching my loft and subsequently following Jack. I was existing in an informational vacuum. I hadn't spoken with Jack so I had no idea what had happened once they had passed from my view. But Sally might know.

The thing was, I couldn't tell anyone else the Venables story and I'd gotten to the point where I had to tell someone. If I'd gone to Jack he'd have gotten homicidal. Harry would have thought I was off my rocker. But it was eating me up. I just couldn't bottle it up any longer.

I had just decided to call her when the phone rang and it was Sally. Things like that had been happening to us all our lives. Our own telepathy. She was bubbling over with high spirits, which were uncharacteristic in the best of times. She sounded almost girlish and I jumped to the conclusion that things must have gotten cleared up on the Harry front. She said she was going shopping and could work her way down toward my part of town. We decided to revisit past haunts, have coffee at Figaro in the Village.

I walked up West Broadway, past the galleries and restaurants, waited for the light at Houston, watched the traffic surge through the heat waves rising from the street. The Village was crowded with hordes of tourists gasping for breath and soaking their polyester. I hadn't been to Figaro in years but it seemed unchanged, a landmark now of the fifties when the Village was synonymous with beat and hip and bohemian. I found a dark corner that was relatively cool and ordered an iced cappuccino.

Sally arrived looking cheery and healthy, flushed instead of pallid. Quite a change from the day she'd summoned me to the Spencer show and told me Harry was in love with another woman. Hardly the same woman. She swept in, dropped a Saks bag, a Macy's Cellar bag, and a small blue Tiffany's sack on an empty chair. She lit a cigarette, ordered something cold, and blew out a long sigh.

"Well, it really is a hit! Can you believe it? The theater parties are buying now, we're selling through Christmas, weekends are pretty well gone into October! Belinda, it's a big hit! God, what a relief! Harry's talking about a Los Angeles company for Thanksgiving. Who'd have thought anybody would give a damn about the Ruffians? And Hacker Welles! Suddenly he's a genius! He's going to do the *Today* show next week! Hacker . . . Well, it's incredible. Peter just can't believe it—he keeps wandering around saying: 'What if I hadn't come? What if I'd missed this?' For that matter, what if any of us had missed it?"

Happy as I was for Sally, I had to work hard to share her mood of exuberance. So I faked it and was too hearty and happy. Normally Sally would have picked up on the act, but not today. Today there was no stopping her and it didn't take her long to get around to the Grangers' houseguest. I listened and felt everything slipping out of my hands, the way you watch a vase slip from your grasp and are helpless as it floats toward the floor and then shatters and there's no getting that vase back.

Peter Venables, it turned out, had made all the difference in Sal's mood. He was a joy!

Peter was in the habit of getting up early, unlike Harry, and the two of them had taken to having breakfast in the garden with the birds twittering and the sprinklers going and the squirrels skittering in the trees.

"Sounds like a Walt Disney picture," I said.

"Laugh at me," she giggled, "I'm having fun. There's no law that says I can't have an innocent little breakfast with an eligible man . . . there we are in our robes and Sarah bringing the orange juice and the toast in a rack and the coffee. We sit there and feel the day coming to life and feel the morning breeze in the trees." She laughed to herself, her eyes flashing at me. It could have been twenty years before. She could have been describing a new boyfriend. She looked at me from beneath raised eyebrows, so black against her forehead, as if to say, *Why not?* "Well, what do you think? He's a kind of dream, Belinda—"

"Yes," I said, "I'm sure he is. A kind of dream. Just so you don't get carried away—"

"I'm not a child to be lectured, Belinda. I know what I'm doing."

"Just so you do," I said.

"Darling, you find yourself in a singularly weak position if you start lecturing me about how to succeed at marriage."

"Oops, score one for Sally!"

"Well, really! I'm just having a good time at breakfast—I'm not . . . *blowing* him. . . ." She dissolved in laughter "Though I'm not saying the thought hasn't crossed my mind. . . ." She had to put her glass down. We were both laughing. She swallowed hard, waved her hand at me. "No, no, I'm just kidding! But you looked so censorious—"

"I'm just so surprised at your flights of romance—"

"Well, seriously, Peter is a wonderful houseguest. Of course, he always did have the most wonderful manners. You remember, Belinda. He never had that hail-fellow-well-met bonhomie the Ruffians specialized in . . . that was always what I liked about him. He was so intense, serious, you remember—"

"You know me, Sal," I said. "I don't remember much about him." I shrugged. No way I was going to get to tell my ugly little story.

"Anyway, Peter's a very sweet guy. Sort of lonely, I think. Full of interesting stories about all the places he's been, I mean everywhere in the world, but based in London. His parents lived there, I guess. And he has a daughter, Delilah. Such an exotic name . . . Delilah Venables. He's crazy about her, carries all these pictures of her—look, he gave me one." She fumbled in her bag and brought out a snapshot and handed it to me. "She's quite the stunner, isn't she?"

The girl was strikingly beautiful. Her thick black hair was cut short, her skin was dark, the brown eyes huge and radiant, the nose short and saucy, tilted slightly. "Indeed, she is," I said. "How old is she?"

"Eighteen," Sally said.

"He should have brought her with him, let her have a peek into his youth, show her off to all his old friends—"

"Maybe he would have, but he just went through her wedding! Married at eighteen! Whew! And you know where she is right now?"

"I can't imagine—"

"In Africa, honeymooning on a safari! Taking pictures. Her husband is a French photographer, they met on a shoot in Brittany. Delilah was a model and they fell in love." She got a misty look and touched my hand. "Think of it, she has all her life ahead of her. Doesn't it make you want to reach out to her, sit down and talk to her, tell her about love . . ."

"I wish somebody would tell me about love." I smiled at her.

"God, I don't know what's gotten into me—I guess it's hearing Peter talking so proudly about his daughter. To say nothing of this concentration on the old days in the show. God, Belinda, I've done nothing but blab! Turn me off, please."

"So where is the lovely Mrs. Venables?"

"A tender point. The late Mrs. Venables. She died a long time ago. He raised Delilah on his own."

"I wonder who he married? It must have been right after we graduated."

"I haven't probed. Look, he speaks very fondly of you, Belinda. Even if you don't remember him. I know he'd like to see you. Lunch maybe. But he's shy . . . he doesn't want to call you. He's afraid you wouldn't have time for him. I told him he was being silly. . . ."

"Speaking of tender points," I said, "Peter must have had something to say about his little encounter with Jack at the party."

Sally made a face. "Peter said that so far as he could tell, Jack still had a pretty good right cross. I mean he took it with good grace, says he knows how tough it must be on Jack and you to have your marriage go bad . . ."

"How magnanimous," I said. "Almost saintly. Have you seen Jack or talked to him since then?"

"Not me. Harry may have. Peter did say something else—he's worried about you if Jack's violent streak is coming out again—"

"Again? What's that supposed to mean?"

Sally shrugged. "Beats me. Ruffian lore, I suppose. None of our business."

"You're right, I suppose. I'd rather not know. But you tell Peter not to worry his little head about me, okay?"

Walking back to the loft, I had the slightly tawdry sensation that I had become a character in a soap opera. I'd heard people observe that life was, indeed, like a soap opera, but I'd never quite known what they meant. It occurred to me that just possibly I was learning.

Because I left the meeting with Sally feeling that what I'd just witnessed was a woman, however foolishly, falling in love. The components seemed to fit. The husband who was fanatically wrapped up in his own project, which— God help us!—virtually forced him to reconsider his happy youth. The gathering of old friends. The wife convinced that the husband had taken a lover. And the arrival on the scene of an old friend with an exotic life and a full complement of good memories. Breakfast in the garden. Squirrels in the trees . . .

It was perfect. How could Sal have resisted?

But there was one grotesque problem.

Peter Venables was a son of a bitch. Maybe crazy. Certainly sick—at least by my standards.

But I was apparently the only one who knew the truth. To everyone else he was one of the Ruffians returned from afar. Hell of a guy. One of the best. Salt of the earth. One of *us*.

But I knew.

And maybe Jack, too. But Jack was halfway around the bend himself.

A soap opera, for God's sake . . .

Chapter Eighteen

They came the next day to crate the paintings. Carlyle Leverett supervised the operation, nervously adjusting a frame here and a bit of padding there, patting his bony forehead with a handkerchief. He came over and stood beside me at the kitchen counter.

I looked at the canvases being swathed in wadding. "My babies," I murmured.

He smiled tolerantly. "Don't be disgusting, dear girl. Far more valuable than babies. Anyone can make a baby, after all."

I watched until they'd finished with the last canvas and lowered two of the largest through the window. Three canvases had necessitated removal from the stretchers and rolling. I felt as if I were watching a triple-bypass operation. And then they were gone and the loft was quiet, sunshine streaming in on the emptiness. The walls stood naked. The paintings were gone, had begun the perilous trek into the art world where fanged creatures waited to rip and tear.

I felt like an infant whose playpen had been taken away.
I was lost and didn't know what I was supposed to do next.
I couldn't get out of my mind what had been the Peter
Venables question and was now the Peter/Sally question.
It came down to the fact that I was still carrying the un-
healthy burden of truth about him: I hadn't been able to
tell the one person I *could* tell. Yet, somehow, I kept
thinking I had to warn her.

Or did I? He couldn't stay forever. Maybe it would just
burn itself out in her mind, and once he was gone, everything would be back to normal.

Why didn't I have any confidence in that scenario?

In that frame of mind I went back to thinking about the
paintings that had just been removed and suddenly I felt a
kind of hatred for them. And I got to thinking that I would
probably never paint another picture. Certainly not a self-
portrait. The very thought nearly nauseated me. I'd had
enough of the whole thing. Three years of painting Belinda . . .

How had I stood it? And why, so abruptly, did I hate the
idea and want no more of it?

Soap opera.

I was listening to a tape I'd made of Zoot Sims,
stretched out on the long wicker couch, reading a
Josephine Tey mystery, when the buzzer from the lobby
rang. I debated for a moment, then decided it might be
workmen or Leverett or . . . Maybe anybody would do,
just some company.

I pushed the buzzer and released the elevator door.

He came in, still rumpled, wearing sunglasses, chinos,
a venerable blue blazer slung over his shoulder, badly
scuffed white bucks. He stood in front of me grinning

broadly. "I'm afraid to say anything. You might start kicking me again."

"You're not awfully neat," I said, "but you are clean. Very clean."

Hacker looked at me, nodded. "I've always been very diligent in matters of personal hygiene. My sainted mother was very clean, as well. Look, for the sake of argument, let's say we're both clean. And you're neat. I've hardly ever seen anyone so neat and clean as you. I wonder how you do it."

"Early to bed, early to rise . . . And I'm glad to see you. They've just carted all my paintings away. To the gallery. It's very lonely without them all around me."

He was mooching around the loft, inspecting the books, the bits and pieces of my life, as if he had some right to do so. "Zoot Sims," he said. "'Isn't It Romantic?' Always makes me think of Bogart and Hepburn in *Sabrina*." He stopped at the wheel-of-fortune. "Wow," he said respectfully, touching it, not spinning it. "I had a wife at one time who read the tarot. Talk about a scary woman." When he put his fingers on something he seemed to soak up the essence, claiming it somehow.

He looked at me quizzically, once he returned to where I was standing. "You and Jack live here a long time?"

"Ever since we got married. Now I live here alone."

"Come have lunch," he said. "Far from SoHo. Get some distance between you and this place."

"That sounds good, Welles."

"I've got something to tell you, Belinda. My little secret. Don't ask why, I just want to tell you."

We got a table outside beneath the red-white-and-blue awnings at the St. Moritz on Central Park South. The horses pulling the carriages slowly through the moist heat clopped on the hot pavement. Beyond the shade of the awning the sunlight was a glaring blindness. He leaned back with a gin-and-tonic and surveyed me with the ingenuous eyes which seemed perpetually amused, as if life were a very good comedy and he'd managed to get his hands on front-row seats.

"I've never seen a man with a Mona Lisa smile before," I said.

"Makes this your lucky day, then. Do you know why the Mona Lisa is smiling?"

"No. Why is she smiling?"

"Oh, it's not a joke. Leonardo had hired some entertainers, a clown, a juggler, a singer, to provide some entertainment while he labored. They worked the area behind him to keep the model's attention . . . and that's why she's smiling. Trying to keep a straight face. But she was amused by a clown, someone taking a pratfall, and the result is the most famous and enigmatic expression our civilization has produced. I like that, it appeals to my view of life—both what was going on in Leonardo's studio that day, which is so gentle and human and real, and all the frantic attempts to understand the Gioconda smile through the centuries since it was painted. Somebody slipping on a banana peel."

"Is that a true story?"

"Said to be an eyewitness account."

"Why hasn't someone told me before?"

"Because you've never told the right man he had a Mona Lisa smile."

"Well, even if it's not true, it should be."

"Life does sometimes need a bit of touching up."

"That's your business, isn't it?"

"Yours too, Belinda, yours too."

It was too hot to eat much, but we shared a sandwich and paid for two lunches so we could occupy the table. "So what was it you wanted to tell me?" I asked. "It couldn't have been the Mona Lisa story."

"Did you hear about the three gay guys who mugged the lady in Grand Central?"

"No."

"Two of them held her down, the third one did her hair. Clavell told me that the other day and now I make it your responsibility."

"You wanted to tell me *that*?"

"No, that was a moment of levity. I wanted to tell you I'm going to write a novel. I haven't told anyone yet, not even my agent. I wanted you to know first."

"I'm flattered," I said, puzzled. "By why me first?"

"It's about the old days. You were part of it. I suppose I just can't let go after spending the last year working on the show, which was really Harry's brainchild, not mine. For me it was like an assignment. Now I want to write *my* version of the story, *my* book about the Ruffians. And you're the first and only person I'm going to tell." His smile curved upward beneath the dark glasses.

"It's different from the show, then?"

"Very."

My mind wasn't working very quickly. "I'd have thought you'd tell the Ruffians first."

"I don't think the Ruffians are going to like it a lot. It's about a woman, one of *those* women, the kind who passes through every man's life at one time or another. If he's lucky. In this case, the woman passes through the life of not one man but a group of men. They all react to her, each guy in his own way." He stopped, waited, and I wished I could see his eyes.

"It's certainly a romantic premise." I was measuring my words. There was something going on in the conversation. I couldn't name it but I felt as if I were on dangerous ground. "Reminds me of Circe turning men into swine. Or is she like Daisy Buchanan in *Gatsby*?"

"I don't think my heroine turns men into swine."

"That's a relief."

"I think maybe the men are already swine."

I laughed. "You always catch me by surprise!"

"But I have some unresolved questions of plot. This woman of mine, these guys are half-crazy about her, but instead of using her power and toying with them and making their lives utter hell, she's quite unaware of her effect on them. She just doesn't notice, doesn't care. Which is worse in a way. Like a slow-acting poison."

"So what's the unresolved plot question?"

"Well, I think there's going to be a murder. Years later. One of the men is killed. And I'm toying with the idea of having her be the murderer. Yet, she's my heroine. I wonder, will it work? Or will the reader reject the idea?"

"Depends on how good her motive is, I suppose. Why does she do it?"

He shrugged his thick, heavy shoulders. "I haven't worked it out yet, although that's not hard to do. But creating such a character, believable both as this totally innocent *femme fatale* and as a murderer—that's tough. What do you think?"

"I think it's a long way from *Scoundrels All!*" I might have added it was also too close to home, too much a warped view of me. Mostly I was wishing he hadn't told me any of it.

"My theory is that anyone can be driven to murder. Put enough pressure on, whammo! My heroine is such an innocent that when she finds out that everybody else isn't innocent, she's in a vise, her illusions demolished, her belief in the rightness of things shot to hell. So she goes off the edge, kills the old friend from college who most epitomizes that shock of reality." He reached across impulsively and put his hand on mine. "Of course, it's just a story. An allegory."

He sank back in his chair, motioned to the waitress for the check. I looked away, back to the trees in the park. Dammit! I couldn't seem to get away from the subject. Hacker was such a bright, calm, reassuring man, but just when I felt I could relax and enjoy him, he came up with this. A little obvious, telling me. And was he right? Was anyone capable of murder if the screws were tightened to the breaking point? How deeply could he see into me? Could he see something there that was still unknown to me? Or had he just taken a shot in the dark? Damn *writer*!

"I hope I haven't upset you," he murmured. He handed the waitress his credit card.

"A little unnerving, that's all. It's closer to life than you might think—no, I don't mean I want to kill anyone. But the way you see things . . . is a surprise." I tried a bright smile which turned out to be a bad fit. *Peter Venables. I could handle him, but if he hurt Sally, then I didn't know what I might do.*

"Yes," he agreed. "Everything that's happened lately has taken me by surprise. Still, I can't ignore the feeling that fate has brought us all back together for some purpose. There's something wrong with the picture, no matter how I fiddle with the knobs. Take Harry and Sally, they've got it all, everything should be great, but there's something funny in their eyes, something hollow, dying fires, they act like strangers sometimes, bruised from some heavy infighting the rest of us haven't seen."

He signed the check. He had nailed down so many of the things I'd been laboriously working my way toward. Just like that. Fast.

"Then there's you and Jack coming apart," he said. "One of those dime-a-dozen sad stories, husband fails to realize his potential, wife goes on past him and he can't deal with it—"

"Where do you get your information?"

"What if I said Jack?"

"And what about you?" I asked. "What's the matter with you?"

"It's obvious, surely. A grown man who hasn't been able to outgrow his fascination with his college days, with all the old relationships that won't die. Isn't that a little weird? Why can't I escape my Ruffian days? Offhand, I'd say it must be unfinished business."

"And the rest?"

"Mike, mooning around you, hoping you'll finally notice him. Even Leverett and Clavell, still trying to figure out if they can set up housekeeping together, two old fairies afraid of the encroaching darkness and the solitude. And now Peter Venables shows up from London with a tragic past and pictures of his beautiful daughter who's the image of his dead wife, a constant reminder of her death, and he just sort of moves in with Harry and Sally." He shook his heavy head and frowned, perplexed. "We're all so unsettled and searching, like people looking for whatever it is that will complete us."

"You sound as if you're talking about Jung's anima figure: whatever will complete us . . . whoever . . ."

"It's like this ungodly weather," he said, standing up. "Everyone sweating it out, waiting for it to break."

He looked down at me and suddenly flashed the smile that crinkled the corners of his eyes. He had a nice California tan. I wished I could see the eyes behind the dark lenses. Maybe his smile was the result of being with me. Hacker Welles, of all people! He *would* have to be the one most interested in poking into the private, forgotten debris of our lives. And that novel he wanted to write . . .

Me. The murderer.

Chapter Nineteen

We crossed Central Park South and headed into the park, across a grassy knoll where people snoozed in pools of shade and kids played catch. I watched him as he began a mock broadcast of the game, dredging up names for the players that he told me were old Yankees from long ago. Snuffy Stirnweiss, George McQuinn, Joe Gordon, King Kong Keller, Tommy Byrne . . .

"How about a ride in a rowboat?" he said.

He led the way to the rental dock, climbed clumsily into the boat, and helped me follow. "I wonder how you do this," he muttered. "Do I sit facing where I've been or where I'm going?" Shade and sunlight dappled his face, full of consternation. "No, don't tell me, I should be able to figure this out. Now, if you pull the oar this way, then you've got to sit this way . . . okay, I've got it. Sit down, Belinda, you're not George Washington and this isn't the Delaware."

He guided us inexpertly, slowly, veering one way and another, out into the bright center of the lake. Reflected sunlight rippled, but there was a hint of mysterious breeze, almost enough to dry the sweat. I lay back as he got the hang of it, felt the easy rhythm of his stroke and the slow movement of the boat beneath me. The sounds of the city were wholly stilled now. The water shimmered. I felt like a character caught in the real story behind the gentle delicacy of a French Impressionist painting. I said something to that effect, squinted through nearly closed eyes at his big shape casting its shadow across the space between us, the sun behind him. He seemed dark, a faceless, featureless shape.

"It's the past again, Belinda. You think of it in a painter's terms, naturally. There had to be a story behind those paintings of people boating and having picnics, and if you look at it just right you can almost see the whole story, all the relationships, in the moment the painter captured." He gave it some left hand and we slowly began to make an arc.

"And you see it as a writer."

He nodded. "I hear a remark, I begin to make a story of it. I see Jack's fist land on Peter's nose and I see your face freeze into a kind of death mask and I can begin to see the whole story rather than just the instant." We were floating toward an overhang of limb and thick foliage, shade. "When Jack hit Peter and you stood watching, I not only knew that you were finished with Jack . . . I knew you were glad he hit Venables. There was a charge of some kind flowing between you and Peter. But I don't know what. I've been thinking about it."

"You are a bastard," I said, after a long pause in which we slid all the way into the shade and I could stop shielding my eyes.

He laughed. "Now you're angry with me."

Closer to the bank I was glad to hear a few of the everyday sounds of the park instead of our own voices, his soft and warm, mine too shrill. Should I tell him all the mischief Venables was causing? I disliked the idea of drawing him any more deeply into that cavern of the past, but I wondered what he would make of Venables' return.

I felt his hand on my bare ankle, shaking me. "Over there," he whispered.

On a grassy bank, Harry and Sally were sitting, deep in conversation. Hacker was right not to interrupt them. I saw that immediately, yet I felt like a peeper.

Sally seemed to be showing him a paper of some sort, a letter, a piece of manuscript; I was too far away to identify it more accurately. Sally leaned forward, pushed the paper toward him, talking intently. He took the sheet, holding it like something dead, hardly looking at it. He finally threw back his head and laughed, the harsh sound floating on the hot summer afternoon.

Sally stiffened as if she'd been slapped; then her shoulders slumped forward, and, kneeling, she began to sob. Harry dropped the sheet of paper beside her, reached across, said something, and gently began patting her back. The signals he was giving—the unkind laughter, the affectionate patting—confused me. But I wanted to reach out to Sally, comfort her. I strained forward, unthinking, about to call out, when Hacker reached out to stop me.

Suddenly Sally got shakily to her feet, stuffed the paper into her bag, wiped her eyes, and walked slowly away, weaving up the slope toward the path.

Hacker caught my eye and shook his head as if to say: See what I mean?

After returning the rowboat, Hacker put his arm around my shoulders and gave me a hug. "You know how these husband-and-wife arguments go," he said. "It's probably nowhere near as bad as it looked. Just one of those things—"

"Don't be condescending," I shot back. "I know Sally better than anyone else on earth, including Harry. And she was really upset. She's having a hell of a tough time these days."

Hacker nodded. "Well, let't hope it's not as bad as it looked."

"Is that really the way you feel? Or would you rather have your theory about all the trouble we're in be proven right? Wouldn't you like it more like a novel?"

"You do think I'm a rat!"

"I don't know what to think about you."

"Usually I'm happy to take life as it comes. There seems to be enough drama to go around. Now, you have the look of a woman who needs an ice-cream cone."

"Oh, stop talking so stupidly!"

We were standing at the statue of Hans Christian Andersen near the Conservatory Pond when I heard the familiar voice behind us.

"Hey, you two." A smile in the voice, a million memories across twenty years. "What's happening? Everybody taking the day off?"

Hacker turned. "Pure entertainment. Showtime. Watch Belinda bathe herself in chocolate-chip ice cream."

"I'm not having ice cream," I said childishly.

"It was hard to look at either one of them, Ruffians forever, no matter what. "Hi, Harry," I said. Memory: I saw Sally's shoulders slump as if she'd received a hammer blow.

Hacker filled the silence. "Why aren't you off somewhere counting the money in the till?"

Harry laughed, shrugged. "I would be, but it's all credit cards these days. So Sally and I came over for a walk. Too hot for her, though. She just went home. She'll be sorry she missed you."

We were strolling back toward Fifth Avenue. Harry seemed utterly at ease, unconcerned, as if nothing at all had happened with Sally moments ago. Roller skaters grunted past, sweat flying. Dogs barked. We stopped at the curb.

I said: "Tell Sal I'll call her."

"Will do." He punched Hacker's arm. "Take good care of my girl."

And then we were alone, looking at each other.

Chapter Twenty

I came awake early the morning my show opened. I was soaking wet, the sheets were wrinkled and clinging, and outside my window the big round thermometer Jack had once installed said it was eighty-eight degrees. It was just past seven o'clock. My stomach was a little nervous. The day stretched ahead like a vast, burning, sandy wasteland.

Venables had left several messages on my answering machine. He wanted urgently to speak with me, kept telling me how important it was. But he didn't have the guts to give me a hint of what he had on his mind. Which assured me that it was just more of his bullshit.

I don't suppose I'll ever know if I could have prevented what happened by simply answering him. It's one of the imponderables you carry with you to your grave . . . but it haunts me.

* * *

Sally called that morning. I was standing mindlessly in the corner like a sailor on a calm sea telling himself there might just be a wind if I could find the right angle. I stood with my foot on the base of the wheel-of-fortune, thinking about the midget Sally always said had crouched inside to control the wheel when it was used for games of chance. Sal wanted to wish me well that night and wondered if there was anything she could do to make the day go faster. She sounded as if all the starch had been taken out of her.

While I listened to her I began to wonder what might have brought her down so badly. What if she really were smitten with Venables? After all, one man's meat just might be another man's poison. Maybe he was a different man with her. And what if Venables were nuts about Sally? And what if Sally went to Harrry and wanted a divorce . . . ? Oh, hell, it sounded too patently absurd! Until you took everything into consideration. Smitten with Venables, Sally also is certain that Harry is in love with another woman. Add Venables falling for her . . . and you might have a woman who wanted out of her marriage. And she might have taken it to Harry in the park that day. Maybe with a letter from Venables. Or to Venables. And when Harry heard her proposal he might have told her to grow up and forget the idea of their splitting up . . . and she might not have known how to handle such an unexpected turn of events . . . and maybe she was going through the agonies of losing Venables, her one shot at romance—which would have had to be the shortest love affair with a sad ending in history. . . .

But, listening to Sally droning tonelessly on, I knew I was letting myself think like a soap opera. And what the heck did I know about soap operas?

Sally didn't mention Venables until the conversation had just about run its course. Then she asked me if I'd seen him. I said no. I could hear a tiny catch in her voice.

"That's strange," she said. "I know he's been wanting to talk to you. Well, he can see you tonight. But that will hardly be the time to sit down and talk about old times, which is what I think he has in mind. Oh well . . ." She seemed to be saying she'd lost interest and who cared anyway?

I decided to chance it. "How are things with Harry? Have you got that idea out of your mind and put to rest?" I tried to sound cheery.

But it was a mistake. Sal flared at me. "I told you. Why do I have to keep telling you? He in love with someone else . . . *utterly lovesick*. The way he used to be, in the old days, that same dumb expression on his face—remember the way he acted when you gave him up for Jack? It's the same look." She was crying. "Who can it be now, Belinda? How can I do anything about it . . . *do I want to do anything about it?* Oh, God, I'd like to brain him . . ."

She mumbled an apology, still crying, and the line went dead.

Harry showed up at the loft in the afternoon.

He came in looking tired and a bit ashen, like someone who'd been put through the wringer once too often. The lines at the corners of his eyes and mouth were deeper and the gray over his ears seemed more visible. He kissed me, leaned back with his arms around my waist, and looked into my eyes. His were bloodshot, adding to the overall appearance of strain and weariness. He sighed and smiled resignedly. "God," he said, "it takes me back. Do you ever think of the dear, dead days beyond recall?" He was carrying a bottle of champagne, which was cold and sweating. He walked toward the table and peeled the tinfoil off the top, began unwinding the wire holding the cork in place.

"I'm not sure what you mean," I said.

"Maybe I'm just in a mood," he said. He dropped the wire on the table and began working the cork with his thumbs. I went to get glasses. "I just got a whiff of your perfume and it made me think of Williamstown, that little bedroom in the old mansion they'd turned into a hotel. Our first time, Belle."

I came back with the glasses and watched the cork pop, fly across the room. The white bubbles ran down the side of the bottle. "I haven't thought about that in a long time." He poured our glasses and clicked the rims.

"To the old days, Belle."

"To Williamstown." I smiled at him, the memory flickering. He'd been very gentle with a frightened college girl who was taking it all very seriously. I'd never forgotten that. The friendship between us was so genuine in later years that Sally and Jack had never been bothered by the fact that Harry and I had been lovers.

He winked at me, went to the window, slipped out of his seersucker jacket, and dropped it onto the sill. Even Harry was sweating. "I was so happy then," he said. "We spent the whole day and night in bed, we didn't even eat." He laughed. "It was never going to end. Well, hell . . . it ended." He sipped champagne.

"It never really ended," I said. "It was just the sex that ended. We've always loved each other. All four of us. Haven't we?"

He turned back. "Sure, sure. And we'll always have Williamstown. As Bogie would have said." He shrugged, as if discarding the past. "I didn't mean to get sidetracked. I brought this bottle to toast your success tonight and ease you into the festivities."

Eventually he got around to telling me what was bothering him. I was glad he trusted me and turned to me. I almost thought I should tell him about Venables.

"Sally and I had a real row," he said. "In Central Park the other day. Right before I ran into you and Hack—did I act like I was coming apart?"

"Anything but," I said.

"Well, I was on the ropes, believe me. She hasn't really spoken to me since. You can imagine it's gotten a little tense with Peter there, too. Poor bastard. The thing is, she's so sure I'm having an affair with someone. She doesn't even have any candidates in mind, but there's no talking her out of it. I don't know what the hell to do."

"Is it true?"

He gave me a startled look and poured us some more champagne. "I'm not having an affair with anyone. No. But have you ever thought how impossible that is to prove to someone who's convinced you are? I mean, I can't do it. She's so sure."

"Maybe it'll pass."

"I sure as hell hope so. That thing in the park—she was just crazy, Belle. I've never felt so frustrated . . ."

"How is Peter coping with all this going on around him?"

"He's okay. Pretty cool customer. He's spent more time with Sally than with me and I'm sure she's unburdened herself to him." He flung himself down on the couch. "I might as well tell you the truth. Sally's made a fool of herself over Peter. Nothing serious, but it's got to be an ordeal for him. But he'll be gone soon. She's very fond of him. I don't blame her . . . but every so often it gets to me—"

"Maybe she's trying to make you jealous. I mean, it is a tried-and-true stratagem."

"You don't really think so, do you? Jeez, that never crossed my mind . . . so I guess it's not working. But she sure has a bur under her saddle. Christ."

"How interested in Sally is Peter?"

"Come on, Belinda. You don't think he and I would discuss that, do you? I don't know . . . how the hell should I know?"

He glazed over on me, as if I'd somehow managed to intrude on Ruffian matters. A no-no, for sure. He didn't say much more and left soon after, telling me to have a wonderful time at my opening and he'd be leading the cheering.

I lay in the tub for a long time trying to see what was really going on deep beneath the surface. There was a pattern to it all, I was sure, but it was so faint, so obscure, that I couldn't make it out.

Chapter Twenty-one

I felt as if I had wandered onto a movie set.

The night was tropical. A marquee had been erected on the streetfront. Palm trees in giant pots twitched in the faint breeze. Clouds had moved in and darkened the late sunlight prematurely, and there was a smell of rain in the heat. Humidity hung like cobwebs. Men in evening clothes and women in low-cut bright gowns, so much tan flesh, the throwaway gaiety of something like a Cairo Polo Club dance. The street was lined with dark limos and gunmetal-gray Bentleys. The chatter of conversation reminded me of a frantic moment at the neighborhood aviary. You could smell the rum and the gin and the fruitiness of the drinks. Busboys in whites fit for a navy composed entirely of admirals were everywhere. Guests sat at rattan tables and glistened moistly.

Carlyle Leverett had shot the works for the opening of *Belinda's Belindas*. The paintings had struck him as erotic and he told me palm trees and tropical gear always did the same. Thus the theme. I had to admit, as theater it worked. I stood inside, looking out the huge windows at the art crowd, the beautiful people, the collectors, all the damned Ruffians gathered together to celebrate the opening. And it seemed a million miles away, nothing to do with me.

Paul Clavell kissed my check. "It's natural," he said, reading my mind, "I've seen it a million times. The artist as lost soul emerges from his studio and realizes the work has become the commodity. The artist has nothing to do with any of this. When Philip Roth publishes a new novel he always makes a point of being in Eastern Europe so he's aware of none of . . . this." He swept his hand at the crowd. "Be of good cheer, Belinda. They'll all be at somebody else's party tomorrow night."

Someone was playing a jazz flute in the shade of a drooping palm. People I knew and many more that I didn't swarmed around me, told me how wonderful I was, and gushed about the huge paintings. The gallery was full of smoke and endless talk. I noticed a few critics in beards and sport coats but it wasn't their night. This was for the buyers, and every so often Leverett would whisper in my ear that another sticker was going up, another painting was sold. Because of their size and the striking quality of the graphics—if not the "art"—he had priced them, in my view, extravagantly. But in that atmosphere, I saw them not as my work but as objects that did have a certain appeal. Someone said: "These people can't remember the last show they saw that the pictures were pictures of something they could actually identify. I mean, look at that. It's a tit, right? Restores your faith." I shook my head to myself.

Looking back on it now, I keep breaking the evening into pieces that I don't seem able to glue back together.

Sally. It's hard to recall what she said because what she said wasn't important. It was the way she looked, the sound of her voice, the dark hollows of her eye sockets— all such a contrast to her attempted gaiety and high spirits. She tried to bubble and was only shrill. She tried to give me confidence and love and succeeded only in making me worry about her.

Hacker. He loomed alone in the doorway, the crowd eddying about him, and I felt an adolescent frisson of relief that he didn't have a girl with him. He caught my eye through the bustle, winked at me, and made a swirling motion with his forefinger, indicating he was going to make a tour of the paintings. Later I saw him leaning against a wall with his calm, moderately dazed expression, as Ruffians and pretty women stopped by to have a word with him. He had, since the opening of *Scoundrels All!*, become known in certain circles. The *Times* had done a feature on him, centering on his use of his own past friendships to create a specific piece of entertainment. The blond from the show had made a couple of columns, her name linked to his—but I was convinced that was the work of a press agent. Now he waited, alone.

Jack, looking tired and tense, moved from one old pal to another. Avoided me. His glass seemed ever full. His hand was shaking as he stood looking up at one of the paintings. There was a fleeting expression of disbelief on his face, as if it had somehow been transformed in the move from loft to gallery.

Harry and Mike were laughing, leaning toward a woman whose large bust was barely contained in her dress. A little paranoid explosion went off in a corner of my brain. Were they laughing at me, my work? But what the hell difference did it make, anyway?

Peter Venables, looking very elegant, was engaged in conversation with a short, round man whose back was to me. They were intent on one another, Peter shaking his head in apparent serious, thoughtful disagreement. When the man turned, I was surprised to realize that it was Tony Chalmers, once again down from Harvard. He was gesturing, his hand on Venables' sleeve. Finally he shrugged, folded his arms, and turned toward me, caught my eye from beneath his gray Afro, and smiled.

Later I stepped outside. I thought I heard thunder. The flute was weaving in and out of my consciousness. I sat at one of the tables and Mike appeared, gave me a Bertie Wooster smile, and sat down next to me. "Must be a relief to get this show on the road," he said. "As you know full well, I love your paintings. Leverett has outdone himself with the setting. I . . . well, I bought one!"

I felt a tear in the corner of my eye. I took his hand and held it to my cheek. And I saw Sally sitting at another table with Tony Chalmers. Her hands were folded in her lap, her eyes cast down, as she listened. She didn't seem to be having much fun. Chalmers was lecturing her, but my mind wasn't really on them. How could it have been?

As I chatted with everyone and watched the passing minuet my friends seemed to be dancing, I felt as if I were behind a protective glass that deflected anything approaching reality. I saw Jack again, sweating, pale, looking

unhealthy, Harry at his side. I felt the tension everywhere, but I couldn't make it stop pulsing long enough to
identify it. And Jack worried me. He looked like a man
building up to something.

It was late and the crowd was beginning to thin out a bit
when I made my way back to Leverett's office to use his
rest room. I stood holding onto the sink, staring blearily
into the mirror, wanting it all to be over. I felt as if I'd
almost finished the course, the ribbon was in sight, and I
had nothing left to give the race. People were calling to
me but I didn't speak their language and I wanted to . . . I
never managed to finish my little excursion into mindless
self-pity because I heard voices in Leverett's office. A
controlled fury that could have gone off the edge at any
moment.

It was all so familiar. It was Jack, but I didn't know who
was with him. I was trapped in the bathroom, just as I'd
been helpless in the rowboat while I peered into someone
else's life.

"Now, listen to me, you slimy bastard." Jack slammed
the office door behind him, blotting out the flute. "I know
why you're here, I know all about you. I know what you've
always been. You can't fool me the way you fool the rest of
them. You haven't changed a goddamn bit—and you know
I know. You were a thief then and you're a thief now. I
caught you at it once and by God you're not gonna steal
anything from me this time. . . ." He was out of breath. I
knew the drill. Fists clenched, face white. "Don't say a
fucking word," he whispered, his voice hoarse. "I know
what you came back for, don't I? I mean, I *would* know—
wouldn't I, old pal, old chum, old sock? I *know*. But if you
try it, if you make another move . . . I swear to God you'll

wish you'd never been born. You hear me?" His voice had risen to a shout. Someone moved, a chair scraped on the tile floor and tipped, clattered. "You hear me? You've been warned—"

There were unidentifiable sounds and I couldn't wait any longer. I opened the door.

For an instant I saw them both, staring at one another, like children who have grown up physically but still operate on their primitive instincts.

Jack and Peter Venables.

Venables saw me first. He started to speak, trying to recover his composure, but he failed. He was afraid.

He turned and was through the doorway, gone.

Jack seemed to come back to the real world, saw me, and scowled. "What the hell are you doing? Spying on me? Trying to catch me misbehaving? Well, good for you—you win! Where does he keep something decent to drink?" He began rummaging in an antique cabinet. "That miserable son of a bitch. Maybe he can take the hint and get out . . . he's after you, sweetheart, the bastard really is after you. Shit! Where's the brandy?" He grabbed a bottle and a snifter, poured with trembling hand, and watched brandy run down the side of the glass, drip onto the immaculate tile. Suddenly he hurled the bottle against the wall. It exploded like a mortar shell, brandy spraying across the room. I felt myself snap.

"You're insane. You're insane! You make me sick! You ruin everything you touch . . ." I was screaming and it kept on. All the frustration and nerves and the wreckage of my psyche came pouring out. "Get out of my life, get out of all of our lives, I don't ever want to see you again, Jack, never, never. . . ." I was sobbing and when he took a tentative step toward me I thought he was going to hold me, comfort me, and I threw up my arm to ward him away.

Then I was reeling backward against the desk.

I'd never been well and truly hit before and I felt the ringing in my ears, the pain radiating along the line of my jaw, the trumpet blast in my ear. My face was wet with tears. I sank to my knees. I looked up and he stood over me, his face a blank, as if he'd just hit a stranger who deserved it.

He walked to the door without looking at me again and went up the hall.

The next thing I knew Sally was bending over me.

Chapter Twenty-two

She was dabbing at a thin trickle of blood from the corner of my mouth. The inside of my cheek had shredded against some teeth. And my head was aching in earnest. I couldn't bring myself to look at the mirror while she quickly stopped the bleeding and mopped up. "Doesn't show," she muttered, wadding up the tissues and pitching them into the toilet. "Now, you'd better dry your wee tears and tell me what in the name of God is going on. Every time I turn around, you seem to be in the middle of somebody getting punched out." She grinned sourly, shaking her head.

"First, why did you come back to the office just then?" I sounded funny to myself. My tongue was swollen and I kept chewing inadvertently on little strings of flesh from my cheek.

"Jack. He was coming up the hallway and I was trying to get away from Tony Chalmers—he was being unduly morbid and I was poised on the ledge of insanity—and Jack said something about your wanting me back here." She shrugged. "I came in and you were down for the count. Please don't tell me it was Jack—he's been looking blue murder at everyone tonight."

I nodded. "None other. I really flipped out at him. I don't exactly remember what I said, but you know how it is, you just boil over sometimes . . . well, I boiled over tonight."

"But why? Everything's been so wonderful for you tonight, it's such a triumph. Really, Belinda—so what set you off?"

"It was Peter again. I mean Peter and Jack. Jack had him here in the office, and I like a fool was trapped in the bathroom while they went at it—"

"Oh God!" she whispered, biting a knuckle. She went back into Leverett's office and lowered herself slowly onto a chintz couch. "They fought?"

"No, no. Peter didn't do much of anything. I just heard Jack yelling at him, something about being a thief, Jack knowing all about it—it made no sense to me. But when I heard a chair tip over I'd just had it. I came out of the bathroom and Peter saw me and he looked . . . well, he looked scared. Scared of Jack, scared of whatever Jack was saying to him, hinting at, I don't know. But he saw me, then just shot through the doorway, and Jack turned on me." I stopped for breath. The room reeked of brandy, and a piece of glass glittered like a deadly weapon on the desktop. The wall was streaked and the floor below wet and littered with broken bottle.

Sally lit a cigarette and coughed nervously on the smoke. She got up and looked at the mess, biting her lip. I was sitting in the big chair behind the desk. I had no idea what to do.

"Well," she said at last, "you look perfectly presentable. Your party is still in progress and you'd better get back out there. God only knows when we'll get this sorted out."

"Sal, I've got to tell you something." I might not have done it under normal circumstances, but normal circumstances seemed to be getting pretty scarce. "It's about Venables . . . he made a very nasty pass at me when he first got to New York . . . we had drinks and he got to reminiscing and we had dinner and he took me back to the loft and . . . it got bad, Sal. I think I was lucky to get him to leave." I hiccuped. Pure nerves. "I didn't want to tell you. He was your houseguest. He was a Ruffian! We mustn't speak ill of the bloody Ruffians . . ." I felt myself losing it and stopped, swallowed hard, and willed the hiccups to get lost. "Anyway, he sent me those yellow roses with a stupid veiled threat about making up for his behavior in person—you should have heard him, going on and on about how it was his turn and he was going to do this and that and I might as well just accept it—Christ, who remembers? But pretty rotten stuff . . . and at your party for the opening of the play he started in on me again. He was obsessed, like he was trying to prove something— and then Jack came and saw him and lit into him." I watched her fingers tightening and untightening, fists appearing and disappearing. "They're both totally crazy . . . but I didn't think any of Venables' bad form was going to come out, just because he was bound to go back to London soon. And then this, tonight. I'm sorry, Sal— none of this is your problem, I'm just babbling."

She shook her head. "We'll sort it out later. For now, you'd better go out and deal with your public. You go ahead. I'm going to tidy up a bit." She went into the bathroom and I took a deep breath and went back down the hallway toward the sound of the flute and the chatter of the crowd.

Tony Chalmers came over to me with two glasses of champagne. "One for you, one for me," he said. "To you, my dear. A wonderful evening! Your work is simply unforgettable—I congratulate. You may turn out to be the famous Ruffian!" He chuckled professionally.

"I'm no Ruffian—"

"Of course you are, you and Sally. Whether you like it or not."

"What are you doing down in New York again so soon?"

"I couldn't miss this. Are you mad? I'm serious about your being a Ruffian—this is yet another Ruffian night, second one of the summer. After what I might call too many dry years? Yes, I think I might."

"Are you still expecting the top to come off the old boys? You were thinking dark thoughts, as I recall."

"All of life is the light and the dark, isn't it? So there's always the chance of the abyss opening and swallowing us, just like that."

"I'm sorry I asked."

"Don't be. It shows you understand more about the Ruffians than most. In any case, all seems well tonight, and I'm just a timorous man as I succumb to middle age at last."

We were winding down mainly to the old bunch. The little jazz group was still playing and the room was taking on that lonely quality. Empty bottles of champagne, glasses, plates with the remains of canapés, caterers busily trying to keep up with the accumulating refuse. I wandered around checking out the sold stickers, amazed at the response, afraid to guess at the money involved. None of that seemed to have anything to do with me at the moment. I just didn't want any more scenes with anyone at all for the next couple of decades.

Mike and Hacker were draining a bottle of champagne and laughing about something. Mike wandered over, weaving slightly, and worked hard at focusing his eyes on me. They swam behind the thick round lenses. "May I escort you home?" he said, desperately sober.

"I've already asked her that question, old lad," Hacker said. "I have in fact beaten you to it. She's coming with me."

"A bold-faced lie," I said.

"Perhaps," he said, nodding. "Perhaps."

"You'll come with me, won't you?" Mike was very solemn.

"Over my dead body." Hacker wore that bemused smile.

"That can be arranged." Mike covered his mouth to muffle a bit of a belch.

"I am going home alone. You are both at liberty." I couldn't face the idea of bantering. I wanted to collapse in the arms of the man I loved. But I didn't seem to love anyone.

Eventually they drifted away. We were all exhausted by the heat and the champagne and the gathering humidity. Beyond the front windows I saw the frequent flashes of heat lightning like strobes on a set.

Everyone was finally gone.

The caterers slowed the pace. Carlyle Leverett stood before me, smoking a cigarette in a holder, looking smug. "We'll go over the accounts later. Tomorrow if you like. But we, my darling, have made rather a lot of money tonight. You have created a very influential market." He suddenly knelt in front of me and kissed my nose. "Now you'll have to get back to work and do a great many more canvases in the same vein. . . . You have started something here tonight and I congratulate you, Belinda." He just looked at me for a while and the ash fell off his cigarette.

When I next noticed anyone, having sat in a daze while Leverett fussed in the debris, it was Harry. I'd thought he must have left but there he was waving to me from the shadows beneath one of trees in the street. He was sitting at a table, leaning back, looking at me through the window. When he beckoned to me I went out. A breeze flapped at the awnings and the rain smelled closer yet, the dark night sky pregnant with it, waiting and overdue.

"Where's Sal?" I stood at the curb taking a deep breath, looking up and down the street. A few tourists were watching the tables being taken inside, wondering what had been going on, what they had missed. I felt Harry take my hand and start swinging it.

"Went off somewhere. In a cab. With . . . I don't know with whom. Said she wasn't feeling all that well. Maybe alone. And I just found myself sitting here watching you sitting by yourself. End of report."

"Was she all right? I mean, okay?"

"I suppose. People usually are, no matter what they say."

"I'd have said just the opposite. They say they're all right but they're aren't."

"You're too deep for me." He sighed. "God, I'm tired. Feels like the final event of Prize Day is over . . . when I was at school, there was this nightmare called Prize Day. Christ, it was such a relief to get it over. . . ."

"This is your day for reminiscing," I said.

"Are you all right?"

"Sure."

"According to your theory, that means you're not."

"Let's not debate the point." I turned and smiled at him. "Harry?"

"Belle?"

"I'm going home. You want to walk me?"

He groaned at the effort and stood up. "I'm your man." He stretched and yawned. "Let's go."

We walked arm in arm the few blocks. We didn't talk. A fine mist made haloes around the streetlamps as we stood below the loft's windows.

"Quite a summer we've had," he said, "you and I." He looked very weary.

I laughed softly and hugged him.

"Sleep well," he whispered. "You've earned a rest."

I watched him walk away. At the corner he flagged down a cab and was gone.

I could still taste the blood in my mouth.

III

Death and the Ruffians

Chapter Twenty-three

Not surprisingly, I slept badly and woke up in the familiar thick gray heat and humidity of early morning. I was still wound up from the pressure of the opening, its apparent success, and its violent climax. My jaw was stiff and my tongue kept seeking out the lacerations in my mouth. I tottered gingerly out of bed, my stomach in knots, put on a tape of the Excuses—loud—and stood under a cold shower.

I wanted the music to drown out thought, but it didn't work. Everything kept coming back.

He's after you, sweetheart, the bastard really is after you. . . .

I suppose I was near hating Jack as I stood peering at my pale green eyes, now murky and bloodshot, in the streaked mirror. Damn him, he'd put the years on my face and I could see every one of them frowning back at me. And in the end he'd finally hit me. What kind of people were we, anyway? The woman looking back at me from the mirror seemed normal enough, if slightly the worse for wear, yet she and her husband had been threatening to kill each other not so long ago . . . and then last night the ante had been raised. From words of violence to acts of violence. What next?

I finished the waking-up process and went to make coffee. While waiting for it to drip through the Krups I wiggled my jaw to make sure it was still properly attached. Jack was really a prime bastard. And maybe worse, maybe he really had slipped off the edge. After he attacked Venables at the Grangers' party he'd seemed so chagrined, so apologetic, I'd thought the shock of his own behavior might have turned him around. I'd been wrong again, as usual, and this morning his state of mind seemed even more alarming than it had last night.

But he was right about one thing.

He sure had Peter Venables' number. I didn't know what in the world his speech in Leverett's office had meant, but when I'd come charging foolishly out of the john, I'd seen the effect it had had on Venables. Jack had this guy figured out, and why, I wondered, was he the only one who did? What set Jack apart from the other Ruffians?

I didn't want to believe it was just that he was crazy.

A little later that morning, working on my second cup of coffee and listening to music, I sat cross-legged on the couch and began noodling on a sketchpad with an ordinary Dixon No. 2 pencil, not really thinking about what I was doing, just letting my thoughts wander, lulled by the sound the pencil made on the rough paper. An unsettling thought was working its way around my head and I knew I'd have to deal with it. It had nothing, thankfully, to do with all the complicated personal interactions which were suddenly so prominent. It had to do with my work. Carlyle Leverett had said something about my having to get back to work doing more of the huge self-portraits, more Belindas. And with a chilling shock of recognition I knew that that was impossible. No way could I go back to shutting out everything else but bits and pieces of me. I could foresee the argument I was going to get; ironically, the more they sold, the more determined Leverett was going to be. But it wasn't a question of artistic judgment on my part: it was pure emotion. Seeing them all on the walls of the gallery, watching the people almost inhaling them, I'd realized that it was over—absolutely over. I was almost literally repelled by them . . . I'd put too much into them, had seen my life turned inside out while I was painting them. I simply had to put them behind me, go on, do something else. . . .

The pencil kept moving, scratching in the stillness now that the tape had run out, and my mind was turning into a kind of theater. Hacker Welles, a riddle, a free-floating spirit in a rumpled jacket, looking at the world from behind his barricades. The shrine Harry had described and the shotgun standing in the corner and the stacks of Jack's manuscript so jealously guarded. The snapshot of Venables' daughter, with her black hair shining like pieces of polished coal. Jack's fist flashing and the blood dripping on Venables' dress shirt. Jack on the couch with his head in his hands. Hacker wanting to make me the murderer in his novel. Tony Chalmers beneath his gray Afro waiting for the top to blow off the Ruffians. The thorn on the bed scratching my thigh. The wheel-of-fortune slowly revolving and Venables grinning at me, asking if he should be bold. The actors onstage doing their slow, infinitely sad soft-shoe as the curtain rang down. Harry's harsh laughter across the water. Sally's shoulders slumping . . .

Hacker's voice.

I see Jack's fist land on Peter's nose and I see your face freeze into a kind of death mask and I can begin to see the whole story rather than just the instant.

I stood up and stretched, went to the window, searched the sky for anything resembling a cloud. Nothing. Nothing but the sun beating down, the stillness of the sticky air, the whirring of the fan in its losing battle. I went back to the couch, stood looking down at the pad, chewed on the wooden pencil feeling old teeth marks with my tongue. I picked up the pad to look more closely at what I'd just done

The lake in Central Park. Two people in a rowboat, a man with the oars, the woman leaning up on one elbow. On the bank, beneath the heavy tree limbs, well in the foreground, a man and a woman undergoing a tense confrontation over something. What? Between them a sheet of paper lay on the grass.

It was nothing more than an illustration. Could I make it more than that? I stood looking at the clumsily sketched figures, the lack of detail. Well, I could try.

I kept thinking about what Hacker had said. There had to be a story behind all those paintings of people boating and having picnics, and if you look at them just right, with your mind in the right place, you can almost see the whole story, all the relationships, in the moment the painter has chosen to capture. . . .

I gnawed at the pencil, threw it down on the couch, gave the wheel-of-fortune an impatient yank, and walked away before it had stopped spinning.

I was back looking at the sketchpad, staring at it almost angrily, trying to look at it *just right*, when the phone scared me out of my wits.

"Belinda . . . something terrible has happened, just terrible." It took me a second or two to recognize Harry's voice, and right away I though of Sally, something had happened to Sally. Harry's voice wasn't shaking but it sounded weak, like a signal from a very distant station, dying as it reached me. "It must have happened last night, I don't know, early this morning—anyway, he's dead and I'd like you to . . . to come over, Sal's gonna need you, she found him—"

"Who? Who's dead, Harry?"

"Oh . . ." He sounded surprised, as if he thought he'd already made that clear. "Venables. Peter Venables is dead. Sal went to the door and there he was . . ." He sighed deeply. "It's funny, we were just talking, you and I, about the old question: Which Ruffian would be the first to go?" I heard him swallow. "Well, now we know." He laughed thinly. "It's pretty awful, Belle . . ."

I had taken the phone back across the room and numbly lowered myself onto the couch. We weren't kids anymore, but death was still a stranger to our group and the result was that rubber-legged shock, the dig to the solar plexus. I won't lie and say that I was sorrow-stricken, but the shock was physical. "What was it? Did he have a bad heart?" It was all I could think of.

"What? Oh, no, no, Christ no, he was shot."

I wasn't being dense, I just wasn't getting it. "A mugger? Robbery? What, tell me what happened!"

"Look, we're not sure what happened exactly and the police are here, they're talking to Sally right now and she's a wreck. Dr. Schein is here, too—Sal's been vomiting and she was hysterical and . . . Look, can you get over here?"

"Of course," I said. "Just tell me where this all happened . . ."

He sighed again like a man struggling to the end of a very long climb. He was speaking slowly. "All we know is that he must have gone to answer the door, the front door, inside the vestibule. He must have just been standing there and . . . I mean, it's really a mess. Belle, there's nothing left of his head. . . . I'm not kidding. Nothing. . . ."

Chapter Twenty-four

My mind seemed to be fumbling and tripping over itself in a kind of frenzy, but I felt as if I were moving very slowly, in a fog. Getting dressed, getting a cab, everything taking forever. Who knew? Had the Ruffians been notified of the decrease in their numbers? Mike in his office at Rockefeller Center, Hacker waking sluggishly in his sublet, Jack hollow-eyed after a night of trashing himself with recriminations—all getting the news that Peter Venables was dead. What kind of gun blows a man's head off? All I could think of was Dirty Harry movies and whatever those cannons were called, Magnums, I guess, like the name of the TV detective with the mustache. So who carries guns like that? Who rings the doorbell and blazes away in Turtle Bay? I was thinking breathlessly, like someone with a carbohydrate rush.

Then I remembered the dream I'd had the night before Harry's show had opened, the yawning black holes of barrels like the guns of Navarone swinging around to point directly into my face, hands steadying the gun, the finger squeezing, the roar and flash in my face. . . .

That must have been what Peter saw, the gun going off in his face. I wanted to throw open the door of the cab and go outside, breathe deeply and calm down, walk before the United Nations Building, which was glaring in the sunshine.

But I didn't. I sat sweating in the back seat, remembering the dream, remembering that it had been Jack's shotgun in it.

We got snarled in traffic in the Forties and I tried to control myself, willed myself not to fidget. I still had a clear picture of the last instant in which I had seen Peter Venables' face. His face. Cracking open in the barrage of Jack's accusations, features fragmenting, the dark eyes staring wildly at Jack, then at me, fear overflowing, something like panic, then the attempt to draw himself together in the failure of that abrupt departure.

I know why you're here, I know all about you. I know what you've always been. . . .

I could hear Jack's voice, the hoarse whisper that meant he was near the edge.

You were a thief then and you're a thief now. I caught you at it once and by God you're not gonna steal anything from me this time. . . .

The driver was honking his horn. Clouds of dust rose from a street-repair gang. There were lots of horns and people shouting.

I know what you came back for, don't I? I mean, I would know . . . wouldn't I, old pal, old chum, old sock?

It meant nothing to me. Absolutely nothing.

There were two uniformed policemen outside the front door and a chubby plainclothesman leaning with his elbows on the windowbox, his round face tilted toward the sun. There were a couple of police blue-and-whites, too, and a small knot of onlookers staring discreetly from across the street. Something was going on, all right, but they didn't know what. The sunbather had been given my name. He moved away from the lavish splashes of red and yellow and white flowers and took me inside.

The entryway was roped off, the doors from the foyer to the entrance hall stood open, and there was no preparation for the dark blue canvas sheet covering the body of Peter Venables. His right hand was flung out, the long thin fingers I'd noticed that day at the bar protruding from beneath the sheet as if he were waving, trying to get our attention or maybe just saying good-bye.

I smelled the blood. I saw the mess sprayed along one wall of the entry, streaks of pinkish blood and clumps of matter on the formal wallpaper. My stomach turned involuntarily, a sudden nauseated surge, and I looked away, ignoring everything as best I could. A couple of men were on their knees in the circular foyer where we'd danced on opening night. They were sweeping bits of God-only-knew-what from the parquet squares into baggies.

I fastened my gaze on Harry standing at the foot of the stairway leading to the balcony where the little band had played. He looked dazed. He smiled faintly at me, hugged me. "Thanks for coming, Belle, you're a sweet-heart."

"Where's Sally? How's she holding up?"

"Well, it hit her pretty hard, coming down and finding him, you know . . . dead. I don't know when it happened, neither one of us heard anything—I fell asleep in the study with the door closed watching a replay of a ballgame on Sportschannel. She was upstairs in bed." He caught sight of the body again, stared at it. Two men were kneeling beside the shroud of canvas and were about to transfer it to a bag. "Christ." He looked away, not really focusing on anything. "Dr. Schein's upstairs with her now. She's done with the cops, I guess. Schein says he's got to give her a tranquilizer or some damn thing. Cop by the name of Antonelli seems to be in charge here, he's using my study. I think he's got the medical guy in there with him . . . it's just like watching *Columbo*." He shrugged. "Funny, but I'm not exactly sure what I should be doing— I keep thinking I should be doing something, but what? Cops have interviewed Sal and me twice each. I told them you were on your way over and I guess they want to talk to you, too."

Dear old Harry, calm under siege, wondering what the proper drill was for *Houseguest, Murder of*. Had I expected more of a Ruffian breast-beating and wailing, more emotion? Well, maybe that just wasn't Harry's way. They had gotten the remains of Peter Venables into the bag and we stood silently, watching them lug him out. Once you weren't a human being anymore, you weren't anything: Venables wasn't threatening me, he wasn't afraid of Jack, he wasn't proud of his beautiful newlywed daughter. Not anymore.

The detective looked like my high-school principal.

"You must be Mrs. Stuart," he said, holding out his hand. "I'm Sam Antonelli. I understand you were a friend of the deceased—I wonder, could you spare me a few moments? Just follow me."

He was a gray-haired man of medium height, stocky, with a gray mustache. His hair was long and combed back from his temples like a matinee idol of the thirties. His voice was soft and very smooth and his manner was deferential, almost courtly. I hadn't seen anyone like him since I was a kid in another galaxy.

He closed the door to Harry's study and sat us down very casually at opposite end of the leather couch. He had the manner of a school administrator embarking on a parent-teacher discussion.

"Just a couple of things, Mrs. Stuart," he said. "I've been trying to get a picture of the late Mr. Venables from the Grangers. Understandably they're quite taken aback by this whole business—innocent bystanders, you might say, plunged into the unhappy conclusion of their old friend's life. You might be able to help me flesh things out just a bit. For instance, what was your relationship with Mr. Venables?"

"We went to college . . . well, not together, but several of us knew one another. Sally and I were at Mount Holyoke, the men were at Harvard. I hadn't seen him since college days."

"And that would be how long, Mrs. Stuart?"

"Almost twenty years. Eighteen, I guess."

"And the group of Harvard men—who made up this group?"

"Harry Granger, Mike Pierce, Jack Stuart, Hacker Welles, Peter Venables . . . I think that's it. I have a notoriously faulty memory, I'm afraid."

"Really? Why do you say that?"

"I'd completely forgotten Peter Venables until he came back. That's all."

"Well, I'll bet you had far more important things to think about these past eighteen years. I understand you married one of this group—Ruffians? Very colorful. You married Jack Stuart, a novelist, I'm told. And you're a painter. And you and your husband have been very close friends, intimate friends even, of the Grangers all these years. Have I got that right?" He smiled beneath the actorish mustache. He wasn't taking any notes. We were just chatting.

"Yes," I said, "you've got that right."

"And was it a great pleasure to see your old friend Mr. Venables after all these years?"

"I wouldn't call it a great pleasure, no."

"Ah. Well, time changes people, doesn't it? A friend of twenty years ago might not be our choice of friend now— we all grow in different ways. The fellow my sister married, for instance . . . But every family is full of such stories. Mr. Venables had changed, I take it."

"I don't really remember what he was like back then. I found him not much to my taste this time around."

"Perhaps you could elaborate just a bit, Mrs. Stuart. None of us likes to speak ill of the dead but, let's face it, this is not an ordinary circumstance. Just fill me in . . ."

He was smiling reassuringly, and it struck me that he knew the answers to the questions he was asking. I'd held off so long in telling Sal about my Venables horrors—if only I'd never told her at all! There was something about Antonelli that gave me a helpless feeling. He was leading me somewhere that I might not like much, but I didn't know how to keep from going there.

"The bottom line," I said, "is that Venables made a very ugly pass at me one night. He was trading on my willingness to accept him as an old friend. It was a nasty scene but a brief one." I sighed and decided to tell the rest of it. "He kept pestering me after that, but only on social occasions."

"Pestering?"

"Threatening me, in a way. Saying that he wasn't giving up, that it was his turn."

"His *turn*? What a peculiar remark."

"I suppose. I didn't attach any importance to it. I certainly left him in no doubt as to my feelings."

"Which were?"

"I thought he was despicable."

"A view that, I presume, was shared by your husband, Jack Stuart?"

"My husband and I are no longer together. I don't feel that I can reliably interpret his thoughts about much of anything."

"Very circumspect, I must say. Most husbands and wives seem so eager to put words and thoughts into each other's mouths and heads." He shifted comfortably, crossed his legs, folded his hands across his knee. "Still, I'm sure you're right about your husband's private reflections. Oh, my yes, husbands and wives. Tell me, did your husband strike you often?"

I blinked at that one. Sally may have been upset, but she'd also been talkative. "No."

"But he did strike you last night? On the night of your gallery opening—that, of all nights?"

"Yes. Jack hasn't been himself lately. Our marriage being in trouble, his moving out . . ." I shrugged helplessly.

"Oh, I do understand. My daughter and her husband." He shook his head. "Sadly, it seems to be the way things go these days, doesn't it? As I was saying, people change over twenty years. You, Mr. Venables, your husband—I daresay you're all different people now. We all are. So, we say so-and-so's not himself. When what we actually mean is, so-and-so has simply become someone else, a different person. It's the process we call life. Why did your husband strike you, Mrs. Stuart?"

"We had words, an argument. I was yelling at him—"

"Do you recall what you were yelling at him about?"

"His temper, I guess. He'd just broken a bottle of brandy, made an awful mess—"

"Good Lord! Why would he do that?" He wore a mask of innocent amazement. Eyebrows raised, head cocked in curiosity.

"Look, Sally must have told you all this—"

"She mentioned something, yes, but I'd much rather hear it from you. She seems to have arrived late, missing the fireworks. Do go on, please."

"Peter Venables and Jack had an argument. They didn't know I overheard them—then I walked in on them and Peter left and Jack and I argued. I just didn't need him getting into the act with Venables. I could take care of him."

"They were arguing about you, then. What did Venables actually say?"

"He didn't say much of anything."

He gave me a puzzled look. "How about Mr. Stuart?"

"I . . . I don't really remember very clearly. Jack was just giving him hell, wanted him to get lost . . ." I was lying and I thought I was being smart. I saw where Antonelli was heading and I'd been right: I didn't much like it.

"Ah. Well, you warned me about your notoriously bad memory, didn't you? Tell me, do you have a clearer recollection of the party here at the Grangers' home? Do you recall any fisticuffs breaking out in your presence?"

"Of course," I said wearily. "I suppose Sally and Harry have told you all about that, too."

"They could hardly do otherwise, Mrs. Stuart. I am inquiring into the murder of Mr. Venables. I have asked them to describe whatever they could of Mr. Venables' activities while he was here. I expect they've done so to the best of their abilities. If you'll think about it, it's surprisingly difficult to ignore a physical attack made upon one of your party guests by another in full view of a hundred or more witnesses—"

"All right, all right, I get the point." I watched him smile at me, sorry that he'd had to reprimand me but letting me know he wasn't going to hold it against me. I wouldn't have to stay after school. Not this time, anyway. But I'd been warned. I told him about the party and the one-punch main event. "And Jack felt just terrible afterward. Really awful. He knew he'd made a fool of himself."

Antonelli nodded slowly. "Yes, I'm sure he truly regretted it. After all, Mr. Venables was an old friend and there is a significant bond between these men. But"—he shrugged—"pressures get to us sometimes, and bang! We suddenly behave in uncharacteristic manners." He smiled. "We're only human. We're jealous, we get angry. We handle the anger in different ways. Well, let me see . . . Oh, yes, where did you spend last night?"

"After the show ended Harry walked me back to the loft. I didn't go out again until Harry called me this morning."

"You were alone all night?"

"I was."

"Well, Mrs. Stuart," he said with the small-town smooth voice, running a thick hand back along his hair, tugging at a pink earlobe, "you've been very forthcoming, very helpful. You know, you really do remind me of my daughter." He shook his head at the resemblance.

"I hope she survives her divorce all right."

"Oh, no. I'm referring to Kate. She's a nun, no need to worry about Katie." He stood up. "If anything else comes up, may I get in touch with you? Just to fill in the picture?"

"Of course."

"And I must take a look at your pictures in the Leverett Gallery. The Grangers are both great fans of yours, you know."

He opened the door into the hallway, held it for me.

"Your husband," he said, pinching his lower lip. He wore a little Rotary Club pin in the lapel of his gray suit coat. His gray-and-red tie was spectacularly unstylish: a thick, clotted material, which I'd have bet had a guide on the back letting you know what color suit to wear it with. He must have been a very reassuring, predictable, understanding father. I stared at him, waiting for him to go on.

"I understand he owns a shotgun," he said. "Do you know this to be true?"

"Oh, good God," I said impatiently. "It's an old thing his father gave him years ago. I don't know where it is."

"Oh, of course, you haven't been to his new place of residence. Well, I'm told—"

"By Harry Granger," I said.

"I'm told that he has this shotgun in his room. I suppose it's important to him as a talisman, you might say. A reminder of his late father."

"And I suppose Venables was killed with a shotgun?" I couldn't stop my voice from shaking.

"My guess would be both barrels, frankly. Close range. Very close range."

He smiled sheepishly and I felt him watching me as I walked back down the hallway toward Harry. Mike Pierce had arrived and was listening to Harry. His face was pink-cheeked and his eyes round as silver dollars. Finally I heard the door click behind me.

Chapter Twenty-five

"What the hell do you think you're doing? You've got that man about ready to stick Jack in a solitary and throw away the key! Good God, are you positively nuts?"

I must have been shouting because Mike started to say *now, now* and Harry took my arm, cast a quick glance at the cops still fascinated by the floor's contents, and hustled me toward the stairway leading down to the kitchen and dining room. The maid in the kitchen was trying hard to be invisible, chopping and mincing intently. She didn't look up as we swept through the dining room and out the French doors to the garden. "Now, just sit down, Belle, and get your breath and stop screaming at me and tell me what's on your mind. Would either of you like iced tea? Coffee? A drink?"

"Sit down, Harry," Mike said. "You sound like a stewardess."

The garden was thick with trees and flowers and shrubs, sprinklers going, a fountain erupting rhythmically, birds flitting in the dark green shadows. The humidity made it all tropical. There should have been big snakes like the roots of trees. The air was so thick it was hard to catch my breath. Mike lit a cigarette, crossed his legs and straightened the crease. He was wearing a perfect fresh seersucker suit and a bow tie.

"Now, Belle, what's the problem? Other than Peter being shot and Sal poised on the edge of a nervous breakdown, that is."

"Jack having a murder case made against him before the body's stiff, that's a problem! I mean, what are you, you and Sally, thinking of? You both must have spent the whole morning dredging up every damning detail you could remember—I mean, seriously, what are you thinking of? You seem to have told Antonelli enough to get him reaching for his handcuffs! And whatever possessed you to start babbling about that old shotgun? Talk about utterly gratuitous! You must have had to work like hell to get that into the story. Harry, I'm just dumbfounded!"

Harry looked at me while I slumped, momentarily exhausted, in the wrought-iron chair. "Well, Belle, you're certainly not speechless. And you're not thinking very clearly."

"I suppose you are!"

"Just listen to me and try to calm down. Antonelli asked me if I had a shotgun, if I knew anybody who had a shotgun, and I'd seen Jack's the other day. You know how strongly that affected me, I told you about it that day at the theater. I told you how it worried me, the combination of Jack's state of mind and the darn shotgun."

"That's all well and good," I said. "We were worried about Jack, we wanted to help him . . ."

"I was worried about Jack using that gun, Belle. On anybody he thought you were getting close to. Hell, I even mentioned Mike here as a possible target, didn't I?"

"Yes, but you also said it was more likely that he'd use it on himself!" I said. "Did you tell Antonelli that? I mean, telling him wasn't the same as just shooting the breeze with me. You should have heard him—everything you told him was coming back at me. He's building a case against Jack and you're handing him the hammer and nails! And Sally—she was at least in shock. What's your excuse? What's going on here, Harry? Is it a game? Let's pin a murder on poor old Jack? Do you really think he'd do this to you?" I stopped talking because my voice was suddenly hoarse and my mouth was dry and I felt like keeling over.

When Harry got angry he always got even quieter than usual. His mouth would tighten and his lips would get white. And all of that was happening. He looked distant and hurt, as if I'd slapped him. I concentrated on a bright yellow Baltimore oriole watching us from a safe distance. Mike leaned forward to hear, Harry's voice was so soft.

"Belinda, you're getting all this second-hand. I didn't hear what Antonelli said to you. You didn't hear what Sally and I said to him. Or how we said it—"

"But you said it!" I croaked. "You just damned Jack and didn't look back!"

"Think about what I said. Has it occurred to you that what we told Antonelli was true? That it might be important? That it might be relevant to what happened here?" The fountain splashed in the silence as if there were no city beyond the garden. Mike flicked his ash into a flowerbed. "He hit you, Belle. He punched you out last night. Do you want to wait for the next—"

Mike said: "He *what*? Who hit you?"

"—escalation? Don't you see the pattern? Are you so blind that you can't see the way Jack's going? I tried to smooth over this thing with Peter at our party, sat you both down and tried to soft-pedal the whole thing, but when I heard Sally say he'd hit you last night—Jesus, Belle, why didn't you tell me then?"

Mike looked from Harry to me, his face flushing. "Jack? Jack hit you? Why, that's . . . that's . . . swinish!"

I said: "Aha, I knew there was a word for it."

"That worried the hell out of me, Belle. First, he hits Venables, he's acting weird as hell, anyway. Then he pops you one . . . and then someone uses a shotgun on poor Peter, poor goddamn Peter—"

"Oh, do stop going on about poor Peter!" I felt myself exploding again and hoped it was for the best. "He was a sick, evil creep! He tried to rape me one night and he's been hounding me ever since . . . he might not have deserved what happened to him, but he was a son of a bitch—"

"He tried to rape you?" Mike looked goggle-eyed. "Not Peter! You must have misunderstood—"

"Oh, shut up," I said. "You're so stupid and innocent. And blind. Both of you, you're the blind ones. He was a Ruffian, *ergo* he was one swell guy."

"Did Jack know this? About what Peter tried with you?" Harry was still very quiet, very tight.

"I don't know, I don't see how he could have. I didn't tell anybody until Sal last night. No, Jack saw Peter hovering over me at the party . . ." Suddenly I was flashing back on something. I must have been sitting there with my mouth drooping open.

"What is it?" Mike said. "Are you okay?"

I nodded. "That same night, the night the show opened, after you had your talk with Jack and me in the study, Jack took me back to the loft. He stayed awhile and then he left and I got up and went to the window, to watch him walk away . . . and somebody stepped out of the shadows and began following Jack. That's it, I thought it was you, Harry, I was sure it was you—and I couldn't imagine why you'd have been waiting outside for Jack . . . and then I realized it was Peter. Peter had been waiting." I shrugged. "I never heard anything about it—"

"But they might have spoken. Even argued—"

"Harry, I simply don't know. We can ask Jack."

Mike lit another cigarette. "Well, he certainly seemed to have it in for Peter."

Harry said, "Tell me, what was this shouting match at the gallery you told Sally about—before Peter left and Jack decided to beat up on you?"

"It didn't mean much to me. But now, the more I think about it . . . Look," I said, "Peter said something funny to me when he was making his pass. He talked about it being his *turn*, he wanted me because it was his *turn*."

Harry looked at Mike and shrugged. "Men talk that way: 'You've had other men in your life and now it's my turn'—no big deal about that. But what about last night?"

"Well, maybe it was about me. Or partly about me. Peter didn't say anything that I overheard. It was all Jack. He called Peter a scummy bastard, something like that, kept saying he knew Peter, all about Peter, knew why Peter was there. He said Peter couldn't fool him the way he'd fooled all the rest of you. Jack called him a thief, said he'd caught him at it and he better not try to steal anything from Jack." I watched Harry and Mike exchange stares again, blank.

Mike said, "Sounds to me like they were getting into some personal ancient history there. I never heard anything about Peter stealing anything from Jack or anyone else—I mean, let's face it, that's pretty farfetched."

"It's nonsense," Harry agreed. "Pure paranoia—"

"Hey, wait a minute," I interrupted. "You forget that Jack was right on the money about Peter and me. He had Peter figured out and was warning him off. That proves Jack knew what was going on."

Harry was shaking his head. "It proves that he may have accidentally stumbled across the truth. And that's all it proves. What we know for a fact is that he acted on his supposition—he attacked Peter physically, threatened later, and . . . well, who knows what else? I think he's paranoid, Belle. I think everything has turned against him—or that's the way he sees it—and he's backed into a corner. Your life is opening up, his is closing down, he's afraid . . . and he's begun to break things."

Mike said, "Belinda, we can't let him break you."

"What are you talking about?"

"I'm worried," Harry said, "and apparently Mike is too. Maybe the same thought's hit us both. If Jack killed Peter, he killed him because of what he believed about Peter and you . . . and if Jack killed Peter, he's terribly sick, terribly volatile. Belle, you could be in a hell of a lot of danger while Jack's running around loose—"

"Harry! You amaze me! It's all right to stick up for Ruffian Peter . . . but whatever happened to Ruffian Jack? What's going on? Jack's out in the cold, is his name stricken from the records? You say he thinks the world has turned against him—well, I don't know about that but I'll guarantee you the last people he thought would turn against him would be you two!" The more I heard myself talk, the more outraged I became. I stood up and headed for the house.

Harry followed. "You're being unreasonable, Belle. You're not looking at the situation clearly—we're not turning against Jack. But things don't look so good right now . . ." He took my shoulders and turned me toward him. "Listen, why don't you stay here at our place for a while? Until things shake out and Jack clears himself with a great alibi or something? I just hate having you alone out there with Jack and the shotgun unaccounted for."

Mike was watching from the table. "He's right, Belinda."

"The hell with both of you!" I shouted, my voice cracking. I stomped back into the house, up the stairs, and outside. I was shaking fit to fall down and I never had gotten to see Sally.

Chapter Twenty-six

I came to rest, feeling sweaty and disheveled, in a coffee shop on Third Avenue, wondering what in the world had gotten into me. I've always tried to control my temper.

But the sudden realization that Mike and Harry were thinking along the same lines as Antonelli had set it off. So I'd blown up in frustration and surprise. Now I was feeling more alone than I could ever remember. Sally was sedated and Jack was doubtless undergoing a fairly unpleasant interview with Antonelli or one of his counterparts and Harry and Mike were in my doghouse. I sat drinking ersatz iced tea and regretted my performance in Turtle Bay. It was a stupid time to cut myself off from two of my natural allies. If I'd been thinking straight I'd have heard them out and presented some alternatives to the circumstantial evidence. And I wouldn't have accused them of selling Jack out.

What could they have done, other than what they did? Were Sally and Harry supposed to lie to Antonelli? If he asked the questions, they had to answer and, as they'd formed those answers, I suppose the obvious was made glaring. Jack had been acting violently. Jack had been involved in at least two scenes involving attacks, both physical and verbal, on Peter. Peter was blown to pieces with a shotgun. Harry knew Jack had a shotgun and he had told me at the theater how worried he was about the combination of an unstable Jack and the gun.

Facts are facts.

The chance that Jack had done it—well, that had me by the throat.

Still, once they had the gun and tested it and heard what Jack had to say . . . then it would all be okay.

I'd forgotten my sunglasses and the blinding glare from the street had given me a headache by the time I gave up on the iced tea and ventured back outside.

Dammit! I needed to talk to Sal.

* * *

Two kinds of fear were eating at me. As the day progressed, they got worse.

First, I was afraid that Antonelli was going to pin the murder on Jack before anything else in the way of an explanation might come to light.

Second, I was afraid that maybe Jack had actually done it.

By the time I had bought some flowers to cheer me up and gotten a bag full of cosmetics I didn't need, ditto, a third worry had taken root, had a life of its own.

I was afraid that if Jack had truly flipped out he might indeed come after me.

I was wandering aimlessly through Bloomingdale's when I thought I saw him watching me, reflected in one of the mirrors. The man moved like Jack, walked like Jack, moved across the narrow width of the mirror in a flicker, and when I turned I couldn't figure out exactly where he'd been. Or if he'd been reflected in yet another mirror behind me. I snapped around and bumped into a half-dead tourist laden with sacks and knocked them out of her hands. We both wound up groveling on the floor and feeling like screaming. When I stood up I was dizzy and the man was nowhere to be seen.

I had to get myself under control. Jack wasn't stalking me. He couldn't be. No more than he could have killed Peter Venables.

It was idiotic, but suddenly I realized I didn't want to walk outside, alone, didn't want to take a subway. Didn't want to be followed. Like a maniac, panic-stricken, I went out onto Third Avenue and got a cab going in the wrong direction.

Back in the loft I called Sally.

Harry answered and said she was still sleeping. He asked me if I was all right and I said yes.

"Are you still ticked off, Belle?"

"I don't know. I just think you're running out on Jack awfully quickly, that's all."

"We're not running out on him. We're just facing some hard questions. But let's not go into all that again. The important thing is just to find out what really happened. And I wish you'd consider staying up here until everything gets—"

"No, really, I'm fine. Have you talked to Sally?"

"Just briefly. She was pretty groggy, which is best. She started to cry—it really was a shock. Not just that he was dead, but the way he looked—well, no point in dwelling on that. Call me, Belle, if you need a thing. Or get worried." He cleared his throat, which, in Harry, passed for nervousness. "And please, please, be careful. Don't take any chances with Jack. Promise me, Belle—"

"All right. I promise."

"Now see you keep it."

I had never been angry with Harry before, not in the twenty-two years I'd known him. He wasn't the kind of person you got mad at. He was too reasonable, too understanding. You had to be looking for a fight. I'd often wondered where he kept his hostilities, all the nasty baggage we drag along behind us. He always seemed to be planning his next three or four moves; he was always willing to listen to your problems. All of which were reasons why his attitude about Jack had thrown me so.

But as I spent the evening alone with a Yankee game dithering away on the television, his observations began to resonate in my head.

He'd always been Jack's best friend. The Ruffians meant more to Harry than to anyone else. He had no ax to grind in blaming the murder on Jack. No, I had to live with it— he just thought Jack was guilty of murder.

Unless Harry had killed him. . . .

Which brought me back to my Sally-falling-in-love-with-Peter scenario. The scene on the bank in the park, the blowup.

Which made it all too convoluted, and I gave up, went to bed with the fan spraying warm air across me and the night paralyzed and still at the open windows.

Chapter Twenty-seven

Twenty-four hours after the murder the newspapers were already having a field day with the story and TV was closing in. It was just too juicy to slip past unnoticed: the real-life friends who formed the basis of the hit show *Scoundrels All!* and the murder of one of their number at the producer's home—you really couldn't blame them for going to town. And they seemed to get things more or less right. Peter Venables was described as a "London-based money-man" with oil interests, survived by his newlywed daughter who was on a "safari-honeymoon in Africa." I was even dragged into the story as a wife of "onetime literary sensation Jack Stuart," and also because Venables was last seen in public at my gallery opening.

It was crazy, as if we'd all become actors in a play of our own that encompassed *Scoundrels All!* I half-expected to read reviews of our performances. I don't know how reporters dig up these things, but they had the names of all the Ruffians in the *Post* the next morning. I called Jack but there was no answer . . . and, so help me, I sighed with relief. In my mind I saw him sitting in his room staring at the jangling phone . . . alone, brooding.

I was working on my Central Park sketch, wondering what in the world Harry and Sal had been talking about, when Hacker Welles called. I'd been surprised he hadn't gotten hold of me and was delighted to hear his voice. I seemed to derive some comfort from knowing that the official chronicler of the Ruffians hadn't folded his tent and stolen away. He asked me if I knew any more than he did about the Venables thing and I told him I really didn't know what he knew.

"Not a hell of a lot," he said. "I was out at my agent's place in Southampton all day yesterday and heard about it on the radio last night. I called Harry right away. He said Sally was a vegetable and he sounded pretty whacked out himself. I came in to town late last night and first thing this morning somebody from *Live at Five* called me, told me Harry had referred them to me—this babe wanted to know if I'd come on the show this afternoon. I guess Harry had been scheduled to talk about the show. I called Harry back, he begged me to go on for him, so— Geronimo!—here I go. Watch me, okay? And meet me afterward. Harry said you and he had a bit of a dust-up yesterday. I want to hear all about it. When I finish making a fool of myself, grab a cab and I'll meet you at Mitchell Place, up on top."

I got dressed and plopped down in front of the set and of course Hacker handled it very well but there was a little kicker right at the end that came out of nowhere.

The woman interviewing him was chatty and intense, pretending she was getting the inside dope on a murder story. Hacker wore a bemused expression. On television he looked a bit balder, which was, somehow, rather endearing.

No, he knew only what he'd read in the papers; yes, he had spoken with Mr. Granger but he was at as great a loss as any of the rest of us; no, he couldn't imagine why anyone would have wanted to kill Peter Venables. Yes, in a broad sense the show was based on the group of college friends a great many years ago; yes, it was a terrible coincidence that Mr. Venables should meet such a fate at just this time; yes, Mr. Venables was an old friend, but Hacker hadn't seen him in many years.

He was typically rumpled in a seersucker jacket and lavender polo shirt. He looked very tan. His voice was deep and soothing, sort of in the Charles Kuralt mode overall.

"Tell us, Mr. Welles, what is *Scoundrels All!* really about?"

He looked vaguely puzzled for a moment, as if he could barely remember the show. "Well, it's about the past, it's about all those hopeful youthful friendships we've all had, but in the end it's about my own imagination—what I mean is, it's about a past that never really was, a past that existed only in my mind. That's a writer's job, isn't it? Turning reality—whatever that actually is—into his own fantasy."

"One last question, Mr. Welles." She looked very proud of herself, anticipating. "Do you think there might be a clue to the mystery of Peter Venables' murder somewhere in your play?"

He looked at her in some considerable astonishment. Slowly, almost imperceptibly, a smile spread across his face, giving him the look of a gigantic imp. "Why, that's quite an intriguing—and certainly unexpected—question. I must congratulate you on originality . . . but don't you suppose it's asking a bit much of my little play? I mean, it's just a piece of fluff, popular entertainment . . ."

She gave the camera a knowing smile and New York heard Hacker chuckling off-camera, muttering, "Well, what next?" But I had the feeling that she'd succeeded in pushing the On button and set him thinking.

The bar took up the whole of the top of the building and gave the most ravishing views of the city I knew. In the heat of high summer you have to sit on the east side with the East River far below and the UN Plaza and Brooklyn and Queens stretching away apparently into infinity. A Circle Line cruise ship moved slowly up the river. The windows beside us were wide open and we were high enough to catch a breeze. Hacker said he wanted a drink that looked like a prize and ordered a gin rickey with some bright red cherries bobbing in it. He gave me a dark grin and asked what I'd thought of his performance.

"All New York is asking the same question," I said. "Is there a clue in the play?"

"That really came out of left field—what a terrible mind that woman has! But I wonder . . . maybe she was onto something. But what?" He plucked a cherry from the drink and ate it slowly. "Tell me about your shoot-out with Harry—he was actually quite upset, said it was all his fault, but I don't think he meant it. I got the idea you were being unreasonable."

"Maybe I was. I thought he and Sally and Mike were stabbing Jack in the back."

He winced at my choice of metaphor. "Do continue."

I slogged through the whole day-old confrontation, including both my interview with Detective Antonelli and the yelling at Harry. He sat listening, chomping on cherries, and getting another drink. Mine sat untouched while I talked. Every time I started to get worked up, my voice sliding up into the higher registers, I'd see him looking calmly at me, nodding, and I'd calm down.

"The point is," I said, "they really planted the Jack-as-killer seed in Antonelli's mind, and I can see the whole thing getting out of hand right away."

"They've still got to build a case," he said. "It's bound to take some time. And maybe Jack can give them satisfactory answers. No, that's not what's really bothering you, Belinda."

"I suppose you know what is?"

"Don't get all bristly. Just think a minute. What's bothering you is that they—all of them, Antonelli and Harry and Mike and the absent Sally—they all have convinced you that Jack probably did it. And *that* has really pissed you off. You fly off the handle accusing them of running out on the old Ruffian and now you're seeing yourself do the same thing."

"Well, it makes me so mad—"

"It also makes you scared. You think Jack's following you and, 'Gee whiz, if he killed Peter over me, then he might just let go a volley at me'—look, I don't blame you. I'd probably feel the same way. You think they've got any peanuts in this joint? That guy's eating peanuts." He succeeded in acquiring a bowl of peanuts, looked up at me guiltily. "So I'm hungry, okay?"

"Okay, okay."

"Anyway, you're scared of Jack and feeling as if you're letting him down. Frankly, that's the healthiest view you can have. After all, maybe Jack did kill him. Maybe . . ."

"But?" I sensed a ray of hope and took a big drink of tonic water.

"But maybe he didn't. If he didn't know about your unhappy encounter with Venables at the loft—well, that might be the kind of thing that a chap would want to avenge . . . No, no, that's crazy too. No, the only thing that makes sense is Jack having to be nuts. Either he is nuts and might have done it. Or he's not nuts and didn't do it. Tell me what you overheard from the privacy of Leverett's powder room—there's something funny about that."

I ran through it again as best I could. His eyebrows drew together in a parody of deep thought. When he drank, his glass dripped onto his shirt. Things like that just happened to him.

He shook his head and yawned. "Nope, I just don't know. I'll have to think on't. We gotta get some real food, the inner man cries out." He got the check. The sun was still glaring on the towers of the city, the Chrysler Building like a graceful spaceship from another civilization. "Thief," he mused as the elevator descended, "so Peter was a thief . . ." He whistled tunelessly, his mind a million miles away. "And now he figured it was his turn. That son of a gun." He smiled at me quickly. "Mexican. Let's eat Mexican. That's what happens to you living in Los Angeles. You get in the habit of eating Mexican. Place called Ports, the chicken mole—and there's nothing in the world like a Pink's chili dog. I've had them air-expressed to me when I've been on location. My wife used to do that for me, bless her heart. Eased her conscience, I think." He winked at me.

An hour later he looked up from the remains of chilis rellenos and beef burritos and chicken enchiladas, poured us each another margarita from a frosty pitcher, and said, "*Arriba! Aribba!*"

"*Olé*," I said, grinning stupidly.

"So you speak Spanish too. I didn't know that. You feeling any better about things?"

"No, but you've taken my mind off it all and I appreciate that. But I'm still worried sick about Jack. And . . . you know, scared."

He nodded.

"I've been thinking," I said slowly, not knowing if I was trespassing on his privacy, "about your book—your version, not Harry's. Someone gets murdered in your book . . . it's a little spooky, isn't it?"

"Life imitating art," he said. "But I haven't written the book yet."

"But it's as if you almost expected something like this to happen—that's what gives me the shivers. That and the way Tony Chalmers told me he always sort of thought the top might come off the Ruffians."

"Tony said that? Hmmm. Well, he should know—he knows more about us than we do, I guess."

"But did you expect some act of violence? Once all the Ruffians were together again?"

He shrugged. "Well, we didn't spend all our time sitting around singing 'Ten Thousand Men of Harvard,' you know. Every so often we'd work off some steam . . . but remember, I'm a writer. I make things up. And in my story the perfect girl was going to be the killer."

"And you said she'd have a reason. And I've been thinking about that, too . . ."

"Fiction," he said. "But I'll tell you something if you'll just keep it to yourself. That interviewer asking me that crazy question, then listening to you recount what you've heard from both Peter and Jack—it all convinces me that

Venables was killed by something from the past, something stemming from a long time ago. It goes back to first causes. This murder didn't just happen, it's the culmination of something that's been building all along."

"Now you're being a writer again."

"You think so? I think we're all the sum of our pasts— life is a kind of process of addition and subtraction, and at any particular time you total something. That night Peter totaled something and the killer totaled something and it added up to a murder. Hmmm. That sounds a bit corny, but you get the idea. And we all came together and the result is somebody murders Peter. I don't believe he died because of something that happened last week or the night he died." He looked mournfully at his empty plate and the nearly empty pitcher. He dabbed at his mouth, then spotted a bit of sauce on his jacket lapel and dabbed at that too. "Jesus, I need a bib. Thank God my personal hygiene is so impeccable."

We were eating in the Village, so we walked south toward SoHo and the loft. Past the Leverett Gallery, where Hacker insisted on looking at the display of my work in the window. I stood back at the curb watching the strollers on the hot night, listening to the endless babble of chatter. People were crowded at the big corner fruitstand. The sidewalks were crowded with moist, lightly clad women and men who were looking on interestedly.

"Have you got a girlfriend?" I asked as we walked on. Well, why not ask? Just making conversation about something but murder.

He did one of those little double-takes, looking over his shoulder to see if anyone else was standing there. "You talking to me?"

"Idiot!"

"No, no girlfriend. I've consecrated my life to my work. How about you?"

"No, I haven't got a girlfriend either."

"Lucky thing. You never know these days."

We stopped at the downstairs doorway to the loft building. He was smiling at me as if he found my every observation hugely amusing. But then, Hacker probably smiled at everyone the same way. Including the woman who interviewed him.

"So," I said, "you're saying that whether or not it's Jack, it's a Ruffian who killed Peter." For some reason that was an unnerving possibility that hadn't occurred to me before.

"Is that what I said?"

He leaned forward, touched my right cheek with the fingertips of his left hand, and brushed his lips across my left cheek. It felt like a shadow slipping across my face.

"Sleep tight, Belinda. And be careful."

"What are you going to do now?"

"Work on my novel. Good night for it."

He waited in the street until I came to the window and waved and then he strolled off down Prince Street, parting the crowds as he went.

Chapter Twenty-eight

It was another hellish night. I kept hearing street noises, the kind you only seem to hear on stifling summer nights when your fellowman has decided he's staying up all night no matter what. I lay in the damp sheets, my legs all tangled up and my hair sweat-plastered against the back of my neck, fading in and out of sleep. I thought for a while that I could still smell the yellow roses, in the air, in the sheets and the pillowcases, as if I hadn't changed them.

I woke again, kicked my way free of the sheets, and sat up wiping my face, still groggy, shaking my head at the thoughts invading my sleep. Carlyle Leverett had been talking to me; I'd been standing alone before the gallery windows looking at my paintings and he'd peeked out from behind one of them, Adam's apple bobbing. He'd started telling me again what villains the Ruffians had been in the old days and how glad he was that somebody had started killing them—the more that got killed, the better: somebody ought to get a medal. *Villains, villains, one and all* . . . He'd been laughing in my sleep.

Then I was back in Central Park, floating on the lake, but I was alone and I didn't seem to have a boat, and it was dark as night. I could hear the carousel music in the background, but when I looked at the bank there were the wooden horses bobbing up and down without benefit of the carousel itself. I floated closer, hearing laughter, and there on the horses were Sally and someone I thought was Harry, laughing and leaning across to kiss, and I felt this immense sense of relief. Then I realized something was wrong and floated closer. It wasn't Harry after all. It was Peter Venables, blood spattered down the front of his white dress shirt, and while he laughed with Sally he looked up, caught my eye, and winked. . . .

I looked at the clock beside the bed. Nearly one. The night was too hot, too humid to be believed. Someone shouted in the street. The glow of the fruitstand filled the windows with an eerie light. A siren worried about something far away. I padded across the floor, stood at the open window, proved unable to convince myself there was a breeze. I went back and adjusted the fan and peeled the top sheet off the bed. Then I lay down gingerly, reducing movement to a minimum, put my arms straight at my sides, and waited for sleep to claim me again.

The clock said it was almost three.

I squirmed around, reached for a glass of once-iced water, now tepid, and gasped. I knocked the glass off onto the floor.

There had been a noise, something in the loft had moved. Something somewhere.

Blinking, rubbing my eyes, panicking, aware of my nakedness, I searched the shadows of the room. "Who is it? Who's there?"

Someone moved at the far end of the loft, in the darkness, in the shadows near the wheel-of-fortune.

A cry caught like a bone in my throat.

A man stepped into the gray light from the window, he was coming toward me . . .

Frantically I fumbled with the bedside lamp. My mind was guttering like a candle in a strong wind, about to go out. It was him, he'd come for me . . .

"Belinda," he said.

I flicked the light on and saw him.

"Belinda, for Chrissakes, relax. It's me. Just me."

"Jack," I said.

I sank back on the bed clutching a pillow across my chest, sighing and laughing, gasping for breath, half-hysterical, but not afraid. He was right. It was just Jack.

He sat on the stool at the worktable. I retrieved the discarded top sheet and wrapped myself, leaned back against the headboard. I watched warily as he toyed with the junk on the table. Erratic, misbehaving, angry, frustrated—he was all those things but it wasn't the same as being crazy. Or being a killer. He yawned.

"Damn air conditioner went out on me tonight," he said. "Good thing I insisted on our exchanging keys—you'll always be welcome to visit my little hellhole. Two windows six inches from a sooty airshaft. To know it is to love it. I miss it already. Anyway, the air conditioner went blooey and I got the hell out. Went to a movie. Revival of *Vertigo*. God, how I love that movie . . . Believe me, I needed a movie. It's been a pretty weird couple of days." He sat staring into space for a minute and I kept my mouth shut. "Then I started walking. Went past Harry's place, the lights were on, I damn near went up and rang the bell . . . but then I got to thinking about this cop, oldish guy, well he seems oldish, Antonelli—well, he said he'd talked to Harry and Sal and you—this Antonelli's been talking to me the better part of these two days and he told me a lot of stuff Harry and Sal had said to him, and while I may have a lock on being an asshole, I'm not an idiot. So I figured maybe Harry and Sal wouldn't be all that happy to see me." He rubbed a knuckle along his jaw. He hadn't shaved and his shirt was none too fresh. "I mean, they seem to have gotten this Antonelli character on my case about the late El Creepo. Which is not to say that I thought he was worth killing, mind you." He shrugged. "Well, let's say it's close, it's a judgment call. Anyway, I took a pass on the Granger residence. I thought about Mike, but somehow, I don't know, but I've got this funny feeling that maybe I'm on his shit list, too . . . is that crazy, Belinda? Or would you say I've put my finger on something rather cogent?"

He slid off the stool and meandered out to the kitchen and I heard him pouring from a bottle of wine. He asked if I wanted any and I said no. He knew me. He brought me a glass of ice water. "Funny, you don't have much to say once you stop screaming."

"I've been listening. You tell quite a story."

"I'm almost done with my picaresque tale. I thought about my old chum and fellow scrivener, Hacker Welles. But the problem is, I'm officially bitter about his making a hit show out of my—our—lives. Seeing the fat bastard would just depress me—"

"He's not fat. He's large. Ample."

"*Ample?* Oh, shit, does this mean you're getting it on with Hacker?" He rolled his eyes and shook his head. "What kind of a wife are you, anyway?"

"Departing. And no, I'm not."

"Well, at this point it doesn't make such difference. He's probably got me ticketed for the big house too. So I just kept walking and sweating and finally I realized my feets was taking me home. Sort of like Lassie." He grinned sheepishly. "So, tell me, what's going on?" His voice suddenly cracked and he whispered: "It's killing me, Belinda. What's going on? Why have they turned on Me? Harry? Sal? Do they really honest-to-God think I killed Peter?"

"I think maybe they do," I said.

"Jesus, you're awfully calm. Or do you think so too?"

"I didn't say that, Jack."

"Yeah. And you didn't say you didn't, either."

"There's no point in getting angry with me—"

"Don't tell me that. I feel angry. And I feel like I'm about to get fucked over but good. Life may be punishing me for my past sins, but this is ridiculous. Do you think I killed the bastard?"

"I don't know."

"Terrific!" He drained his glass and went back to the kitchen and filled it again.

"Jack, listen to me. When two men have as much trouble as you and Peter were having and then one of them gets killed—well, the question *does* arise. You're the natural suspect. What did you tell Antonelli?"

He came back and ignored me. "I must admit I didn't expect the warmest reception in the world, but this—well, I'm amazed. Marital discord has not previously added up to a willing acceptance of a murder charge." His hand was shaking.

"I'm scared of you, Jack."

He frowned at me. "Oh, by the way . . . I really am sorry for slugging you. But what's a quick right between a homicidal maniac and his wife? You're lucky I didn't blow your head off too. Come on, Belinda, get serious—we're talking murder here, not my being a dickhead. There's a difference."

"God, I hope so. I hope you can prove it."

"Proving it to Antonelli is one thing. But why should I have to prove my innocence to the goddamned Ruffians? And to you? That's what baffles me."

Slowly, like a rather worn-out doll, he came over and slumped down on the end of the bed, hands on his knees, head down. It was Harry's study all over again. And I wanted to help him, comfort him, make it all better. His shoulders were shaking. I remembered the football hero. The novelist in the flush of success too soon. The guy coming apart and losing his wife. Just Jack.

He lay back across the foot of the bed and put his palms over his eyes. His jaw was clenched. He was struggling with all the demons and he was for the moment holding his own.

"I don't think I did it, Belinda."

"What does that mean exactly?"

"I got loaded. Really loaded. Somehow I got up around Gracie Mansion . . . maybe Mayor Koch can give me an alibi. I woke up on a bench with the sun coming up over the East River right in my eyes." He rubbed his eyes and took his hands away. They were red and empty. "It's a miracle *I* didn't get killed. Anyway, I don't know any more about what happened that night." He coughed, exhausted. "I don't think I killed him, Belinda. That's all I can say."

I reached down and touched his hand, felt his fingers tighten around mine.

"The shotgun, then," I said. "If you didn't go home, the gun must be clean, or dusty—dusty, that'd be perfect. Unfired—there must be tests. It's the gun, Jacko, that's what made it all seem so plausible . . . the gun will prove you didn't do it."

"No, I don't think it will, honey."

"What do you mean? Why not?"

"It's gone. The gun's gone."

I just sat there looking at him, and finally he turned over on his side and went to sleep. I felt like all the horrors of the night were closing in on us.

Chapter Twenty-nine

Jack left early, after a piece of toast and a cup of coffee. He went quietly. He said he had no idea when the shotgun disappeared from his apartment: it had been there the day Harry had stopped by. He never paid any attention to it and wasn't at all sure if he'd have noticed it absence. He shrugged, said he knew it looked very bad—but what else could he say? Antonelli was drawing his own conclusions and Jack just didn't have much more to tell him. *Que será, será*. I told him I didn't know he spoke Spanish. He laughed weakly and left.

I took a sketchpad and made a list. I had to try to get things straight in my mind or I'd go under for sure.

Sally. I wanted to know how she was. And I had to try to figure out if she was in shock because (a) she'd been horrified at finding the body or (b) that it was the body of her lover. I couldn't begin to imagine how I might dig that out.

The Past. If Hacker was right about the killing of Venables stemming from the events of our joint past—and therefore that the murderer was a Ruffian—then how best to excavate the past? How secretive would the Ruffians be about reasons only they might know for a murder so many years later? Bloody damn secretive, if I knew my Ruffians. If only I could remember more!

Jack & Venables. What did their words mean? What about that "thief" conversation? What about Venables saying it was his "turn"? This probably related to *The Past*.

Betrayal. Were the Ruffians betraying Jack or was that no more than an illusion in my overly protective mind? Was Jack as dangerous as they thought? Or was he the pussycat he'd seemed last night? Or could he swing between those two poles? I had felt myself being lulled by his condition during the night but I'd also been down that particular garden path with Jack before: the next time I saw him he could give me that white-hot stare as if he wanted to kill me.

I scribbled some marginalia and drew some arrows and made some connections and wondered if this was how Hacker worked on his plot.

The mind works in curious ways. One moment I was working on my own list, the next I was thinking about Hacker's novel . . . and the next I'd had a stroke of genius.

Jack's novel! That stack of pages that Harry had casually touched and Jack had rushed to protect. He was writing again. And Jack had always written about his own life, had worked and reworked his own experience, both in the first successful novel and in the later unpublished work. The past. Jack's version of the past. And something he didn't want Harry to see . . . So far as my inspiration could carry me, it seemed like a wonderful source of information. Well, if not wonderful, it *was* a source, and I couldn't seem to think of any others. All I had to do was get a glimpse of it.

"He was really down," I said. "You can imagine how he felt. He'd spent two days with Antonelli's hinting he was a murderer and he figured Harry, Mike, and Sally had thrown him to the wolves. And his air conditioner broke—I mean, he was in the pits. The least you could do is try to reaffirm his faith in his fellow Ruffians. Call him, take him to lunch—"

"I thought you said I was on his shit list too. He won't go."

"Be charming, loyal, friendly. Sympathize. Be curious, tell him you want to know what the hell is going on. Look upon it as research for your novel."

Hacker cleared his throat at the other end of the line. "Antonelli called on me today."

"And?"

"You were right. I felt like I should raise my hand to go to the bathroom. Then I bought an insurance policy. Anything to get him out of the house. He's so *kind*. Sort of guy who means it when he says this is going to hurt him more than you. I told him the unvarnished truth. Sanded down a bit to make it as innocuous as possible, but no varnish."

"So will you call Jack?"

"Sure. I'd like to see the old bastard, anyway."

"Then call me back, okay? Let me know if you're going to see him."

Three hours later I was sitting at the counter of a flyspecked coffee shop so far up on the East Side that I felt I should have brought my passport. A fan sitting at the end of the counter was blowing more out of habit than a belief in itself. I'd been working on a Coke and a tuna-salad sandwich for half an hour while I watched the entryway of what had once been a rather grand old building across the street. Now torn curtains hung limply in the tall windows. The front doors into the darkened lobby stood open and unmanned. But flowers bloomed in windowboxes. The building wasn't dead yet, it was putting up a fight, although the end looked to be near. Jack lived on the second floor rear. I was waiting to see him leave to meet Hacker for lunch. Two guys at the first booth were talking baseball with the proprietor. Baseball and the heat. A little girl on a trike kept riding back and forth on the sidewalk ringing the bell on the handlebars. I waited.

At one-fifteen I saw him come out, check his watch, and head off up the street, past the green plastic sacks of trash and a gushing fire hydrant where some kids were having the time of their lives. I went out, watched him hail a cab, and crossed the street. I had the key he'd forced on me when he moved. The lobby was dim and the floor of cracked white tile was uneven, as if a giant had been trying to hammer his way out of the basement. There wasn't a soul in sight. The walls were freshly painted and huge old-fashioned floor fans stirred the leaves of a couple of potted palms. I saw the broad stairway and went up one flight, feeling furtive, regretting the whole idea.

I needn't have brought the key. The door was unlocked, as I'd half-expected it to be. Jack refused to remember to do things like that: it was part of his nature, an almost studied casualness. He figured that any burglar stopped by a simply locked apartment door hadn't yet worked his way up to New York. So I'd always been the official door-locker in the family. There was no one in the hallway. I smelled burned fried eggs, but the frayed carpet was neatly vacuumed, the standing ashtrays full of clean white sand. I took a deep breath and went inside.

The room was small and stuffy and badly lit. There was a tiny bedroom, more like an extension of the corridor off which the bathroom opened. The sink in the galley kitchen was full of dishes soaking in gray water. The square of countertop was cluttered with the white card-board containers from a Chinese takeout. A couple of coffee mugs rested in a spindly wooden drying rack.

There was a couch, a small TV on a hassock, its antennas shooting out at crazy angles trying to bring in a better signal. An almost full bottle of Glenlivet sheltered beneath a lampshade on the end table. A dropleaf dining table had been turned into a desk. A couple of boxes of books he hadn't unpacked and a glass-fronted bookcase full of those he had. It wasn't a depressing or filthy place, just a small New York apartment, maybe five hundred dollars a month. Maybe more. No evidence of mice or roaches. Neat. It made me feel just a little better about Jack.

I turned on a lamp and there it was. The shrine Harry had told me about. Dozens of snapshots of me. They were arrayed on the finely figured flowered wallpaper, fixed with thumbtacks. Belinda at the beach, Belinda squinting in the sunshine at a lodge in the Adirondacks, Belinda at twenty-eight on the boardwalk at Coney Island, beneath a gate into the Harvard Yard at twenty-one, Belinda in a bikini and in jeans and in an expensive suit he'd bought for her in Paris, Belinda looking up at Big Ben under a gray London sky, Belinda holding a mug of ale outside a pub in the Lake District, Belinda making faces at the camera in some forgotten moment of hilarity—every time he looked up from the typewriter he was confronted by all these images of Belinda . . . of happiness lost . . . of the past.

I sat down in his chair before the typewriter. I swallowed hard. There wasn't a solution that would satisfy Jack. We weren't going to dance a soft-shoe into the wings together. No matter how many snapshots he tacked on the wall, no matter how I felt my heart wrenched, that wasn't the way it was going to work out.

I felt like a shit of the worst sort. Here I was, with no claim and no right to be there. I was premeditatedly intruding on his privacy, just as voyeuristically as someone watching through a peephole, like Anthony Perkins in *Psycho*. I sat still as a little girl listening to her parents fighting, afraid and fascinated. Jack deserved his privacy, his solitude, his secrecy.

A faucet was dripping into the dishwater. Boy George singing "Karma Chameleon" in the airshaft, no ray of sunshine, just the heat like an oven and the dirt-encrusted, defunct air conditioner. No wonder he'd gone for a walk. I was dripping wet.

God, I felt like a traitor! One of the worst, far worse than Harry could ever have been. But I wanted to help. I wanted to help Jack and I didn't want to be afraid of him anymore. I wanted to find something in his work that would explain his state of mind, his view of the past . . .

something that might explain what was going on between him and Venables. I desperately wanted to be convinced that Jack was all right, that he hadn't killed anyone and wouldn't kill me. I was doing a wrong thing for a right reason, that's what I'd told myself as a little girl. *A wrong thing, Mommie, I did a wrong thing but I didn't mean it.*

The manuscript was neatly stacked beside the typewriter. Not a long work, if it was complete. Maybe 250 pages. I knew the drill. Twenty-pound bond. Squared edges. A blank page on top.

I peeled it away. No title page yet. Page one.

She woke to the fluttering curtain, blowing across the bed, stroking her leg like a lover's touch.

I began to read.

An hour later I laid my head on the table, my face slippery with tears, sobbing, trying not to scream.

I had never read anything like it.

It was the vilest possible pornography. An American woman visiting her lover in Paris, betrayed by him, drugged, made to perform in an erotic theater . . . her body and her thoughts and reactions described in minute detail, page after page after page, as she grows to accept her role, then to enjoy it, and finally to develop a voracious, insatiable need for all the perversions.

Normally I'd have read a couple of pages, leafed through the rest of it with vague sexual curiosity, and thrown it away. No, it wasn't the fact that it was a dirty book. It wasn't even the fact that Jack had written it.

No, it was the way Jack had dealt with the woman, The vicious enjoyment the writer had taken in her fate. The exquisite detail of the descriptions of her body, the textures of the orifices, the flexing of her muscles, the sounds she made . . . the things she said . . . the things she did.

She was me.

Every bit of her, every inch and every syllable, she was me.

And he hated her.

I don't know how long I sat there. I didn't finish the manuscript, God knows. I lay half-sagged across that old dropleaf table, sobbing like someone who's been hit hard in the stomach, which was just how I felt.

Someone who could write this, who could use his wife as the model, could also pull those triggers, kill a man. He could kill me. He had symbolically killed me on those pages.

I had to get out of that room.

I stood up weakly and knocked the manuscript off the table in the process. It splayed across the worn carpet.

I went out the door and shakily negotiated the stairs. At the foot I stood in the semidarkness and took several deep breaths, squared my shoulders. The inner chill had dried the sweat on my skin. I felt brittle.

A cab. I needed a cab. I stood on the sidewalk, blinking in the unearthly brightness, spots dancing before my eyes. I felt light-headed. Where was a cab? I began walking toward the park. I wasn't thinking, I wasn't watching for anything but a friendly cab. And some twig of memory scratched me: I focused on the man coming down the street toward me.

It was Jack.

Sick with a weird complex of reactions, terror and fright and disgust, I turned and dashed across the street, hearing him call my name. A cab was coming toward me and I waved at it frantically. Jack called to me again. The cab stopped, back door locked, the driver had to reach back and punch it to get it open, and Jack was coming toward me. He couldn't figure out what was going on. The door popped open and I got in, slammed it as he reached the side of the cab.

"Go, hurry up, just go," I shouted, and being a New York cabbie, he got the point.

I looked back. Jack was standing in the middle of the street staring after us. He didn't move until we got to the corner and began to turn, and then he looked up at his building and began to run toward it.

Chapter Thirty

I stopped shaking about half an hour after I got back to the loft. That kind of primal fear is a terrible thing. I think I must have sat catatonically on the couch staring out the window, not moving, waiting for it to pass. It was so visceral. What did I think he was going to do to me there in the street? Why had my heart felt like it was going to burst in my chest? How could the words he'd written—and which he had never intended me to read—have brutalized me so completely?

I didn't have any of those answers. I only had the crazy fear. I'd done something I shouldn't have done, I'd found something awful, and I'd nearly gotten caught at it. Sitting there waiting for the tremors to pass, I knew I'd already begun paying for it.

I finally got to the telephone and called Hacker. No answer. I had to tell someone, I had to shift some of the burden of knowledge. I called Sally but I got Harry.

He sounded distant, exhausted, as if life were ashes for him. "Belle," he said, "how are you? Are you still upset with me?"

"No," I said. "I know you were thinking of my own welfare. It's okay." But I couldn't bring myself to tell him what I had found in Jack's apartment. "Is Sally up and about?"

"Oh, hell . . ." His voice trailed away. "She keeps taking those tranquilizers or sleeping pills, whatever they are. I don't know . . . the doctor says she needs rest, says she's very upset, he talked to me about whether or not she might be willing to go back into therapy—how the hell should I know? Oh, dammit, Belle, I don't know what to do. . . . I wish you were here, we could sit in the garden and have a drink and listen to the fountain and just be happy." The phone went silent and when he spoke again he'd gotten himself back together. "Anyway, she's dead to the world—do you want me to ask her to call you when she comes to?"

"Please, yes. And, Harry? Have faith in her and in your marriage, okay? It's just one of those bad times. It'll all come around."

"Sure it will," he said. "God knows it is one of those bad times. Funny thing is, I don't feel much about Peter—I mean, I don't really seem to care. I don't even notice he's gone. I feel shitty about not caring . . . the first dead Ruffian. I said something to Hacker about that, and you know what he said? He said maybe I'd feel better if we had him stuffed and stood him up in the foyer! What a crazy bastard! I'd say nothing's sacred to old Hacker . . ." He was rambling again. "Of course Peter hasn't got a head, he'd look weird stuffed . . . look, Belle, I'd better go look in on Sal. I'll tell her you called."

I called Mike but he wasn't in his office. I was about to call Leverett just to come over and keep me company when I heard the elevator start banging and wheezing. Someone was coming up.

Jack came off the elevator and stood staring at me. His face was empty. He wasn't carrying a shotgun. I looked at him, then looked away.

He walked past me, crossing the loft and going to the window in the corner by the wheel-of-fortune. He was looking out the window when he started speaking. He sounded like a man talking to himself.

"Don't you think that was a pretty cheap trick? Did you ask Hacker to buy me lunch just to get me out of the apartment? Was it a kick, spying on me? Real Nancy Drew stuff? Sneaking in and poking through things? You really give me a pain in the ass, Belinda. What am I going to have to do with you? Why do I keep trusting you? Why do I come to you when I'm down to the last bit of guts I've got? . . ."

I sat down, trying to get my bearings. He felt wronged. *He* felt wronged. He had written that manuscript and he felt I was a pain in the ass. He kept talking but wouldn't turn to look at me. His voice was as expressionless as his face had been.

"Venables came back for you—you were what he wanted. He told me that, just told me to my face. So what if I hit the bastard? What's the big deal? It's not the first time I've made a bit of an ass of myself. Suddenly I'm a goddamn untouchable, I'm a murderer. Well, maybe I did kill him. Maybe I loaded up the old blunderbuss and let him have it. But maybe I didn't. My friends all seem to think I did. And my wife seems to think I did. And she knows me best." Slowly he turned around and folded his arms across his chest. "Whattaya think? You poked around in my place, looked in the drawers—how does it look to you, Belinda? Your hubby a shotgun murderer?" He smiled at me.

"I read your manuscript," I whispered.

"Like it? Did it capture the true essence—"

"I think you're very sick."

"Ah, I see. Does that mean I blew Peter away, then?"

"It means you're capable of anything."

"Really? One dirty book makes me capable of anything?"

"You raped our lives, our marriage. That's me in your book, Jack. *Me.* You were watching all that happen to me in those pages. I can't even talk to you—"

He looked at me as if I'd begun speaking in tongues. "Whoa! What's that book got to do with you? What are you talking about?"

"Please, leave me alone. I'm begging you . . ."

"Christ, don't start crying."

"I'm not. I just want you to go."

"That's not you!" The color suddenly fired his face. He came toward me, his voice slipping away, out of control. "It's not you! Damn you, listen to me—"

I grabbed the telephone, some hopeless idea about dialing 911. He yanked the phone out of my hand, pulled it with all of his strength, and I heard it rip out of the jack. He grabbed my bare arm and twisted. I screamed. He threw me back on the couch. All I could think was that he was going to start hitting me, he was going to kill me. His eyes were bottomless with fury. I tried to squirm away but he pinned me down, staring at me, the black hair hanging across his forehead, the memory of his boyish good looks still lingering on his face. He might have been in the grip of sexual passion. But suddenly he loosened his grip and stepped back, still staring at me. The anger and frustration faded, his eyes widened.

"My gosh," he said, the innocent expression characteristically indicating a dawning recognition, "you really do think I wrote that crap about you! Oh, Belinda—what an idea! My heroine, if you'll pardon the expression, doesn't even look like you—she's a character given to me by the book packager—no, I'm not kidding, Belinda . . ." He came tentatively toward me and held out his hand. "Come on, upsie-daisy. You're not hurt—God, look at the phone. Well, here comes apology ninety-nine-oh-three. I'll plug it into another jack."

I watched him fumbling around and fixing the phone. He picked it up and nodded. My head—or more accurately, my psyche—was spinning. The swings and shifts of his behavior were like nothing I'd ever seen before, not even from him. Almost childlike. If it was the pressure building on him, he'd had more than enough. But for the moment I thought the danger had passed. I pulled my knees up under my chin and stayed put on the couch. He perched on a stool watching me, shaking his head slowly.

"It was me, Jack," I said. "Maybe you didn't mean it, maybe it was entirely subconscious, but it was me. There was a lot of hatred in those pages and it was all directed at me."

"Why don't you look at it this way," he said reasonably. "Better to work it out on paper than on you."

"Seems to me you've had it both ways. I haven't exactly escaped unscarred lately."

He nodded. "Yeah, I guess that's true."

"It's a question of how much rage you're working on. I'm scared now, Jack. One minute you look like bloody murder, the next you're calm and collected. I'm scared of one of you. I'm scared of the one who attacked Peter and hit me. The one who wrote that godawful book—"

"The book," he said. "Thereby hangs a tale, if you'd like to hear it." He wiped his forehead with a crumpled handkerchief. I was so used to sweating I no longer noticed it.

"Sure, tell me."

He looked at his watch. "I need a drink. Need. You want one?" I shook my head and he went to the kitchen. It seemed as if everybody was living on gin-and-tonic and iced tea that summer. He was clinking ice and talking to me.

"I'll try not to let this sound too pathetic, but the fact is it's a pretty pathetic story. I'm an expert, as you know. Fellow I know, used to be an agent, now he's a packager—he has ideas for books, usually book series, he makes deals with writers to write them from basic plots he comes up with, he sells the whole package to a publisher." He came back in, took a long drink, and sat down at the other end of the couch. "This guy, Harvey, spotted me in a bar one day and came over and made his pitch. It was all bullshit but the upshot was I could make a fast seventy-five hundred dollars if I'd write a book for him. He said he wanted a real writer, not one of the hacks he worked with on some of his other stuff. He told me that he wanted a 'classy porno,' and if it worked out there was another project he'd like me to consider, not a porno, but a World War II series about a 'spy behind enemy lines.' Well, I had a brainstorm—I'd at least be writing for money again, I could polish off the porno quickly, and then—remember, I'm a dreamer—maybe really make something out of the spy series. Maybe craft was where my talent lay, I reasoned, not finely wrought autobiography." He sighed and gave one of his sheepish smiles. "And I had another thought which will no doubt make you laugh. With the seventy-five hundred dollars . . . I was going to win you back. The money was going to buy us one helluva second honeymoon, a return trip to the Lake District and then a month in Italy, Venice, Florence, the works. I was going to be irresistible and you were going to be beautiful and we were going to get our show back on the road. . . . And if the girl in the novel reminded you of yourself, all I can say is that when I think of sex and pleasure and masturbatory fantasies— well, I think of you." He stared down into his drink. "Now, this little confession leaves me pretty naked, Belinda. But it is true and I might add that you had no business going into my place and reading that manuscript. You shouldn't have done it. I'm not at all sure I can forgive you for doing it. And maybe you can't forgive me for the way I've been acting. And for all I know, that's the way it should be. Look, I think I'm going to get out of here." He stood up and took his glass back to the kitchen.

"I'm glad I read it," I said. "Otherwise I'd never have found out."

"Found out what?"

"That you didn't kill Peter Venables. If I hadn't read it, we'd never have had this talk. You didn't kill—"

"I still could have. You know how I wanted you back. He wanted to take you away . . ."

"You didn't think he could do that. You know me too well. Not Peter Venables—it's a joke."

"Not necessarily. There was a time I didn't think you'd ever want to be rid of me. If you're wrong once, you can be wrong again." He was walking away from me. He looked tired but hanging on. "Look how wrong I was about the people in my life. They turned on me with the first whiff of provocation . . . Well, forget it, Belinda. I still don't know where I was when he was getting his just deserts—and the gun hasn't turned up. So it looks like I'm still the man . . ."

He left me then. I heard the elevator yelling and screaming.

He hadn't killed anyone. And he'd wanted to win me back and I was the one he thought of when he thought of sex . . . At just that moment life struck me as even more complicated than usual. But I had learned one thing from my foray into detection.

Jack Stuart hadn't killed anyone. No one else could be as sure as I was, but that didn't matter. He hadn't killed Peter.

Which meant someone else had.

Chapter Thirty-one

People who don't seem to know what's going on have always driven me nuts.

But one of the things I was learning that summer was that I'd spent most of my adult life being one of them. I'd always made a point of paying attention only to what I thought was my own life, and then mine and Jack's, but it was turning out that just about everyone had thought I was wholly wrapped up in myself. And now they had *Belinda's Belindas* to prove it. The funny thing is, I think they were right.

Even now when I look back on those baking months I wonder what I was really seeing, what I might have been able to understand if I'd been quicker and less wrapped up in my own life. Everything surprised me. I was continually off balance. The last thing that had made sense to me was Jack's moving out of the loft. Once he was gone, everything came springing out of the box lickety-split and I was always flinching and backing up and trying to get my bearings.

I kept thinking back to the day Sally had summoned me to the gallery and told me Harry was in love with another woman. I think about my reaction and I wonder. That was the first bolt from the blue, the first of my post-Jack assumptions that proved to be without foundation. From then on it was just one thing after another, all summer long.

I was sitting in the dark wondering if I could work up an appetite for dinner. Burgling Jack's apartment and then getting caught at it were not the kind of events that make you hungry. Hearing Jack's explanation had left me feeling cruel and useless and drained of both emotion and energy. The whole day amounted to simply the latest of the surprises. Surprises, I reflected, can wear you out.

I was still sitting there, dangling between the twilight zone and a nap, when Hacker called wanting to know what I'd found at Jack's. I told him and he whistled slowly. I could hear the Yankee game in the background, Phil Rizzuto yelling "Holy Cow!" To be a Ruffian you had to have been a baseball freak. Over the years the Yanks had practically become relatives of ours. I told him how terrified I'd been when Jack saw me outside the building. I had Hacker on the edge of his seat. And then I told him what had happened when Jack had shown up at the loft. I had to tell somebody and Sal was out of the picture and Hacker was left.

He listened patiently while I rambled on. When I'd finished he said: "So Peter actually told him he'd come back for you. Well, what do you know about that?"

"Not much," I said, wondering why he'd picked that out of the whole recitation.

"Rhetorical question," he said. "You'd better get some sleep. But tomorrow I think we should get together and solve this sucker. Sound good to you? Antonelli stopped by for a chat today. He wants to arrest Jack so bad he might just go ahead and do it. But you and I know Jack didn't do it."

"Are you still thinking about the past?"

"A little."

"Why do you think Jack didn't do it? Really."

"Because he convinced you."

I was sound asleep when the telephone woke me up. I don't know how many times it had rung by the time I fumbled it out of the cradle. I didn't recognize the voice at first because I'd been dreaming about Carlyle Leverett telling me I had to paint more and more pictures of myself and I was crying and cowering while he yelled at me. I wasn't making much sense when I answered. Eventually I figured out it was Harry, but he sounded even less like himself than he had earlier.

"I'm sorry to wake you up," he said. "But I need you. I'm at the hospital, NYU Medical Center—"

"What? Where? Are you sick?" I was shaking my head, trying to force myself back up to the surface. I looked at my watch. It was only eleven o'clock. I'd been so tired. Was I still dreaming? "What's going on, Harry?" All I could think of was surprises. More surprises.

"No, I'm fine. It's . . . it's Sally."

"Oh no, what? Tell me?"

"She tried to kill herself, Belle. I found her, I thought she was dead . . ."

* * *

He'd given me directions and ten minutes later I was in a cab. On the way there it began to rain and I watched the wipers slapping back and forth. I kept the window open trying to cool off and felt the spray on my face. Sleeping pills, he'd said. No way to tell when she'd taken them. He'd gone into her bedroom—their bedroom—to say good night. She'd asked him to sleep elsewhere and he'd been staying in the study rather than the spare bedroom. So he'd gone in to kiss her good night and she'd been lying on the floor in her nightgown. "Her face was white, Belle," he said softly, "white as if it were all bone, no skin." By some miracle Dr. Schein had been at home. An emergency call had brought an ambulance, and Schein was waiting at the hospital when it got there. They were working on her now and Harry didn't know anything.

I got out at the nearest entrance and of course it was the wrong one. It was pouring outside, thundering, that low cracking rumble of summer storms. You could feel everything shake. I had to go downstairs and wind my way through an endless subterranean passage past kitchens and ominous examination rooms, past orderlies and patients in wheelchairs and other wanderers like myself, all zombies, looking drained and tired and speechless at the fates that had brought them to these corridors.

I found Harry in the lobby looking out at the rain pelting down. He was eating a Mars bar. I touched his arm and he pecked my lips. I tasted chocolate. "I don't know a damn thing," he said. "I suppose I'll be the last to know. I guess they're pumping her out. . . . What am I gonna do, Belle? What if she doesn't come out of it?" He looked as if he wanted to cry but was too tired.

"If they're doing that it means you got her here in time," I said. I didn't know what I was talking about, but it simply had to be true. I couldn't lose Sally. It just couldn't happen.

I got a Coke and we sat and waited. Harry dozed and I watched the rain and the cabs whisking past. It seemed important to watch the rain. Harry roused himself in mid-snore and looked around as if he didn't know where he was. Then he stood up and paced for a while.

"Why do you think she did it?" I imagined a note, some cry for help. But then, Sally had been crying for help ever since that day at the gallery. She'd needed help while Hacker and I floated in the rowboat watching her pain. I'd tried to help but I knew it hadn't mattered. She'd been coming apart inside where I couldn't go. I knew why she'd tried to kill herself. Had it dawned on Harry?

He looked at me. "Why do people do things like that? They slip off some high ledge. They're not themselves anymore, their reason fails them." He shrugged. "You know Sal. You know there are mysteries inside her."

"That's a bit metaphysical," I said sharply. But it was true. I just didn't want him to wriggle away from the truth that mattered, the everyday truth. People don't kill themselves over metaphysics. Or do they? What did I know about it, anyway?

Dr. Schein came down to the lobby about midnight. He was a short man with swarthy, bulbous features, a deeply lined, deeply tanned face, and long wispy gray hair. He threw himself down in a chair opposite us and closed his frog's eyes.

"Harry," he said, "that was too close for me. She'll be okay. We'll keep her overnight. But, Christ, what's going on with her? Didn't she give any hint? Was she acting weird or depressed or what?"

"Nervous, tense." The good news had turned Harry into a rag doll. He looked at his hands. They were shaking and he grabbed his knees. His knees were shaking too. I felt exactly the same way. "You know the shock she had. But suicidal? No, I didn't see any signs of that. None."

"So we'll call it a wash. I'm saying officially that it was an accident. That saves some reports getting made that you wouldn't like dealing with at all. But, Harry, I'm telling you to keep an eye on her. She's got to get free of all this stress. Take her someplace. Go on a trip. And get her thinking about therapy . . . Ah, hell." He stood up and flexed his thick, powerful arms over his head. He was wearing a polo shirt tucked into rumpled seersucker slacks. "I've known Sally a long time. She's got a will of iron. She wants to close herself out, she'll do it. But don't make it easy for her, okay? I think she'll be so scared of what she almost succeeded in doing that she'll never take another sleeping pill as long as she lives, which should be another forty years. But you never know. We'll keep her here tonight. She's already sleeping just fine. You go home and have three or four martinis and go to sleep. Come get her in the morning. Bring her flowers or something, be very tender with the lady. Baby her a little. Think about getting her away from the house and thoughts about Venables with no head and all the rest of it. Okay?"

"Okay," Harry said. "You're sure I shouldn't go up and see her?"

"I'm sure. Go home. Just go home. Make him go home, will ya, Mrs. Stuart? Our boy needs some sleep."

I said I would, and Dr. Schein went away.

Harry looked at me. "Home, James," he said, and tried to laugh.

I went outside and got a cab for us.

Chapter Thirty-two

The city was quiet in the way that only rain or snow can make it. It was nearly one o'clock and we were sitting under the awning in the garden. The only light came from the night sky, and I couldn't see Harry's face. The tip of a cigarette glowed before him. Rain fell steadily, bouncing and drumming on the flagstones, dripping in the thick foliage. Turtle Bay seemed to have gone to sleep.

I had known Harry so well for so long, trusted him so implicitly, but still I wasn't sure of saying what I knew I had to say. Sal was an even older, even closer friend and she had just about succeeded in killing herself. The debt to her was the greater and someone had to speak for her. I couldn't let it rest with what Dr. Schein had said. There was more. There was no one but me. And I had to trust Harry. Still, at that point, if I couldn't trust Harry I was in pretty bad shape.

"Schein gave you some pretty good advice," I said. I heard the ice in his gin-and-tonic. I sucked on my piece of lime.

"He's a bright guy, a very caring guy, as they say." He puffed the cigarette.

"You're really going to have to put everything else out of your mind now and get Sal back on her feet. You've got to make her feel very safe and secure with you. She's been through a lot. You know what I'm saying?"

"What are you saying, Belle? Words of one syllable—it's been a long day."

"Look, I'm not prying, I'm not asking any questions, I'm not picking on you—"

"Okay, now we know what you're not doing."

"But Sal is my best friend and you know how it is with best friends. I worry about her, I want it to be okay, and tonight scared me half to death."

"I'll bet." Clink, clink with the ice.

"So that's it, I guess," I said lamely.

"Come on, Belle, that's not it. What's on your mind?"

"You've got to understand I'm not asking for details, I'm not asking you to deny anything—"

"There you go again—"

"You've got to forget the girlfriends," I blurted.

I felt him smiling at me across the dark space between.

"I know about the girlfriends, Harry. The late Peter Venables told me about that part of your life."

"Oh, he did, did he?" He didn't sound angry.

"And Sally told me, too, about the tarts. I can't figure it out, but she accepts all that. Or she says she does . . . but she says you're really in love with someone else now."

"You know Sal," he said. "She latches on to an idea and you're stuck with it."

"Well, if you are in love with someone, then you are, but right now you've got to think of Sally. How much can this other woman mean to you when you put her in the balance with Sal and with Sal's life—"

"So you think Sally tried to kill herself because I'm in love with another woman."

"Don't deny it, Harry, you don't have to say a word—"

"I'm not denying it, Belle."

"What?" I heard something scurry in the shrubbery and hoped it was a squirrel. "What did you say?"

"I'm not denying it, Belle. I am in love with another woman. There's nothing I can do about it. It's one of those things, it goes back a long time. I've fought it for so long

it's part of my everyday life. Like breathing and eating and
sleeping. I'm not going to fight it anymore, that's all. Life's
getting shorter all the time . . . it's time to admit the truth
and do something about it." He sighed and I saw the
glowing cigarette arc through the darkness and land with
a tiny shower of sparks on the flagstones.

"What are you saying? Who is it?"

"It's you, Belle."

He left me alone and I heard him moving around the
kitchen making fresh drinks. My head ached and I made
him bring me four aspirin to have with the second drink.
He brought a candle in a hurricane lamp and put it on the
table between us. It was still raining and it was still hot
and I felt like a character Somerset Maugham would have
loved.

He came back out and sprawled in the chair, held the
tall cold glass to his forehead. He crossed his long legs.
His sneakers were flapping loose, the laces long gone. His
little toe was visible through a spot that had worn
through.

"I love you, Belle. I've always loved you, I've never
stopped loving you. The problem is, it's gotten bad, really
bad since you and Jack called it a day."

"Oh, no, Harry," I said, "no, no, that's absurd, we've
been friends all these years, I'd have trusted you with
anything. Oh, please don't tell me this now—I . . . I can't
quite take any more surprises."

"It's been more pronounced this summer. I've done
everything I could to push it out of my mind, I threw
myself into this show, I've said the hell with any little
girlfriends—and our lamented chum Venables was all

wet, anyway. Well, never mind. But you must know from my behavior that I've fought it."

"It's just not true," I said. "Why, you tried to get Jack and me to patch it up—"

"I *had* to, Belle. I couldn't have lived with myself if I had just leapt into the situation gleefully, figuring now was my chance. You and Jack had to have every opportunity to get all the way back together. Now it looks like Jack isn't going to be doing much patching . . ." He looked at me for a long time when I didn't speak. Maybe he was expecting me to cry or laugh or throw a fit. But I just sat there, feeling his eyes on me.

"What's going on in your noggin?"

"I wonder where there's a safe place for me to hide," I whispered. "Nothing's the way I've thought it was. I feel as if I've been living my life all these years with my eyes closed to reality. Oh, it isn't just you . . . it's everything. When Jack used to play football he'd tell me how important it was for a player to keep his head in the game . . . now I know what he meant. I just didn't keep my head in the game, I guess. Everything's an illusion. I guess that's what Venables was trying to tell me." I looked at Harry, who was staring at me, unmoving. "Venables tried to make me go to bed with him, he got pretty nasty—it just came out of nowhere and I was shocked, horrified. He was a monster, Harry. He seemed to think he had a right to me. I don't know." It was late and I was tired and I bit my lip because of all the things I didn't want to do just then, crying was first on the list.

"I know, I know . . ."

"You *know*?"

"He told me he'd come back to New York for you."

"And you didn't think of telling me?"

"You don't need me to be your keeper. That was between you and him, wasn't it? He didn't tell me he was going to try to rape you, if that's what you mean. He said what he said and it wasn't my place to interfere." He smiled almost shyly through the candlelight and he might have been Harry of twenty years before. "You're talking about hiding. You want to hide from me?"

"I don't know, Harry. My God, I don't know what to say or think. What am I supposed to think? Men are such romantics! It's infuriating! After all these years, you're trying to tell me you're in love with me all of a sudden—"

"Always. I've always been in love with you. Jack just interrupted everything for a while."

"Quite a while, I'd say."

He nodded. "I'd have to agree with that. But I've never changed my mind—"

"Venables said the same thing about you." I remembered the conversation, Peter saying that Harry had spent all these years looking for another one of me. I remembered how crazy I'd thought it was.

"Well, he was right."

"But why? Women don't do that, women don't love someone for twenty years, carrying a torch—I think you're just under a lot of pressure and worn out and . . . I don't know what. But you're going to regret all this in the morning."

"I only regret Jack's being a Ruffian."

"Now, what's that supposed to mean?"

"I should think it's obvious. I couldn't make my feelings known when you were married to a Ruffian."

"Now I've heard it all," I exclaimed. "You didn't do anything all this time—not because of Sally, mind you, your *wife*—but because Jack was a *Ruffian*? That's the absolute end!"

"Belle." He sounded hurt but patient. "You just don't understand. You're not going to understand. But it's all right."

"Well, that's a relief!"

"In any case, that's the whole truth and now I've got to do what I must."

"How ominous-sounding."

"Well, it is ominous, in a way, I guess."

"What are you going to do?"

"When things have calmed down," he said, measuring his words in the stillness, the rain dripping steadily, "I'm going to leave Sally."

"No," I whispered, "you must not do that to her!"

"And then I'm going to have to deal with you, Belle."

That was when I began to cry and Harry very gently put his arm around me and held me for a while. Then he got the car out of the garage at the corner and drove me home. His lips brushed my hair when he left me at the door, and that was all.

IV

The Last of the
Ruffians

Chapter Thirty-three

Things, they say, look different in the morning.

Well, they're right. The next morning things looked worse.

It was hotter, over ninety by midmorning, and the humidity hung in the air like mist, not quite rain. Sally's suicide attempt hadn't been a bad dream, after all, and my conversation with Harry had been an oh-too-true nightmare. He really had said all those things, and try as I might, I couldn't replay the talk in my mind and make it come out differently. No matter how difficult things may at times appear, I can usually come up with some kind of plan—certainly not a good plan in every case, but a plan. But the talk with Harry had me over a barrel.

What could I do? Ignore it? Not easy to pretend it didn't happen. So how to face it? Was he really going to tell Sally? Would he leave her? What if I told him to forget it, I wouldn't be waiting for him? But he didn't seem to expect that: he just sounded as if he were determined to change his life one step at a time. What kind of toll would it take on Sally? What kind of toll would it take on *me*? The whole thing made me dizzy, as if things were slipping, as the world spun off its axis.

I'd always thought I'd been lucky to have one man in love with me. Suddenly I seemed to have two men in love with me, both apparently obsessive about it, neither one of them in the least interested in whatever my feelings might be. And a third who may not have loved me but came under the heading of Dead Sex Maniac. The funny thing was, they had all been friends for a quarter of a century.

I tried to figure the odds on that. They had to be very long, indeed. Three old pals converging on the same woman after all those years. What in the world to make of it? And why did it have to be me?

How did Harry fit into the whole picture? His role—as confidant, dependable friend, husband of my closest friend, one of Jack's fellow Ruffians and indeed the founder of the Ruffians—his role had changed completely. He had to be seen through an entirely different prism.

If Harry thinks he loves me, I reasoned, and Jack and I break up, then Harry decides to go after me . . . and suddenly there's Venables lobbing a monkey wrench into Harry's plans, telling him—announcing to him, really—that he, Venables, has come back to New York *for me*! The egomania of it all left me dazed and infuriated—what could these men, the two of them, have been thinking of? What could have made them think they had any right, any chance with me whatsoever? God, I wanted to punch somebody!

Back to my equation. Venables throws his monkey wrench. Now, if Harry is obsessive, as monomaniacal as he seemed last night, if he has bided his time for so many years and has finally gotten his opportunity, has decided to leave Sally, what might he do to Venables, who comes along and threatens to louse up what Harry's waited for so patiently?

Well, somebody killed Venables. Once he was dead, he didn't pose a problem to Harry's plans. If Jack didn't do it, and I was sure he hadn't, why not Harry?

I'd wound up where I was last night, only I was calm now and didn't have shock and barely controlled hysteria as an excuse.

I was so shaken by all the twists and surprises that had leaped at me from the dark, I was beginning to think I was learning something, getting smart. Harry had been the last one to betray my trust and he'd done it by loving me. I couldn't believe it, I couldn't cope with it . . . but I could resolve not to be fooled again by any of them.

I prayed to all that's holy that he wouldn't be stupid or brutal enough to tell Sally now. What had he said? He was going to have to deal with me? I didn't even want to imagine what that might mean.

But I couldn't stop chewing at the questions. Harry could have been enraged at Venables' presumption about establishing something with me . . . after Harry had been not only my first lover but a close, close friend for all the years since our affair. If Venables had behaved to Harry with the arrogance he had with me, I could see a man killing him. And if Harry had killed Venables, it might explain his willingness to put the blame on Jack . . . which would also have gotten Jack absolutely out of my life. . . . No, I couldn't believe it.

Wait, correction. I couldn't have believed it a few days before. Now I could believe almost anything.

But Harry? Impossible. I'd known him forever. Of course, I'd also known Jack forever, and he'd turned into someone else. Harry might have too. He had been to

Jack's apartment. He would know how seldom Jack locked the door. He knew all about that damn shotgun . . .

He could have walked me home after the opening at the gallery, then have gone to Jack's and gotten the gun, knowing that Jack would have gone anywhere in the world but directly home that night.

Suddenly I'd managed to throw a real scare into myself.

Real life intruded for a moment when Carlyle Leverett called. He asked me if the cop Antonelli, who reminded him of "a maiden uncle of mine," had been snooping around me and I said not since my first conversation with him. Apparently he'd visited Leverett twice, centering most of his questions on Jack but not skimping the rest of us, either. "Do you think he's serious about Jack?" Leverett asked me.

"I suppose. It would help if they could find the murder weapon, but from what I've heard, they haven't."

"Frankly, I'm rather worried about Jack. Antonelli has something serious in his eyes, behind all the avuncular trappings. How is Jack? What do you think?"

"I think Jack's pretty fatalistic about it. They'll either charge him or not. As for me, I had some doubts . . . but, no, I don't think he did it. I'd bet on it."

"Oh, hell, I know he didn't kill that asshole. Though I wouldn't mind shaking the hand of the chappie who did. Helping to keep New York clean, in my opinion. No, I just hope to high heaven they can't pin it on Jack . . . what a mess that would be! Well, another bit of news on a happier note. I've heretofore neglected to tell you the results of the opening and the purchases since . . . Brace yourself, my dear—"

"Oh, Lord, don't tell me everyone backed out and decided they were drunk when they had you put those little stickers up."

"Hardly. Forty-six thousand dollars thus far, dear girl."

"You're joking! You must be! Oh, Carl . . ."

"And we're not done yet. You really are established. And I am now officially clamoring for more."

"Ah. Well, we'll see."

"It's a seller's market, let me remind you. Don't be foolish now. Another show in January or February. Mark my words. This is no time to take a vacation, Belinda. I hate to be stern, but I'm being stern. We'll talk next week. I'll be cracking the whip, I assure you."

Once he'd hung up I skipped briefly around the loft thinking of the money, stopped and slumped over the wheel-of-fortune at the thought of fighting with him over moving on to a new series of paintings. I didn't see how I could paint one more self-portrait, but I'd have to go carefully, work out one or two of the story paintings, and ease him into them. Tell him maybe I'd return to the others later. Ha! When I was ninety!

I called Hacker. I had to tell him the way my mind had been working. It didn't occur to me that doing so was an expression of precisely the kind of trust that had been blowing up with such regularity in my face. So I called him, but there was no answer. Dammit! I suddenly had to get hold of him. I didn't want to wait. I called Mike Pierce and my instincts were good. He'd spoken with Harry and wanted to talk about Sally's escapade of the night before—"Was it an accident like Harry said? Or . . . what?" Hearing the party line, I acknowledged that as far as I knew it was an accident, a case of somebody who'd been under a degree of sedation just forgetting how many pills she'd taken and taking a few too many. Mike didn't sound as if he were absolutely convinced. But when I asked him if he knew where I might find Hacker, it turned out that he did. Or didn't, rather. He'd had dinner with Hacker last night, who'd said he was going out of town to do some research for a few days. No, he didn't say where he was going but he'd be back well within a week. Mike asked me if I was still angry about his thinking that things didn't look so hot for Jack, and I said no, I understood how things must have looked to him. He, too, asked if I'd seen any more of Antonelli, and when I said no he seemed rather surprised. Apparently Antonelli was seeing the gentlemen in the case and writing off the ladies. In other words, he was presumably working on the same idea that I was—a friend of Venables must have killed him. Mike wanted to have dinner to talk things over.

"There's really something I've been wanting to tell you," he said. "Now seems like a good time, all things considered."

"Oh-oh, that sounds like trouble," I said.

"Well, maybe. I don't know. But it involves you and me and . . . gosh, it's fairly complicated, Belinda. We'll have to talk—"

"I've got some things I have to do," I said. "But I'll call you. Give me a few days to get a couple things straightened out."

"Okay, but there is a kind of urgency."

"I'll call you," I said. "Really. I will."

I proceeded to take the bull by the horns and called Harry. He sounded much as ever when I asked him about Sally. "Oh, sure, Belle," he said, "I picked her up this morning at the hospital. She's feeling fine. Acts as if she doesn't even fully remember what happened last night. Do you think maybe she did take an OD by accident?" He sounded vaguely hopeful.

"You never know," I said. "Maybe. Can I talk to her?"

"She's not here right now. But, listen, Belle, I want to see you, I've got to see you. After last night we really do have to talk. There are a lot of things I want to say to you, things I have to explain—"

"Not now, not yet. Anything you've got to say to me can wait, it's waited twenty years. Now, tell me where she is, Harry. Do you realize I haven't spoken with her since Venables was killed? I didn't even see her at the hospital. I *miss* her, Harry. I need to see her."

"Well, there's a problem. She's not here. She's not in the city, I mean. You know what Schein said last night—so she went up to the cabin. It seemed like a good idea."

"She went up to the mountains? By herself?" I couldn't believe it.

"Listen to me. I couldn't have stopped her if I'd wanted to. She was perfectly happy and absolutely determined. We didn't have a fight, she wasn't accusing me of anything, and I promise you, I didn't say a word about last night."

"If you did, Harry, I'll . . . I'll . . ." I wasn't exactly sure what I'd do.

"You'll be mad at me, I understand that, Belle. But I didn't. It's going to be good for her to get away. It's quiet up there, it's pretty, it's maybe even cooler, she can swim—"

"It's crazy. She shouldn't be alone. Schein would have a fit if he knew."

"Goddammit," Harry exploded, "she's still my wife and I was not about to argue with her, okay? You're going to have to accept that. And if you don't like it, Belle, you can

223

go up there and keep her company. And anyway, her being gone will give you and me a chance to talk. You owe me some time, Belle—"

"I owe you absolutely nothing," I shouted at him. "Last night you betrayed the trust I've always put in you. You have needlessly complicated your own life, and mine too, to say nothing of poor Sally's."

"The hell with poor Sally! What about poor Harry? *I love you!* Now I want to talk to you about it. I put myself on the line last night, I'm risking a lot, you can't say you won't talk to me! What's the matter with you, anyway? There's so much past between us, so much we've got to deal with. I've got to see you, I'm going to go right around the bend if I can't hold you, Belle—"

"All right," I said tiredly, my anger waning: just one more person I couldn't trust. "All right. But I can't do it now. Let me call you in a couple days—"

"Don't leave me hanging too long, Belle. I'm warning you . . . please, for all our sakes, please. Think of the past, Belle—"

"I am, Harry." He was warning me. Harry was warning me and his voice sent a ripple of fear along my spine. He sounded like someone else, not the Harry I'd always known. Suddenly I wanted to stay out of his way. "That's exactly what I'm thinking of, the past."

When I finally got off the phone, I went to the closet and dragged out an overnight bag and started throwing clothes at it. I checked to make sure I had my credit cards and counted out my cash. Luckily there was a couple hundred dollars so I wouldn't have to stop at the cash machine, which was virtually always out of commission.

All the answers lay in the past. What had Hacker said? We're all just the sums of our pasts?

There was only one thing left to do. Only one thing I could think of, anyway. Hacker had chosen to disappear. Jack had his hands full with Antonelli and his own psyche losing one wheel at a time. Mike had just faded into the woodwork and I didn't think I wanted to hear what he had to tell me. Harry was simply impossible and I couldn't get away from the fact that he was scaring me almost every time he opened his mouth. And Sally was off doing God only knew what in their Adirondacks cabin.

So I was finally alone. At last.

I was alone with only one place to go.

The past. I was going back. . . .

Chapter Thirty-four

I was fast but I wasn't fast enough. I was heading along at top speed, wanting to get through the doorway into the past. I was packed, I'd run around giving the flowers and plants drinks, unplugging the fan, when the elevator began its racket and I heard voices. Naturally the door downstairs was open and someone had come in. I was set with a million excuses but I let them all die when I saw my guests.

Antonelli and Mike Pierce came in looking faintly discomfited to be together. Antonelli said: "Mr. Pierce and I happened to arrive simultaneously, Mrs. Stuart. I saw no reason why he shouldn't join us. What I have to say may also have some meaning to him. Do you have a moment? It is rather important."

He was smiling his principal's smile and I had the feeling that somebody had been caught smoking in the john. Or worse. He had a flower in the buttonhole of his gray suit and I could smell his after-shave. Old Spice, just like my grandfather's. I told them to come in. Mike didn't explain his presence beyond raising his eyes at me and mouthing something I couldn't decipher. Antonelli looked around the loft and nodded approvingly.

"A lovely setting for a painter," he said softly. "By the way, I did manage to stop by Mr. Leverett's gallery and had a very nice guided tour of your work. Most impressive, absolutely delightful. I fully intend to bring my daughter down to see it—your focus, the concentration on detail, is amazing, Mrs. Stuart. The sense of proportion, the shadings . . ." He had spotted the wheel-of-fortune in the corner, stood surveying it from its base to the top of the wheel itself. "May I?" I nodded and he gave it a spin. Mike looked at me, shrugged his shoulders. Antonelli watched the wheel spin but didn't wait for it to stop. He turned around. "But, to business, Mrs. Stuart."

I sat on a stool at one of the worktables and Mike folded himself into a wicker chair.

"We have continued our investigation into your husband's possible involvement with the late Mr. Venables. I'm sorry to say that Mr. Stuart has not provided very satisfactory answers to some of our more pertinent questions. And we have found—"

"Not the shotgun!" I exclaimed.

"No, not the shotgun, though I expect he'll eventually tell us where it is. Sooner or later. No, we found a rather interesting entry in your husband's diary. I have a copy and I would like to read it to you, if you have no objection. Let me assure you that your husband provided us with the diary in the course of giving us access to all his belongings.

And of course we had a warrant. It's all very proper." He smiled reassuringly, as if that would make all the difference.

"Go ahead," I said. Mike shifted nervously, as if the whole invasion of privacy made him uncomfortable.

"I quote, then," Antonelli said, reading from a typed sheet. "'Venables has come back and it was grand seeing him, until I realized why he was here. He's still playing the old game and he just laughed when I confronted him with it. He's totally insane on the subject and the whole thing just keeps getting worse. At first I thought he'd come back for Sally and I didn't know what to tell Harry. But I was wrong. It's Belinda he's come for, all right. He says there's no way I can stop him. Well, he's wrong on that score. I can stop him but I may have to stop the son of a bitch once and for all. What a mess! What idiotic, foolish children we were!'" Antonelli cleared his throat and folded the page, replaced it in his inside jacket pocket. "Now, I ask you if that passage means anything to you, Mrs. Stuart." He tugged at his earlobe, then crossed his arms on his chest, which I took to mean that the pleasantries had been pretty nearly exhausted.

"It seems self-explanatory," I began, then stopped when his eyes clicked up from the floor at me.

"Hardly. Or perhaps it explains itself to you. But not to me. 'The old game'—now, what does that mean? Why might Mr. Venables have come back for Sally? Why, indeed, would he have come back for you? What was Mr. Venables' rationale, I wonder. Stopping him 'once and for all,' I grant you, doesn't need a great deal of interpretation." He stared at me, waiting.

"I have no idea what game he's referring to except that Venables was a good friend of all of these men in college. As to Sally . . . well, Venables stayed with them and maybe Jack drew that conclusion. Why he might have come back for me passes all rational understanding, but isn't that what Jack's saying, that Venables was 'totally insane on the subject'? And as far as I'm concerned, stopping him for good could just as easily have meant punching him in the nose."

"Not, however, in the light of events, eh? Well, I would ask you, Mr. Pierce, what does any of this mean to you as an old friend of both Mr. Stuart and Mr. Venables?" The arms remained crossed impassively, the comforting face not very comforting anymore.

"Oh, God, I don't know. He could have meant almost anything. It was such a long time ago." Everybody was changing now that the pressure was being put on. Mike didn't look at all like Bertie Wooster anymore. He looked worried and his eyes behind the thick lenses darted from Antonelli to me to the floor.

"But what," Antonelli persisted, "could this subject be that Venables was totally insane about? Surely it must ring a bell of some sort? What old game would Stuart know about that you wouldn't?" He tugged the earlobe again. "Think, man."

Mike furrowed his brow, scowled, pursed his lips, and succeeded only in looking more innocent and hopeless and foolish than ever. "I'm thinking, but nothing comes," he said. "It's a mystery to me." He sounded like an amateur actor reading his lines for the first time, and badly at that.

"Why," Antonelli said quietly, "would there be this confusion about Sally and Belinda in his mind? Or does it matter? Who cares? Mrs. Stuart doesn't seem to be involved at all—except as a possible motive. And the unfortunate Mrs. Granger merely found the body."

"Why don't you just ask Jack?" I said.

"Oh, we have. But he doesn't seem to have much to say. Curious, isn't it? Says he was just writing, a stream-of-consciousness he calls it—well, I'm only a police officer, Mrs. Stuart, but I've dabbled in my James Joyce, and your husband's idea of a stream-of-consciousness and mine are worlds apart, I'm afraid.

"Well, where does that leave you?" I said.

"It isn't so much a matter of where it leaves me, Mrs. Stuart, as where it leaves your husband."

"And where's that?" Mike asked.

"We've taken Mr. Stuart into custody. We're charging him with murder."

If Antonelli had wanted to shut us up with his quiet bombshell, he must have felt enormously satisfied. He left immediately thereafter, thanking us for our time, and Mike and I sat looking at each other like two fools. Somehow the murder seemed more real than ever in light of Jack's arrest. It had gone from the abstract to the concrete in a lightning flash and my first thoughts were of what it must be like for Jack. In a cell, deprived of what life really means to any of us, the freedom of movement. I wondered what it would do to him, how he would take it, and I feared the worst.

Mike was staring into space, still scowling.

"Why did you lie to Antonelli?"

He jumped as if I'd stuck him with a needle. "What? What are you talking about?" His eyes flickering past me, his voice brittle and tense. He wouldn't look at me. Poor Mike, so transparent. It was so easy to forget that he ran the publishing company. Maybe the appearance of innocence was something he could use to his advantage. I hoped so, for his sake.

"You know what that diary means. You must. I just want to know why you lied to Antonelli, that's all."

"Why would I lie to a cop? Be serious, Belinda—"

"I don't know. That's what I want to find out. Why *would* you lie to a cop? What could be so important? But it's none of my business . . . except insofar as it affects Jack."

"Well, there you are!" he cried, leaping to his feet and striking a Bertie Wooster pose, hands on hips. He was wearing an elegantly wrinkled white linen suit with a French-blue shirt and a lemon tie. "Jack won't even tell what the diary means."

"But what has that got to do with you? Jack's not here right now, you are, and I'm asking you why you lied—"

"I don't know what it means! It's Jack's diary, not mine. And I'm damned if I see where you get off calling me a liar, Belinda. I mean, it's me, you know, Mike . . ." His look of innocence seemed suddenly tired and forty years old, the big round eyes not quite so bright, the hair a little thinner, the complexion not quite so pink. He was right, of course, he was Mike. Mike Now, not Mike Then. I kept confusing the two. If he had lied to Antonelli, I had to remember that Mike Now might have pretty good reasons.

"I don't think Jack killed Venables," I said. Mike dabbed at his forehead with a handkerchief. Shouts from the street rose, battered at the silence we'd built for ourselves in the loft. The bare wall where all the Belindas had once hung looked down on our little dialogue, rose around us like the treacherous North Face of Greenwich Village. Full of faults, chasms, betrayal, and sudden death. "Somebody knows what was going on with Peter and Jack and all the rest of you—you may not know who killed him, you may know but not realize it, for all I know you killed him, Mike—but somebody knows what the subtext of all this is. And that somebody isn't telling. I'm afraid the result is that Jack's going to be convicted of a murder he didn't commit."

"Subtext! If you don't mind my saying so, you'd be better off keeping your theories to yourself—what does subtext mean? Somebody shot Venables and it looks bad for Jack. What else matters?" He shot me an exasperated look. "Really!"

"Why did you come down here now, I told you I'd call you. What was so important that it couldn't wait?"

"Well, I don't know . . . I just wanted to talk to you." He brushed a long wedge of lank dark blond hair from his high, noble forehead. "No big deal."

"You sounded pretty urgent on the phone," I reminded him.

"I don't know, Belinda, all right? I was antsy in the office, I wanted to see you, I came down. Is that all right? Did I need a permit, for God's sake? What is it with you? You act like a cop—is all this because you think Jack is just some harmless and misunderstood delinquent who needs our sympathy?" The face I'd smiled on for so many years had taken a new turn, had sprouted a kind of petulance I hadn't seen before. "He beats you up, he acts like a perfect fool, malevolent and stupid . . . and still you carry this pathetic torch? What in the world's the matter with you, Belinda? I've been watching Jack for the past year or so and I always wind up with a face-ache from trying to stay civil while he gets drunk and dashes about insulting people, mainly you—I cannot stand to see him treat you that way, Belinda. You're too decent and sweet and . . . well, you know what you are. And now you insist he's innocent! He's been heading for this for a long time, and why can't you admit it? Don't you want the responsibility? Can't you handle the idea that you drove one man to kill another over you?"

"That's melodramatic and imbecilic!" I was shouting and Mike was staring at me, his face white and shaking.

"It's the truth! You'd better just grow up and accept it!"

He knew a decent exit line and that was it. I was barely aware of his departure. I was rooted to the spot, like someone planted with Krazy Glue, and my mouth was so dry I couldn't swallow. I felt as if he'd driven a skewer of truth through my heart.

Chapter Thirty-five

It was early evening by the time I got out to La Guardia and the Eastern shuttle terminal. As always, there wasn't an empty seat. All the passengers had that dazed, glassy-eyed, helpless look, and one and all they glistened like creatures who'd been rained on. I sat with my eyes closed, willing myself not to open them until we landed, except for the moment when they stopped the cart at my seat and I produced my credit card.

I almost made it, not looking until we were sweeping low over the water lapping at the edges of the runway. Logan Airport in Boston looked blurred through the heavy, dirty fog swelling up where the city met the ocean. The lights of the city pulsed behind the humidity. I waited stickily for a cab, took the quick five-minute ride into the heart of town, curling off Storrow Drive and up into the Back Bay. I'd been lucky and gotten a single in the old part of the Ritz-Carlton on Arlington Street.

The shower was a dream come true. I threw the windows up and looked out on the Public Garden, the globes of light on the poles, the willows waving gently. I dressed slowly, feeling almost crisp, and walked up Newbury Street, found a café with tables outside, and ordered a light dinner and a glass of Beaune, almost ice cold. I began to feel myself relaxing for the first time all summer. It was Boston, I suppose, the contentment I always found in the unique solitude the city provided.

I tried to organize my thoughts without getting upset. I shifted through the men involved in the death of Peter Venables, summing up whatever struck me as pertinent. Jack: a personality in trouble, a man losing so much of what was important to him, awash in self-pity and luckless middle age looming ominously on the horizon; recent violent outbursts against both me and Venables. But he was trying to turn the corner, fight his way back; he'd taken the job of writing the dirty book, but he'd had his reasons. Two things really mattered: First, did punching someone and threatening him imply the capability of killing him? And, second, where was his shotgun?

Harry: obsessed with what he believed was love for me, having decided to leave his wife once he'd satisfied himself that I really was at the end of my marriage; then learning that Venables had his own plans for me . . . and possibly benefiting by the removal of both Venables and Jack—for the murder—from the scene. What really mattered? How serious were his feelings for me? And would he actually have used Jack's shotgun, thereby not simply betraying but framing a fellow Ruffian?

Mike. Well, yes, Mike. He was a Ruffian. He was an old friend of mine. But no matter how I turned the crystal ball, I couldn't discern a motive. Working on the Theory of the Least Likely, he'd be the perfect murderer, driven by something I knew nothing about. But that was absurd, surely, and made a total hash out of the whole ghastly business.

And Hacker Welles. Fascinated by the past, immersed in Ruffian history for the past year while writing the show—but not terribly involved. More of an observer. Then, there was his idea for a novel, which involved a figure based on me murdering a Ruffian. Had he told me why she was killing a Ruffian? I couldn't remember.

I drank a brandy with my coffee and suddenly felt very tired. I walked back down Newbury. A breeze had come up and for the first time in weeks I was able to shut my mind off and sink thankfully into a deep sleep. The last memory of the night I had was the curtain swaying in the draft of balmy air swirling through the willows across the street from my window.

I was having breakfast when I remembered why Hacker's heroine killed the Ruffian-type, the ones she didn't turn into swine because, as he said, they were already swine. It was because she'd been so disillusioned by them—because she was such an innocent. She'd killed the one who most epitomized the shock of reality.

Now, how could I make that fit in?

Wondering got me through much too large a breakfast, with the sun streaming down outside the Ritz-Carlton's dining room. Then I made a telephone call and set off across the garden, past the great statue of George Washington on his horse, through the flowerbeds, over the little humpbacked bridge with the elegant white swan boats bobbing beside the pier. It was going to be ungodly but the heat hadn't yet hit and the morning was crystalline, every color defined and perfect, every sound clear and almost musical. I tried not to think what I was actually doing in Boston. For a moment I felt a long way from murder.

Tony Chalmers lived in a narrow house on Joy Street, half a stone's throw from the State House, which sat grandly beneath Bulfinch's gold dome atop Beacon Hill. He greeted me with a smile, a wreath of smoke from a long curved pipe circling his head. He was wearing a seersucker jumpsuit dabbed with mud and he apologized for not shaking hands because his hands were dirty. "When the time comes to repot, by God, there's nothing to be done but repot. But," he said, "your call was a most pleasant surprise. Though it does occur to me that there's probably something rather serious on your mind. Hacker called to tell me that Jack seems to be a suspect in Peter's murder . . ."

He led me through a mid-Victorian apartment with gilt-framed paintings and Boston ferns and heavy settees done in rich blue and red upholstery. The wood shone, smelled of furniture polish. A couple of cats watched my arrival, not without a slight air of misgiving. They lay in blobs of bright sunshine. There was an opulence to the professor's surroundings which intimated that the collection of furniture and trappings long predated him.

He led the way through a long crowded dining room and out onto a deck, which I'd recognized from the street as the top of a carriage house. He'd made a grand mess with huge terra-cotta pots, countless trowels and bags of earth and plant food and watering cans and a hose curling like an emaciated green snake in search of a tiny mouse. The furniture was white wrought iron mixed with old-fashioned yellow-red-and-green-striped canvas chairs.

Chalmers was wearing a seersucker hat, with his gray Afro bulging out beneath it. He looked like an aging, pint-sized Bozo the Clown. He poured me a cup of coffee and nudged a basket of sweet rolls toward me. "Let's sit in the shade and reminisce. If that's what you have in mind, of course." He settled into one of the canvas chairs and I perched on wrought iron and found myself looking down at him. He took off his hat, dropped it on the wooden planking, and sipped noisily at his coffee.

"Well, you're right, reminiscing is what I have in mind. And I naturally thought of you, not just because you were what I've heard described as the Ruffians' gray eminence but also because of what you said to me that night at the Grangers' party—when you spoke, sort of worriedly, of always having a funny feeling about the Ruffians. Something unhealthy in the closeness . . ."

"Mmm." he nodded, nibbled at a roll. "So I did. But I thought I was being a mindless old worrier. I take it you've come to think I was onto something—I'm not at all sure you're right, mind you. From what I've heard, Venables' death may have been pretty straightforward."

"The police certainly think so. Jack's been arrested."

"Good Lord!"

"And I don't think he did it. It's not because I'm his wife or because I've suddenly realized what a prince he is and how much I love him. I haven't. But I'm convinced that I know him pretty well, I know how screwed-up he is, I know he gets angry. I also know he didn't kill Venables. His reaction has been all wrong. It's difficult for me to explain and I surely couldn't convince the police. But I am convinced Venables was killed because of the past, something back there that's hidden. I was hoping you could shine your memory into the darkness and let me see what it is."

I told him about the things I had heard Jack say to Venables in Leverett's office. I told him about what Antonellii had found in the diary. I told him about the evening I had spent with Venables and what Venables had proposed for the two of us.

He listened and ate his breakfast and when a cat joined us Chalmers put his cup down and let the cat finish off his coffee. He lit his long swooping pipe again, puffing contentedly, listening.

"Belinda," he sighed, "for the last twenty years you've had what amounts to a Ruffian overdose. I can't help but feel you've earned the right to pick my brain. Which is something I've never let any of the Ruffians do." He absentmindedly tickled the cat's ears and it hissed at him. He pushed it over on its back and scratched its tummy and it went to sleep. "As you know, I've always had that nasty little fear that something ugly might come out of the Ruffians. They were so wrapped up in romanticism, the one-for-all-and-all-for-one thing. They were *so* close. I've sometimes wished I'd discouraged Harry when he brought up the idea of a club. He was thinking about the old Rakehell bunch, Merrie England and all, but then I was smitten by the spirit of youth, that spirit of camaraderie they—*we*—all felt. They were going to be my pipeline to what was happening, to the sixties." He laughed abruptly, his eyes wrinkling to slits. "God, did I pick the wrong bunch for that! One of life's little jokes, I guess. But it was fine for a while. Took me back to my own undergraduate days, somehow. I should have known better, I was the grown-up, so on and so forth, but what's the good of saying all that now?

"The thing is, I knew that life was bound to treat them unevenly, that it would strain their golden, happy love for each other. Still, who'd have thought the whole idea wouldn't just have evaporated after college? I can't help but think that would have been the case with virtually any such collegiate group—but not these characters. But maybe I knew it wouldn't just go away.

"What I did know is that there was a damned good chance that the dark side of the Ruffians would show itself sooner or later. There was bound to be a stain of sheer bloody-mindedness before they were done. For that matter, there were signs of that darkness long before they ever left Harvard, Belinda."

The sun was climbing higher and the shade was receding across his roof garden. Chalmers struggled out of the canvas chair and started moving from pot to pot with the hose, standing squinting, puffing his pipe, telling me the story as I followed him. It all had hinged on my leaving the relationship with Harry and beginning to date Jack. In any kind of normal situation it wouldn't have amounted to anything, wouldn't have made a story to remember more than a day or two. But Harry and Jack were Ruffians, a fact of which I at that time had been utterly unaware. So far as I knew, they might have been nothing more than casual acquaintances.

Jack had been the one to break the code. He knew that I was dating Harry but he'd asked me to go out anyway. I had enjoyed meeting him at a mixer. I suppose I thought I was being a trifle naughty, but on the other hand, Harry and I weren't going steady—that is, though we had slept together, nothing had been said about exclusivity. I knew I was taking advantage of a technicality, as it were. Among the people I knew, if you slept with a guy there wasn't any doubt about it, you were definitely going together. We may not have been representative of the sexual revolution of the sixties but we knew our own rules. Still, I had liked

Jack Stuart and gone out with him, more or less behind Harry's back.

But Harry wasn't angry with me, or if he was, he was a hell of a lot angrier with Jack. A girl couldn't be expected to understand the code of the Ruffians, but Jack had helped create it.

Harry put up with it for a couple of weeks, asked me just what the score was, and I told him that I thought we needed a break from each other because we'd been getting too intense. The sort of things girls say to guys at times like that. And I told him I intended to date Jack if Jack wanted me to. Harry took it like a man, told me he hoped we would remain friends, and I breathed a sigh of relief and said I hoped so too. But Harry wasn't about to let Jack off so easily.

As Chalmers told the story, Jack and Harry were living on the third floor of Eliot House then. Harry spent one evening that Jack and I were out working himself into a fit of temper. When Jack pulled in about midnight Harry was waiting for him. They argued. The argument escalated into a shoving match. And Harry wound up going for Jack with a lamp and breaking it on Jack's head. Jack, streaming blood from scalp lacerations, went over the top, methodically knocking Harry down the three flights of stairs, stopping at each landing to straighten him up before knocking him down the next flight.

Mike had found them. Harry was unconscious and Jack couldn't see through the blood. Mike had called Chalmers, who had appeared at Eliot House in the middle of the night, gotten the combatants back up to the room, and checked for damage. It was a stupid risk to take, Chalmers acknowledged, but they'd waited until morning and then gone in his car to a doctor near Central Square in Cambridge. Chalmers had never seen anything like what they'd done to each other, but at the time, secrecy seemed of the utmost importance. The doctor had taken some stitches in Jack's scalp. Harry had three broken ribs, a broken bone in his left hand, and a hairline fracture of a bone in his foot. And lost two teeth. The doctor observed to Chalmers that Harry looked as if he'd been worked over by a couple of professionals.

Chalmers finished soaking the last of the trees on his deck. He turned off the water tap and rolled the hose up on a rickety old stand. "Quite a dust-up, quite a lot of very bad feeling. Neither one of them was prepared to forget it. Harry made a good many threats and Jack welcomed them, said he'd be glad to keep dishing it out if Harry wanted to keep taking it. For a few weeks I didn't think we'd ever mend it. But, corny as it sounds, it was the Ruffian spirit that carried the day. Mike and Hacker and Venables brought them together right here, in my parlor, and we talked for a long time. We talked of life and love, of men and women and the troubles and jealousies we're all heir to, and in the end the lads shook hands. You, my dear, were awarded to Jack and that was the end of it."

I stood there in a state of amazement. "I was *awarded* to Jack . . ." The absurdity of it overcame my anger at the very idea. I burst out laughing. "That's incredible!"

Chalmers looked at me, nodded. "Times change, don't they? Yes, now it does seem rather quaint. Yes, I see your point. But that's the way it was then."

"Crazy, to think this happened and I never knew anything about it. Nobody said a word."

"Well, no, they wouldn't, would they?"

I followed Chalmers inside. "There's also a story about the unfortunate Venables," he said, busying himself at the kitchen sink, rinsing cups, washing his hands. "I've never told a soul. I never break a confidence, Belinda, which is why I'm such a repository of odd information. Now, with Peter shot to death and Jack arrested for the murder, it may be that the sanctity of the Ruffians needs to take a back seat. Let me change out of these filthy duds. Then we'll go for a walk and I'll empty out the vault for you."

Chapter Thirty-six

We walked down Joy Street, crossed Beacon, where the heat shimmered off the pavement, and entered the Common. The leaves of the trees were dulled by a patina of dust, the grass before us had a skinned and browned-out look to it. Hundreds of kids were splashing in the huge shallow swimming pool, a band was playing music from Gilbert and Sullivan in the quaint little bandstand, and the shouts of a ballgame or two drifted lazily up the hill from clouds of dust far below. Old men wearing straw hats and suits and ties sat reading newspapers on benches and black mothers in spandex shorts wheeled tots in strollers and tourists seemed weighed down by the cameras draped from their necks like millstones. They were headed for the Freedom Trail and Old North Church and the redeveloped waterfront and Locke-Ober and the Quincy Market. But Tony Chalmers and I were headed deeper into the past, an antique place centered on Harvard Square where I'd once lived life so blissfully unaware of the currents all around me. It was an odd feeling, like a swimmer in the Charles realizing he's being towed under not by an icy undercurrent but by the *memory* of one, drowning in something that happened a long time ago.

We stood watching the band playing and the crowds surging around the Park Street subway station. He leaned against a tree and we tried to catch a breeze to dry us off.

"Venables came to me at the end of senior year," he said, knocking a different chipped and blackened pipe against the heel of his hand. Then he was scraping inside the bowl with an old penknife. "He was a secretive fellow, quiet, and I'd never been quite as close to him as the others. Still, I was the one he came to at this point, the one he confided in. By this time you and Jack were thinking about marriage and Harry and Sally were a fixture on the scene. Sally had just announced that she was going to Europe for the grand tour . . . everything was going quite nicely. And alone comes Peter late one night, right there to the Joy Street place, it was a warm spring night and we drank beer and sat out on my deck . . . God, almost twenty years ago and now he's dead. Well, he had quite a story to tell.

"He had been seeing this girl, he said, but for a variety of reasons he'd had to keep it quiet. Couldn't tell a soul, and positively not the Ruffians. But now he had a problem and he didn't know whom else he might turn to—but me. Well, I knew what was coming and sure enough, I was right. It didn't take a genius, and you have to remember that things were different then. He'd gotten the girl pregnant . . . at least he thought it was his doing and the girl said she was sure. She had another boyfriend they both knew about, Peter accepted the situation, but she said she knew the baby she carried was Peter's. She was pretty upset, she hadn't been able to tell even her closest friend, and she'd finally decided to have an abortion. Somewhat more involved then than now. Peter wasn't so sure she should. He came to me to ask me what to do. He wanted me to talk with her. He wasn't asking me to apply any pressure, he just wanted me to talk with her. My feeling at the time was that he loved her, wanted her to have the child for that reason, even though she was apparently going to marry this other boyfriend. It was a delicate situation."

Chalmers leaned back, took a pouch of tobacco from his pocket, and crammed the pipe full. "This is all very interesting," I said, "but I don't see the connection, you know? What did it have to do with Jack? Or the rest of the Ruffians?" I watched the breeze blow out two matches before the third one got his pipe going.

"Well, there is a connection," he said, puffing. "But I had to see if you already knew the story. Apparently you don't."

"Of course I don't. Venables would hardly have confided in me."

"I realize that. But Sally might have."

"How would Sally have found out about Venables' tawdry love life?" I couldn't keep the impatience out of my voice.

"Sally was the girl in question, I'm afraid. She was pregnant by Venables."

I sat down on the grass and leaned back against the tree. Chalmers told me I looked like I'd seen a ghost and went to get us hot dogs and Cokes from a vendor. He came back and sank down beside me. I looked at the hot dog as if I'd never seen one before.

"Go ahead, eat it, drink up," he said. "You've had a shock."

"I ought to be getting used to them," I said weakly. "But somehow I just keep getting caught off guard."

"You don't have much guard," he said. "Never have had. It's your nature. Anyway . . ."

I sat chewing my hot dog without tasting it, listening to his recreation of the events so long ago. They had all met in the old rooftop bar at the Parker House. The sun had been setting across the city, burning off the golden dome. Sally had been so pretty, so pale and intense with her straight black hair and dark, deep eyes. Venables dark and fine-featured, worried, so attentive. It was all true, as Venables had told Chalmers. Sally and Peter had begun an affair almost by accident. She was drawn to his introversion, his darkness, his mystery, all in such contrast to Harry. He had simply fallen in love and to hell with the Ruffian code. He'd been through Harry and Jack beating hell out of each other over me, he knew Harry might have gone even further had it happened again, so he made sure the affair was kept secret. Chalmers thought Peter hoped the pregnancy would change Sally's mind about marrying Harry. But Sally was committed and Venables struggled to understand. But he begged her for the baby. He wanted the baby.

"It all may have turned on my Catholicism," Chalmers said, carefully balling up his wrappers and dropping them into the empty Coke cup. "I'd left all that behind me, hadn't been inside a church in years, but this atavistic thing came out—I didn't want her to snuff out that baby, that life inside her. Call me what you will, but I—subtly, I think—orchestrated the pros and cons of the argument in such a way as I knew would shift her toward Peter's point of view. She could have it both ways, she could have their baby and in that way always retain a tie to Peter, to this passionate love affair she'd already decided must be a temporary thing . . . and she could have Harry, too, the life she'd committed herself to." He shrugged his round shoulders and ran his hand through the curly gray puffball of hair. "So in the end that's what she did. She went off to Europe, looking at museums and whatnot, hanging around Florence and Venice, staying longer than she'd planned . . . and having the baby in Switzerland. Peter was there. He took the baby. He and his parents raised the child in England—"

"And," I gulped, "she just got married . . ."

He nodded. "After she had the baby, she came home and married the man she really loved, Harry Granger. She and Peter somehow managed to put their romance behind them and got on with their separate lives."

"And the baby? Sally just forgot about the baby?" I was shaking my head, like somebody having a spasm. "No, I can't believe that, a mother couldn't do that."

"Sally? Oh, I think Sally could. The bargain was her own. How is it different from adoption?"

"Incredibly different! The baby was with a man she'd had deep feelings for, the baby was growing up, she knew she could have seen her, watched her grow up . . . and she just turned her back and walked away? Impossible."

"Not for Sally," Chalmers said. "Very strong-willed woman, Sally. Don't you think? It may have cut her to pieces inside, but she'd handle it, that's her way. She'd made her deal, she was going to live with it. And she had Harry to think about, they had a life to live . . . She didn't know Peter anymore, nor the child, and the years went by and life went on and it somehow wasn't connected to Sally anymore." He dug the pipe out of his pocket again, knocked it against the tree, and the ashes sprinkled down into the dry, brown, dusty grass. "Remember that wedding at Sag Harbor? That was quite a life too, Belinda. That life mattered too."

The afternoon wore on but I wasn't paying much attention. Chalmers had run through his classified memories, spilled what he knew. The rest was just generalized chatting, reminiscing, and a refusal on his part to speculate on who might have killed Peter Venables. We finally walked across the Common and stopped. He looked up the path that led to Beacon Street and Joy.

"I've told you what I know in confidence, Belinda. You do with it whatever you think is right. Ruffian secrets don't seem to have much priority anymore. At least not in my mind. They—we—did some stupid things. Who doesn't? But somehow we all clung together for a long time, still are. Clinging to the wreckage at this point, I guess. But . . . but it's what we wanted. Back then, anyway. We saw it differently then. We didn't know how complicated things might get. . . ."

I watched him trudge up the path. When he reached Beacon he turned around and waved to me, as if he knew perfectly well I'd be watching. Then he went across the street and out of my sight. He'd unloaded a lot excess baggage. But somehow he looked more weighed down than before.

Chapter Thirty-seven

There was no question of not believing it.

Tony Chalmers was utterly convincing. And now that I knew, I didn't really know what to do with the knowledge. What most amazed me, I suppose, was the fact that Sally carried it all off so perfectly when it was happening. I had never dreamed she might be having an affair with someone else while she was seeing Harry. And to have gotten pregnant! By one of the Ruffians, yet!

I was simply stunned and it took me several hours and a long bath back at the Ritz to begin pulling myself and my reactions together. Quite a few things made more sense now, at least superficially, but I still couldn't imagine what Sally must have been going through all these years . . . let alone the period since Peter Venables had come back to New York.

I remembeed most of all the moments over coffee in the Village when she'd shown me the photograph of Delilah Venables. The shine in her eyes and the happiness on her face as she'd talked about the girl, her marriage, and how she and Peter had been breakfasting together in the garden, enjoying the renewal of their friendship. Delilah Venables. Sally's daughter. God, it was so obvious! At least it was once you knew. The hair, the eyes, they were so utterly Sally. And the coloring, of course, was Peter's.

The way she'd spoken so pleasantly about Venables, what a nice boy he'd always been. It made sense now, almost as if she'd been trying to hint something to me. Afraid to just tell me. Why, I wondered, had she been afraid? Wasn't it just the kind of thing you confided to your best friend? I should have known the truth all these years, been able to help her through the hard times and the sense of loss, abandonment. But she hadn't told. Why? Had she simply not wanted to burden me with the truth? That might have been Sally in one of her flights of nobility . . . yes, that was the only real bet. Sparing me the lie and its moral imperatives.

What must it have been like in that house? At the party for the show? Seeing him every day? Managing to keep Harry in the dark? Had she made love with Peter after so many years? Had they been strangers or friends? Or lovers, still?

Had Jack been right on the money with his first assumption? That Venables had indeed come back for Sally? Perhaps all the rest of his diary entries meant nothing. Maybe he had put his finger on it right away.

When Hacker and I had been floating in the rowboat and seen the terrible confrontation between Harry and Sally—what had that been about? There had been the sheet of paper fluttering between them and Harry had laughed, and later, at the ice-cream stand, he'd been so calm. And later still, telling me the fight in the park had been over her accusations about his having a girlfriend, had Harry been lying?

How much had Harry been lying, anyway?

I seemed to have no appetite. Everything seemed to have conspired to leave me feeling gaunt and dry and old. I got dressed and sat at the scarred old desk looking out over the Public Garden in the evening's slanting sunlight. I went outside and went into it, the garden and the sunlight, smelling the flowers and watching the children tugging at parents and young couples sitting in the grass kissing and touching one another. I walked down to the little wooden jetty at the Frog Pond and went aboard one of the swan boats, waited for it to fill up, then stared off at the haze and the soundless people on the banks, felt the coolness as we slid under the footbridge, heard the children beside me chattering, only as if they were far away, at the end of a long tunnel. My God, I felt so old. And I didn't have a man I loved, or a husband, and I had no children, and I couldn't believe I was going to start having them now . . . and my best friend had been someone else all along, someone who hid things from me, who couldn't share her life with me. And all I had to show for any of it was a bunch of paintings. Of myself. Christ, the whole thing was making me fairly sick just then.

What had Hacker Welles said? I know I didn't have it all exactly right, but he'd taken a fairly dim view of us, all of us, and had called us all guilty parties.

What were we guilty of? I'd wondered.

Maybe an answer was taking shape in my mind. Maybe we were guilty of self-absorption and insulating ourselves and keeping too many secrets and not just letting go and being kind and decent and loving. Maybe. I didn't know and probably never would.

I left the swan boats and the Frog Pond behind and walked along Arlington Street, past the offices of *The Atlantic Monthly* and the corner of Commonwealth and then turned and headed up Beacon Hill. I wanted to reach the top and stand by the State House and look down over the Common and Park and Tremont and the Parker House and pretend for a moment that Jack and I were kids again headed for a party at somebody's place in the Back Bay where you could hear the music from the open windows six blocks away.

Of course, I couldn't stop thinking. Nothing Tony Chalmers had told me led me to believe that Jack had any reason to kill Venables. No reason from the past.

The fight between Jack and Harry—now, that must have been something. Jack was lucky he hadn't killed Harry, if it came to that. And breaking a lamp over Jack's head—my God, what a pair. I dug around in the corners of my mind, through the oldest rubbish, to see if the fact that they were apparently fighting over me provided me with any retroactive satisfaction. It didn't seem to. Would it have then? I couldn't answer that question. I didn't know how stupid I might have been in those days.

So that was how Harry reacted to having his girlfriend pinched from under his nose by another Ruffian. Not a pretty picture. No wonder Venables had taken such care to keep it quiet. Maybe that was why Sally hadn't confessed all to me. Maybe he had told her about the lamp and Jack's head and Harry and the three flights of stairs at Eliot House.

Then, nearly twenty years down the road, Peter had come back to see Harry and Sally. And maybe Jack had been right.

And maybe Harry had found out. . . .

I saw him and for a moment I was afraid he'd seen me. I'd been leaning at the fence surrounding the Common, the State House right behind me, and I hadn't been paying any attention to anything but what was going on in my head

Suddenly I'd seen something I or my subconscious recognized, a man coming up the steep hill from Tremont Street toward the top of Beacon Hill. The light had pretty well failed in the western sky and the streetlamps were on. First he was just a big dark shape; then I focused on him and heard myself gasp. I didn't do what a normal person who hasn't been kicking through the past and fights and murders and illegitimate babies and whatnot would have done: I didn't call his name gladly and happily and grasp for something on the bright side—oh, no, I let myself shrink back into the shadows beneath the trees while I watched him cross the street and pass in front of the State House.

What the hell was he doing here?

And don't give me coincidences, not now. I was there, Tony Chalmers was a few blocks away, and there *he* was striding determinedly along like a man who knew exactly where he was going.

I waited for him to pass; then I followed along on my side of the street, ready to dart down into the Common and God only knew what awful fate if I thought he'd spotted me. I must have been going quite mad.

He pushed onward and I kept him in view. He wasn't looking around and he wasn't dawdling. I knew perfectly well where he was going to stop and turn.

Joy Street.

I stood well out of the penumbra of a streetlamp's glow and watched him, as if he were a robot and I was controlling the handset. Turn, I thought, and he stopped, looked at his watch, and turned.

I crossed over and stood in the shadows at the corner. He made his way up the street. He didn't need to check any house numbers. It was familiar territory.

He went to the door of Tony Chalmers' house, pushed the buzzer, and the light over the door clicked on. The door opened and in a matter of a minute or so I heard, then saw their shapes, as they came through the dining room and out onto the deck.

I heard the clinking of glasses in the summer-night stillness and if I'd wanted to I suppose I could have gone closer still and heard their voices.

Tony Chalmers and Hacker Welles.

Chapter Thirty-eight

I went to bed thinking my journey into the past was over, figuring that it was all too deep and muddied for me to deal with, figuring that I'd never get my tired brain wrapped all the way around Harry and Tony and Hacker and Jack and Mike and poor dead Peter. They'd lived in their own little world and I was a woman. I wasn't even going to understand it and no matter how hard I tried I was never going to gain admittance. It was a men's club and time had locked the door and thrown away the key.

That's what I'd thought when I went to bed that evening, still seeing Hacker in the shadows of Joy Street, waiting at Tony Chalmers' door.

But when I woke in the morning and had a fine breakfast of eggs and croissants and marmalade and hot coffee brought to my room—then I began thinking that maybe the journey wasn't over quite yet. If I hadn't actually been a Ruffian, I'd been, along with Sally, as somebody had once said, one of the Ladies Auxiliary. Somewhere inside I was part Ruffian. What was happening now proved that. As the Ruffians had come to grief, as the old edifice had begun crumbling, Sally and I had gotten trapped inside too. We were paying the same price.

So I had one more call to make and I knew I had to do it in person.

* * *

Guilty Parties

I rented a brown Chevy, loaded my overnight bag, and drove west into the summery Berkshires, dark green and thick as a forest in a fairy tale where the trolls lived, and connected with the New York State Thruway. I turned south. It was perfect for August, hot and pale blue, almost white, and the highway shimmering in the heat like a fluttering ribbon. I played the radio and half-heard the Top Forty and the news on the hour and all the commercials and the hiss of the tires and the whoosh of pasing trucks, half-heard it because I was thinking again.

Hacker had told Mike he was off to do some research. Only one kind of research you do with Tony Chalmers. But what could be left for them to talk about? They'd researched the Ruffians for a year, getting the show down on paper.

Hacker had wanted to talk to me after the caper at Jack's apartment, but somehow we hadn't gotten to it. I'd been through the Suicide Night and Harry with his off-the-wall declaration of unrequited love, and when I'd called him he was already gone . . . and now he turns up dogging my tracks in Boston.

What was going on? I felt like a spy, a secret agent, but I didn't know what I was doing. Spooky feeling.

But not as spooky as thinking about Harry. Harry and his fight with Jack. Harry still determined to love me. Venables coming back and telling Harry he'd come for me.

Everything kept coming back to Harry. Harry betrayed almost twenty years ago by Sally and Venables. Harry, Harry, Harry.

Harry in the Turtle Bay house while Sally slept. With a sleeping pill, I'd bet. Harry confronting Venables . . . Harry with a shotgun solving a lot of problems. . . .

* * *

I knew the turnoff.

Everything slowed down once I left the thruway. I could hear the sounds of summer that summer, not man, made. It was a relief. The road wound up into the green mountains, where I left a trail of dust swirling behind me. A dog barked at me from beside the road and the trees were full of little sounds, whiffs of breeze, a stream tumbling along beside the dusty road. The heat clamped a kind of bell of stillness over everything. I'd turned the radio off once I'd left the racket of the highway and the quiet had swallowed me.

The forested hillsides closed around me as I climbed, and the road got narrower. Then I came upon a clearing, a turnaround where the road petered out. I parked the brown Chevy, which had grown a thick covering of dry countryside, and sat for a few minutes, afraid to leave and knowing I had to. It finally got too hot in the car and I had to get out.

I stood at the top of a narrow path looking down at a flat, absolutely placid lake so still it resembled a giant coin at the bottom of a thick green carpet. Halfway down the hill an A-frame cabin sat amid the trees. A balcony faced the lake. The quiet was overpowering. The buzz of insects, the occasional call of a bird, the leaves rustling in the wind. I felt the sweat drying on the back of my neck as I stood looking down on the tranquillity.

Far below, a gray dock jutted out into the lake. A small motorboat bobbed at the end of its tether. A woman sat at the end of the dock with her knees drawn up to her chin. She was staring out at the water. A couple of large, elegant birds swept through the heat over the lake. I stood watching the stillness and the isolation for what seemed an eternity. Then, without warning, the woman on the dock stood up, turned toward me, and waved, as if our minds had signaled one another without a sound, through all that empty space. It had always been that way. The unexpected phone call when I'd most needed it, my turning up on her doorstep just when she'd begun to cry and throw pillows at the wall. I waved back and went down the hill.

She hugged me but she wasn't the same Sally. Something was different, but it didn't become clear to me until she's made us gin-and-tonics and we'd gone to sit on the balcony and I saw her face as she stared out over the water again. I looked at the water and it occurred to me that it was a perfect place to die, to leave the world behind you, to just slip away and pull the hole in after you. That was what was different about Sally. She was quiet and composed and at peace, which wasn't like her. The tensile strength, the fierceness that had always lain beneath the surface, was gone. There was a coolness, a calm, as if she'd glimpsed the end and wasn't afraid of it. Peace. I watched her and I looked out at the water and I thought it was the peace of death.

"Are you all right?" I said at last.

"That's a funny question. Harry's trying to convince people I took an accidental overdose, he even tried to convince me. What a silly man. No, I'm not all right but in a strange way I'm better off than I was." She turned the lamps of her black eyes on me. "How are you, Belinda? How's it all going? I've been wanting to talk with you, needing to."

"Now's a pretty good time," I said, looking around at the blanket of isolation. "No interruptions."

"I've been thinking. Since, you know . . . Peter's death and my typical flubbing of my own. You're so well-mannered you'd probably grow old and gray and die yourself before asking me why I did it—isn't that the truth?"

"I don't know. I've wondered, naturally . . ."

"Well, I've wondered if I should tell you or if I ought to just let it go. What do you think? Does it interest you?"

"Talk about funny questions," I said. Her eyes bored into me in a curiously disinterested way, as if none of it really mattered much anymore. Her voice held the same lack of concern, as if a vampire had bled it of all emotion.

"I've asked myself so many funny questions. I came up here to ask funny questions and then I thought I might go swimming and just not come back. You wouldn't believe how deep this lake is. Or how cold, even in summer. Icy. I went out in the boat and shut it off and just floated one day, looking up at the sky, watching the clouds go by, seeing the faces and the animals and countries the cloud shapes make, and I dangled my hand over the side—God, it was so cold—and before I knew it my hand was numb, and I thought, hmmm, that's not such a bad idea, all I'd have to do is just slip over the side and in a matter of seconds, a minute at most, I'd be numb and that would be it. Sound crazy to you, Belinda? Am I crazy or what? Or am I sane? Maybe I just want to make everything come out right, even everything up . . . and that'll be the end of people getting hurt." She poked her finger down into the drink and twirled the lime slice around, licked off her finger. We might have been sitting by the pool at a country club talking about the sex lives of the members. "I've got a daughter. I never told you that."

"No."

"No, I don't have a daughter, or no, I never told you that?"

"I know you have a daughter."

"Really? Is it common knowledge, then?" She sipped her drink. Emotionless except for maybe a slight curiosity.

"No. But I wish you'd told me yourself."

"But I just did, Belinda. I didn't know you already knew. Be fair. I had to tell you because I want to sort of clear up accounts. I want everybody to know the stuff that matters. Is that stupid? Oh, I suppose it is. Who cares, right? Well, I guess I care. How would you like to hear the story? I'll tell you. Horse's-mouth stuff, and I'm the only horse left."

"I'm glad you brought it up, Sal," I said. I reached over and took her hand, squeezed it softly. The answering pressure was so faint it might not have happened at all. "I wish you would tell me the whole story. Get it off your chest. Then we can begin life all over again."

"Can we, Belinda? What an extraordinary idea. But you've always had terrific ideas. As far back as I can remember."

I wanted to get her talking. I didn't want Sally to head out into that lake and not come back. Talking her way through the whole story might be just about the only way to keep that from happening.

"You can imagine what it's been like," she said, "sitting on a page-one story for nearly twenty years, not being able to tell my very best pal. Not being able to tell anyone, not even talk about it with the man. Having a daughter. Never seeing her, never hearing from her, knowing she thought her mother had died. It's been a chore, Belinda. Painful, so painful I pretty well managed to convince the daily me that it had never happened at all. There have been days during those years when I never thought of Peter Venables, nor Delilah Venables, even one time. Not many days, but some. God, there were so many reasons why it could never come out. You see that, don't you?"

I shrugged. "I don't know. It was up to you, I guess."

"Do you realize what it would have done to Harry? Just think of it—Harry would have clouded up and rained all over everything, every inch of the life we had. And God has no idea of what might have happened between him and Peter. I could have dealt with it. But it might have ruined Harry's life. He's a romantic guy, love means a lot to him . . . but then, you know all about that. Sometimes I forget that . . . that prehistory of ours. Love means a lot to most people, but I've asked myself, does it to us, Belinda? Or is it really the day-to-day living that matters? How far can love take you? That's the way I used to feel about things—oh, I think I probably delivered myself of those sentiments to you at one time or another in girlhood. That's the way I thought when the thing with Peter started. Romance and passion were one thing, an ephemeral thing, and what I had with Harry was for the long run. Then Peter came back to New York and I was positive all that was behind me, all those fires had died out a long time ago. Maybe Harry could still work up some grand passion for a woman, I was sure he had, but not me. I was scared about seeing Peter again, scared in a vague way, but I hadn't seen him in such a long time—I didn't believe in passion anymore, so what harm could seeing him do? And he didn't seem to have any qualms about coming back. I made myself ignore the question of Delilah. She was a young woman I didn't know. I might not even have liked her." She stood up and went to the railing, turned her back to the sun so she had no face when I looked at her.

"Then he came back, he was in the house," she said, "and I discovered I'd been wrong. Wrong about just about everything I'd been so sure of."

"I know the feeling," I said, but she didn't seem to hear me.

"I was crazy about him, Belinda," she said softly, "and, better yet, he felt the same way about me. It was magic. Does that sound stupid? Do we believe in magic anymore, Belinda? I was so sure I didn't. But I did. Oh, goodness, I did. Do you still feel passion, the real thing? Have you felt it lately? Or is it a memory?" She looked at me expectantly.

"I don't know," I said. I felt lame, half a person. The passions I'd felt lately hadn't had much to do with love.

"You don't know. Belinda doesn't know. Do you know if you'd like something to eat, then? That's an easy one."

I tried to laugh but it's hard to laugh alone. I followed her into the kitchen and watched her slice some cold chicken for sandwiches. It was a very quiet process.

Chapter Thirty-nine

Her mood remained constant throughout the afternoon as she told me the story of her affair with Peter Venables. She might have been talking about someone else, had I just been hearing her tone; but the story she told was as personal as things get. The story was as real as sex and love and all the other messes people make of their lives. It was just that Sally's story sounded like the plot of an old Lana Turner movie. Yet I had moments when I wanted to cry and take her in my arms and feel her sobbing. But she wasn't sobbing. She was beyond sobbing and I could only hope she could find her way back to safety, the safety provided by familiar emotions.

She started by recounting yet again how she had been going out with Jack when Jack and I met and Jack dumped her. And how I had left Harry in my haste to take up with Jack. And how in the aftermath of hurt and depression she and Harry had found one another. She wouldn't have heard me if I'd tried to interrupt to tell my version of the story, so I didn't try. She told me how her needs and Harry's had correlated, how they had fallen in love and begun making plans for the future. She felt a tremendous security with Harry and she knew she made him happy. Everything had been going so well . . .

Then she spent an evening with Peter Venables, just an accident, waiting for Harry, who got held up and couldn't keep the date for some stupid reason, and something had clicked, something she couldn't define, something she couldn't bring herself to tell me about. It sounded like yesterday as she talked about it, recalling what she'd worn and what he'd said, as she saw something in him, something romantic and bruised and sensitive, almost a doomed quality. She had never seen such things in a man before. She'd been thrilled, as if she'd discovered a new and unknown country, a new kind of creature, and she couldn't seem to help falling in love. And Peter had loved her, too, youthfully and earnestly and forever and ever and ever.

But she'd felt horribly guilty about going behind Harry's back. And for Peter it was a question of two Ruffians, just as Tony Chalmers had told me. They became obsessive that last winter—their first winter—about keeping everything absolutely secret. Then she had gotten pregnant.

At first Peter had wanted to face up to it, tell Harry. But Sally had grown timid. She told herself that what she felt for Peter was infatuation, that her feelings were too intense to prove durable. She just wanted to have an abortion. But Peter had fought that idea. It was their child, the product of their love—oh, he had been such a romantic, one of love's fools. So she had agreed to talk with Tony Chalmers, just to hear what he had to say, and the result was that she'd gone to Europe and had the baby and Peter had accepted her going back to marry Harry. Had he believed she'd crack and come back to him? Sally didn't know. She vowed to go on with her life as planned and had lived for a bit as a tragic heroine, and then her feelings had begun to fade. She had never seen the little girl, had never been told that Peter had named her Delilah. There had been nothing after the pain of labor. It was as if she had had an operation and a period of recovery in the Swiss clinic and then she'd gone to Paris and reshaped her life and gone home to her parents and to Harry. And she had married Harry and I had married Jack and we had driven through the Pennsylvania countryside and Sally had found the wheel-of-fortune and our lives had continued.

The afternoon was gone. It wasn't like spending it with another person. It was more like dwelling in an echoing archive peopled with memories and feelings and events that were little more than shadows. But shadows that made themselves felt at the core of your soul.

Sally suggested a walk at sunset down beside the lake. There was a rocky shoreline and the breeze across the water was cool and clean. The smell of the trees was everywhere. Bats wheeled in the purple, darkening sky where the clouds lay thinly like strips of paint drying on a canvas.

We sat on rocks and pitched pebbles into the water, hearing the plunk and creatures scuttling behind us in the dark woods. Sally told me the rest of the story.

She did have one terrible fear about Peter's coming back to New York. She was afraid he might not, after such a long time, still find her attractive. But he had been so sweet, so eager to touch her face and kiss her. So full of stories about their daughter and the life he had led and, always, about how much he had missed her, how he had never married, how he had never stopped thinking about her.

They had spent hour after hour talking about how much they remembered of one another, how they had longed for the touches they recalled.

And they had realized, Sally told me, that they were still in love. Or in love *again*. Peter wanted her to come back to England with him, to come and live with him and get to know her wonderful daughter. What a wedding present, he'd said. Her mother!

Sally knew she had to tell Harry. She asked Harry to go for a walk in Central Park. It had been hideously hot, but they'd found a shady spot beneath a tree, on the bank of one of the lakes. She had shown him the picture of her daughter and told him the whole story and Harry had sat quietly and listened.

"But he didn't believe me, Belinda, he didn't believe me when I said that Peter wanted me to go with him. He thought I was making it up. He laughed at the idea and said he didn't mind my having an affair with Peter at this late date. He told me to go ahead but he wouldn't give me a divorce. I could play around as much as I wanted, for all he cared, if I'd be discreet. After all, he said, he'd been discreet. . . ."

And finally, staring out at the dim light reflected off the lake, Sally began to cry. I didn't realize it at first but then I heard a sibilant moaning and I went to her, put my arms around her and cradled her, comforted her. It was what I needed to do. I didn't know how much to believe of what she'd told me about that conversation in the park and I didn't think it mattered. I couldn't make it square with what Harry had said to me about his feelings for me, and Venables—well, Venables defied my understanding. Having dinner with me, attacking me, telling me it was his turn—and all the time telling Sally he loved her and wanted her to come back to England with him? None of that made any sense, but maybe it didn't have to, maybe it just didn't matter. What could it have to do with anything?

Venables was dead. And Harry . . .

Sally leaned back, away from me, and wiped her eyes with a fist. "He's dead now, Belinda, and all that matters is that I loved him. I bore him a daughter and now he's dead and we'll never see our daughter together . . . I'll never see my baby . . ."

"Who killed him, Sally?" I held her steady by the shoulders and tried to penetrate the darkness, tried to see her face.

"What? What do you mean?"

"You know who killed him, don't you?"

"How could I know. . . ? Jack, it must have been Jack. It was Jack, wasn't it? Or somebody else . . . I don't know . . . It doesn't matter, does it?"

"Don't lie to me, Sally," I whispered, holding her close, feeling her breathing, her body pushing against me. "Please don't lie to me. Not when they think Jack did it . . . please!"

"I don't know what you mean," she said close to my ear. But her voice was slipping away from me again, the emotion draining away like the color from the night sky.

"You know perfectly well who killed him, Sally. You can't lie to protect him, you can't let Jack be blamed . . ." But it was no use. She was nodding against my shoulders, humming to herself, a song I didn't know.

I took her hand and led her up the path, surrounded by the sounds of the night. Mysterious splashes in the lake, the cracking of twigs in among the trees where the trolls were coming to life.

I put her to bed and went to the kitchen, sat looking at the telephone, wondering who should be called. I didn't know what to do with Sally. I didn't know what she would let me do. I'd have to see how she was in the morning.

I made myself another chicken sandwich and found some oranges and peeled them and ate them and realized I'd just whetted my appetite. I looked in the freezer and found some pepperoni pizza and some ice cream. In the cupboard I found some chocolate sauce. I heated the pizza, ate it, poured a beer to drink with it. Then I made a chocolate sundae and ate that. I felt like I was making up for not having eaten all summer.

It was cool on the balcony. I put on one of Sally's sweaters and sat with my feet up on the railing.

What was I going to do?

I needed help.

Harry Granger had killed Peter Venables.

But what good did knowing that do me? What good did it do Jack? And where the hell was that gun? It was so frustrating. Jack's motives were so public, so widely observed . . . and Harry's were so private, just so much hearsay. But I'd finally gotten smart. I kept telling myself that. Things weren't what they seemed. No matter how bad it looked for Jack. There was another story under the surface and if I didn't think of something, Harry Granger was going to get away with murder.

* * *

I finally went to bed in the small second bedroom where Jack and I stayed on visits in the past. The scents of the trees seeped in at the windows, sweet and evocative. I could see the moon, blue and nearly full, through the window. I stood looking down at the reflection of the silvery globe in the face of the lake. It looked like a painting of the Maxfield Parrish school and I expected to see a jester in cap and bells sitting at the end of the railing. No jesters, however.

I don't know how long I'd been asleep when I heard something, a creaking noise, that wakened me. Or was it just a tree bending? Then I heard it again. A footstep on the balcony, the wooden floor complaining.

The skin on the back of my neck crawled. It was the sheerest kind of fear, heart-stopping. It was Harry. It had to be Harry. He knew we knew. He'd found out where I'd gone, he knew I'd gone to Boston and seen Tony Chalmers and figured it all out. He knew I'd come to see Sally. To tell her the truth. It was all on top of me, crushing down, driving the breath from my body. I heard another step. Outside my window. Then silence.

I slid out of bed and crouched beneath the window. Slowly I raised my head. Through the screen I saw a shape, then heard something.

A tuneless humming. And I saw the red tip of a cigarette and remembered sitting in the dark garden with Harry.

But it wasn't Harry. It was Sally, humming to herself and staring out at the lake, alone in the middle of the night with her sorrows.

Chapter Forty

"So you just got up in the morning, calmly had some scrambled eggs, and went away so she could drown herself before lunch?"

"Cornbread, too. She got up first and made fresh cornbread. Not the act of a woman who's going to kill herself. Hot cornbread presupposes a willingness to enjoy it, to finish the pan at breakfast tomorrow. Anybody knows that."

Hacker had left a couple of messages on my machine, and ten minutes after I'd gotten into the shower the phone was ringing again. So I dashed out and stood there dripping wet, water washing road dust out of my hair and down into my eyes, answering questions and impatiently wanting to ask Hacker some of my own but not knowing how to start.

"I don't know, it seems to me you're taking a hell of a chance, leaving her alone up there with the bats and the squeaks in the middle of the night and that hypnotic sun shining on the lake—that could drive a sane person to suicide, let alone Sally."

"What are you talking about?" I yelled at him. "Who says she's not as sane as you or I? I hate this easy psycho-analysis—"

"You and I didn't just try to kill ourselves," he said patiently. "But okay, sane and insane are stupid categories. I stand corrected."

"About time!" I heard him laugh quickly. "But really she seemed all right," I said. "She was livelier and wouldn't talk about anything . . . ah, upsetting. She sounded done with that. Nothing about the woman Harry's supposed to be in love with . . ." I wondered if he could hear the sudden spurt of tension I felt. "And she insisted that she wouldn't do anything dumb. She said she'd be back in town in a few days." I hadn't told him anything about Venables and Sally because I'd gotten smart about things like trusting people with bits and pieces they didn't need to know. I didn't know what he'd been doing in Boston and he wasn't offering any information about that.

"Where have you been?" he asked. "I thought we were trying to figure this out together."

"Indignation and hurt feelings! That's beautiful. I tried to call you and you'd gone off on a research trip. Whatever that might be. And I had to call Mike to get that little crumb. You could have left a message on my machine—"

"I know, I know, but I'm a hell of a swell guy, in case you've forgotten—to say nothing of being almost supernaturally clean."

"Don't try to soft-soap me!"

"That's good! Soft-soap . . . clean? Get it? Well, I had a lot on my mind. I had to find out a couple of things. And the upshot is, I've got to see you." He reminded me of Mike telling me he had to see me urgently, arriving with Antonelli, and then lying. "Dinner? The thing is, I . . . ."

"Yes?"

"I've got this thing figured out."

"So have I," I said.

There was a long pause, long enough to make me think we'd been cut off. Then he said stiffly: "What do you mean?"

"I know who killed Peter Venables. Isn't that what we're talking about?"

"Ah. We'd better compare notes, then. Meet me at Emilio's. Thirty-third and Third. Early. Six-thirty? I don't want to wait, Belinda."

Hacker was at the long bar. He bought me a drink and sighed a lot, as if he'd been thinking and hadn't slept in a while. There were dark circles under his eyes and his seersucker double-breasted jacket was even more rumpled than usual. He was wearing a shirt with broad pale blue stripes and a bow tie that was floppy and knotted a shade off center. He looked at his watch and nodded at my punctuality. "Drink up," he said. "You're gonna need it. You're in for a long night."

"Wonderful. You know how to lift a girl's spirits."

He grunted and I followed him up the few stairs with the piano on the right where the elderly black guy was playing "Perfidia." A riot of flowers sprawled gorgeously straight ahead and our table was toward the back on the left, out of the main flow coming later. I slid in against the wall and Hacker sat down facing me, ordered two more drinks, and settled in with his elbows on the table, his palms supporting his face on either side.

"Harry Granger shot Peter Venables with Jack Stuart's shotgun, which he stole and hid God only knows where. Probably dropped it off the Brooklyn Bridge and nobody will ever find it . . . unless, of course, he's not quite through using it. A thought which scares the hell out of me. And I have the feeling that Sally may know he did it." He took a deep breath. "I think he killed Venables . . . because of you, Belinda. I don't expect you to

268

swallow all this right off the bat, but I'm right, I'm sure of it." He blinked tiredly.

"Yes, I think you are too," I said, and watched his brows raise and his eyes grow a fraction less tired.

"You do?"

"Yes, I do."

He took a man-sized gulp of his fresh drink and swallowed hard, like a man taking some very large pills. "Because of you?"

I nodded. "During my memorable evening with Venables he said some things about Harry's feelings for me that I've been thinking about these past few days. He thought Harry had never gotten over our relationship—though Venables thought Harry was trying to find a duplicate of me, not thinking about getting the original back. At least that's what he said—and he, Venables I mean, was the one who wanted me personally."

"And you've decided," Hacker said slowly, "that they both wanted the one and only you. I salute you!" He lifted his glass and touched it to mine. "No shrinking violet, our Belinda."

"Are you a bit drunk or just very tired?"

"Both. So you've deduced that Harry killed Venables because they both wanted you and he happened to be the one holding a shotgun. Makes sense to me." He smiled sourly. The waiter appeared and Hacker brushed away the menus. "Sliced tomatoes and mozzarella, a dozen oysters, then we'll see." The waiter nodded gravely and departed. "You are such a smarty-pants," he said shaking his head. I noticed the gray in his sun-bleached hair, strands of gray against his tanned face. He massaged his lower lip, squeezing it. "Such a smarty," he repeated.

"Try not to be so condescending and don't use your tiredness as an excuse. Work up a little sympathy and think—do you have any idea how hard it is for me to talk about myself the way I'm having to do? Believe me, it seems just as ridiculous to me—all these men thinking they're in love with me—as it does to you. But I think—"

"It doesn't seem ridiculous to me. The fact that you find it ridiculous makes it seem all the less ridiculous."

"Don't even try to translate that for me. The point is, however you came to your conclusion, you're right. The night Sal tried to kill herself, after I met Harry at the hospital, he took me back to Turtle Bay for a drink. He told me he loved me, had always loved me, and that he was leaving Sally. I didn't know what the hell to think, it was just getting crazier and crazier—"

The waiter arrived with the starters and Hacker speared an oyster, dipped it in horseradish, and savored it for a moment before swallowing it. Then he attacked the tomato slices, which were about an inch thick, alternated with thick rounds of cheese. I was too intent on getting the story out to eat just yet.

"It was crazy, Hack," I said. "First Venables parachuting in and telling me how determined he was to have me. *Have* me, babbling on about how it was his *turn* . . . then out of a twenty-year friendship Harry decides to commemorate Sally's suicide attempt by telling me he's never stopped loving me and is leaving Sal because I'm now back in the marketplace." The drinks and the heat of the drive home from the cabin and not eating enough were all conspiring to loosen my tongue. It was waving like a semaphore and I knew it but it all seemed to be out of my control.

Hacker was munching steadily and the oysters were disappearing but I just kept on talking. "And, listen, you're a guy," I gabbled on, "and you don't know what it's like to be treated like a prime filet mignon. Everybody seems to have all these plans for me, but nobody consults me . . . you wouldn't believe what Tony Chalmers said, he told me about a fight Harry and Jack had a thousand years ago and I was the *prize!* I was *awarded* to Jack! I've got to tell you, it's a joke, it's craziness! So what's—"

I suddenly realized that Hacker was casting nervous little glances at the next table, where I'd developed an audience, both of whom were grinning broadly. I worked up a dirty look, laid it on an elderly woman with a mustache, who slowly returned to her triple martini.

"Well," I whispered, leaning across the four remaining oysters, "what is going on with these guys? Do they know what they're doing or what?"

"Just a minute. Tony Chalmers? When did he tell you this?"

"Oh-oh," I said, covering my mouth and reaching for my oyster fork. I slipped one into my mouth, then another, while Hacker sat and stared at me. So I told him the story of my trip to Boston, my visit with Chalmers and — extracting the deepest promise of secrecy—the story of Venables and Sally.

Hacker's eyes slowly widened. His fork slowly made its way back and forth between the last of the oysters and his mouth and then they were gone and he looked surprised. He'd never known anything about Sally and Venables and he couldn't quite fit it into the big picture. But he wasn't sure it mattered.

"And now," I said, "having been caught because you purposely have plied me with strong drink, I have a question for you. What were you doing skulking around Joy Street two nights ago? What was the nature of this big research trip?"

"What are you, some kind of detective?" He flashed me an admiring glance. "Well, yes, I guess you are. I had a long talk with Tony and that's what I want to tell you

about. I can explain everything, but not here. I think
Mike should be in one this, too."

I finished the bread while Hacker paid the bill.

I prayed for sobriety and deliverance from the past.

Chapter Forty-one

Mike Pierce was perspiring heavily despite the arctic air
conditioning. He was the only man I'd ever known who
apparently wore a sport coat while puttering around his
own place by himself. But tonight it lay like an exhausted
pet on a blue print couch. Mike was turned out in white
slacks and a pale yellow shirt, forest-green suspenders,
and a gray, unhealthy face. He was making drinks and I
shook my head enough to make it ache. Iced tea, please,
and he went to the kitchen to make it. He'd given his man
the night off and seemed slightly unfamiliar with where
things were in the cupboards. He brought me the tall cold
glass and we followed him out onto his balcony, which
looked northward from Central Park South. The park lay
moist and green behind a curtain of humidity. To the left
Lincoln Center glowed like the aftermath of a bombing
raid.

"Christ, it's hot," he mumbled, leaning on the railing.
The traffic pulsed below us but the density of the atmosphere killed the sounds. Geraniums, bright red and
soft pink, filled windowboxes, and a couple of palm trees
sat in large terra-cotta pots.

Hacker lit a cigar and said, "It's time, Mike old sport.
We're going to tell Belinda and then duck." He chortled
to himself. Mike didn't seem to hear. I sat down and

sipped my tea and wondered what was going on. "You have the floor," Hacker said.

Mike finally turned around, looked plaintively at me, and hooked his thumbs through the beautiful suspenders, dragging them downward toward his waist. "I told you I wanted to talk to you, urgently, the other day, but then I arrived with Antonelli and I couldn't talk . . . and then he told us they'd arrested Jack. That gave me second thoughts—such as, why drag out the dirty laundry if the whole thing is over and life is just going to struggle on? You told me I was lying about not understanding Jack's diary. Well, hell, I was lying, but in a good cause. Or so I thought. Saving everybody some pain and unhappiness. Then Hacker and I spoke, he told me Antonelli was just fishing around and probably couldn't hold Jack long, certainly couldn't make a murder charge stick with the kind of extremely circumstantial evidence he had. No gun, no witnesses, nothing that really added up to anything—except Jack's blowing off steam and punching a guy for messing around with his wife . . . well, that made sense, too. If Jack didn't do it, who did? And Hacker told me what he thought. I damn near fainted. But Hack's a smart cookie, right? And he's been digging through old Ruffian crap for the past year."

Mike took a sip of his drink. Hacker puffed and looked off into space.

"I'm a cowardly man, Belinda," Mike said. "I wanted to be as little part of this mess as I could. I'm good at picking up the pieces and sweeping everything under the rug and holding people's hands, but I'm not good at breaking things. Try to understand that." He looked at me again and I nodded. "You may recall Jack's accusation that Peter was a thief and that Jack had caught him at it—you wondered what that meant. So did I, so did Hacker . . . and then I woke up in the middle of the night, jolted out of sleep by a memory. I asked myself if it mattered—I didn't see how it could. Until Hack told me who he believed killed Peter." He kept skirting Harry's name, as if there was no way he could bring himself to mention it in such a context.

"You see, Peter had always been sort of obsessed by you." His eyes were round, as if he'd peeked into the past and been alarmed by what he saw. "Some men are like that. He hardly knew you, but it was the way you looked, what your appearance said to him. There's no point in quibbling—write it off to impressionable youth, whatever you like. Fact, these are facts. Peter watched while Harry went with you, and Harry was bound to tell us about some of his . . . you know, exploits. With you. And it really got to Peter. We used to kid him about how you were his sex object, his centerfold, and he'd just smile, shake his head, and tell us he'd be glad to wait for you. It was just talk, the way guys talk." He looked desperately at Hacker, as if for help in developing his narrative, but Hacker just smiled and waved his cigar at him—go on, go on.

"Well, Harry was known to keep a journal. He was always telling us how important it was to keep a record of everything important, everything that mattered, so we could remember it when we were old and gray. Harry was always sitting around the room scribbling away and it was his little eccentricity. We got so we didn't pay any attention . . . all except Peter, as it turned out. He got the idea that Harry had to be writing down everything that happened between you and him—he didn't tell us, but apparently he couldn't get it out of his mind. If only he could read Harry's journal, then he'd get the whole story, every detail." Mike sighed and took another drink. "Christ, Hack, this is so embarrassing!"

"Press on, lad," Hacker said. "It's gonna get a lot worse before it gets better." He grinned at me through the smoke and didn't make me feel any more confident. I didn't know what was coming next but I'd have bet I wasn't going to enjoy it.

"Well, to make a long story short. Peter got the journal one weekend when Harry went home and forgot to take it with him. I don't know the details, maybe nobody does. Anyway, Peter got it and had it for a couple of days, and then had to get it back to Harry's desk before Harry got back. The upshot is that Jack caught him bringing it back and Jack got very moral about it—you know Jack's temper—he raised real hell with Peter and it got pretty rough, pretty humiliating for Peter, and Jack wouldn't let him off the hook. I walked in on them and Jack told me all about it and Peter was so stunned and ashamed—I can see him now, his face absolutely scarlet, then he started to cry, begging Jack not to tell Harry, and Jack was saying: Harry, hell, I ought to tell Belinda what a creep you are, what a pervert—on and on. I played my usual role as peacemaker, sweeping up the wreckage, and we put the damn journal back and, you know how it is, Jack and I sort of had something on Peter ever after. I forgot it, or repressed it, it was so ugly—I mean, I felt humiliated just having seen the way Jack laid into Peter . . . but Peter went through the tortures of the damned and then some, I guess. Not long after that you and Jack got together and Jack and Harry had their big ruckus . . ." He let it trail off and turned away from me, looking back out into the night.

"For guys who were so close, such pals," I said, "you had a hell of a tough time getting along—"

"Well, you're just hearing about the bad parts, Belinda," he said. "Ninety-nine days out of a hundred all that was forgotten and we'd have done anything for each other. And that includes Jack for Peter and Peter for Jack. It was forgotten. Totally. Absolutely. When we'd had it out that day and put the journal back, I'd bet my life that Jack never mentioned it again to Peter, never thought about it again. It didn't fester, it didn't infect us. Not until now, not until Venables came back and started paying attention to you . . . and *that* was what I wanted to talk to you about the other day, when I chickened out. Why Peter was suddenly back and coming after you."

He stopped and I knew his recitation was done. Hacker cleared his throat. "Which brings us, dear one, to my research trip to Boston. I had to verify a thing or two, make sure my memory wasn't playing tricks on me. I had to check Tony's memory about the goddamn Belinda Pact . . . Buckle your seat belt, Belinda, and try to remember that boys will be boys."

The Belinda Pact.

It lay there at the bottom of everything for all these years. No one had ever told me, no one had ever hinted, not until Peter Venables took me out for drinks and dinner and set his foot upon the road to death.

They had all been a little in love with me. College-boy love. And they loved to make commitments. Hacker said he thought it was Harry who had started it. After he and Jack had beaten the hell out of one another and Jack had won me. The idea was that there wouldn't be any more opposition, no more stealing of girlfriends, no more bull-shit.

"You were the turning point," Hacker said. The lamps in the living room cast shadows toward us on the darkened balcony. I smelled Hacker's cigar. I was conscious of my senses, felt my scalp tingle and gooseflesh rise along my arms as he talked, telling me about the secret life I'd had without knowing it.

"You were the turning point and we were all different after we decided what to do about you. You were the golden girl. If that's corny, and it is, well, we were corny guys, I guess. But you were it. You became something less than a woman, but also something more than a woman. To all of us. We made you a kind of icon, the woman we wanted. It sounds pretty sick now, but what can I tell you? It wasn't sick then. . . ." Hacker took a deep breath and I smelled the jet of cigar smoke.

My own thoughts squirmed around inside me. I remembered Hacker at another time, telling me something else. *She doesn't make them swine. I think they were already swine. . . .*

"You became a kind of trophy in our minds," Hacker continued. "I can remember Peter saying something, he made some remark about a traveling trophy. Anyway, when you had passed from Harry to Jack and Jack reported that he not only loved you, he'd finally slept with you, we had a party. A Belinda party. We took food down to the banks of the Charles at midnight one night and drank some beer and ate and celebrated. Oh, God, it was all in good fun, a ritual was being established, and we wondered if we'd ever live to see another Belinda party. Tony Chalmers said that it would make a wonderful novel, the story of a group of men loving the same woman, and through the passing years by whatever turn of events that might befall them . . . passing the woman from one of them to another. That's how we looked at it. You had passed from Harry to Jack. You've got to realize, Belinda, it was because we all cared so much about you . . . ."

I bit my lip and clung to the chair. I wouldn't have wanted to see myself in a mirror. Wrath of God.

"We all began to wonder," Hacker said, "who would have Belinda next. We talked about it quite solemnly. Mike remembers, I remember. Tony remembered."

Mike interrupted, still with his back to us. "We were kids, for God's sake . . . it was crazy."

"But we were in earnest," Hacker said. "We weren't joking about it anymore."

I listened to Hacker talk about me as if I were a statue, something that couldn't hear, something to be admired and valued and passed from one owner to another. They had jointly monitored the situation, solemnly congratulating Jack when he told them he'd decided to marry me. It was Venables who had said that he knew he spoke for all of them when he said they had found an archetypal woman. So he wanted with their permission to suggest a long-term plan—that they make an oath, a pact, that Belinda would remain a kind of Ruffian herself, *the last Ruffian*, that they would always see to her welfare, that she would never be allowed to pass into the hands of anyone but a Ruffian.

"But I suppose we'd all forgotten it as the years went on," Hacker said almost wistfully. "I sure as hell did. I know Mike did. You and Jack got married and stayed married and we all went on with our lives. No one ever mentioned the Belinda Pact again. So far as I know, not until now, tonight, here. But Peter didn't forget. When he got word of the show he also got word from Harry that you and Jack had broken up. And the bell rang. The Belinda Pact, the last Ruffian. Was he crazy, Belinda? Or just one of love's fools? Well, whatever he was, he came back to get Belinda . . . he told Jack and predictably Jack went crazy and slugged him and threatened him and broke a blood vessel in general. Peter also told Harry, and I'll bet the world that Harry didn't say much, just started to think. Because that was Harry's way. Old Harry just started figuring out what he was going to do about it . . . because he'd already decided he wanted Belinda for himself. He wanted her back . . . *and Peter wanted his turn.*"

We sat quietly for a long time. I didn't trust myself to say a word. I don't know if I was angry. I don't know what I felt. But I think it went way, way beyond anger. What they had done—for whatever reason—was so monstrous, so incalculably perverted. They had used me as an excuse. They had suffered a kind of group madness and they had used me as their justification and there was nothing I could do about it. I couldn't go back and undo any of it. What I felt more than anything else was a kind of grief-stricken frustration. Helpless . . . and one of them was dead and there was another who had killed him and I was the excuse.

I wasn't entirely aware of having gotten out of the chair and gone back through the living room. Not one word, they didn't say one word.

I realized I was crying as the elevator descended. I couldn't see. I was making awful stupid sounds. The doors slid open and I went into the lobby. I must have looked drunk and disorderly and then I began to run. Binded by tears of rage and frustration, I ran. I ran directly into someone coming in the door and I felt strong hands grab me to keep me from falling.

I was sobbing and I heard someone calling my name and I wiped at my eyes and my runny nose and looked up gratefully into a pale, haggard face I knew.

"Harry!"

I don't know if anyone could even understand me.

But I began to scream something, maybe his name. I yanked away from him, pushing him, pulling away at the same time. He held on to me. I don't know what he wanted to do with me. Maybe he'd have killed me there and then. . . . My mind wasn't working. I was going on adrenaline.

"No, no, don't come near me, you stay away—"

He looked like a man having a heart seizure.

"I know what you did, I know all about it, it was you, it was all of you—"

"What, Belinda? What are you saying?" He looked like a man of sixty. A sick man. I began to cry again, trying to get away from Harry. Good old Harry. He looked like a dead man.

I backed into someone, a doorman in a brown uniform with gold braid and epaulets. He didn't look happy.

"Get me a cab! Please!" I clung to his arm.

"Are you okay, lady?"

"Keep him away from me, just keep him away, don't let him get me. . . ."

Harry stood there with his arms out in front of him, palms up, frozen.

Then I was in the back of a cab and it was dark and we were pulling away from the curb and Harry had come outside and was standing alone, staring after me, a zombie.

And I just let go. I couldn't stop crying. It seemed as if there were nothing left. Nothing and no one.

Chapter Forty-two

I got myself well under with two sleeping pills and slept dreamlessly, but I came awake with a startled cry, heard it in the echoing loft, and the image before me was Harry's

terrible, agonized face, the staring eyes. I blinked and
blinked until they faded, then reached over and turned on
the radio to help drive the fear away. I was groggy still, lay
quietly under the single damp sheet, then finally forced
myself up and into the bathroom.

It was a dark day, no sun anywhere, clouds low and
streaky gray. The humidity felt like a clammy hand and
the radio said it was eighty-three heading for ninety-five. I
showered and thought about Harry, lowering myself into
the muck of last night with considerable care. Something
had slipped all the way out of kilter inside him: I saw it in
his face. Something wasn't working anymore in there, but
it wasn't that he looked crazy. It was pain. I don't think I'd
ever seen so much pain in anyone's face before.

I had to stay calm, I had to think. I made toast and filled
the coffeemaker and let myself think about the Belinda
Pact. I had to proceed carefully. I couldn't talk to anyone
about it or I'd lose it, just the way Jack was so prone to do.
I had to keep a clear head. How hateful was it, anyway,
this Belinda Pact? How ambiguous was their concern for
me? They had wanted to protect me, they had thought
they were my insurance policy, swept up in the romantic
idiocy of their youth and passions.

But that wasn't the way it had worked out, was it? No,
twenty years later it was something else altogether. Something evil, something wicked. Twenty years later they
were prisoners, victims of their own mindless obsession
about a girl who didn't even exist anymore, a girl who had
turned into a woman and had a life of her own. But that
hadn't mattered, not to some of them, and there had been
a murder.

Murder. Tony Chalmers had been worrying about it for
a long time, this seed growing in the heart of the Ruffians.
It had grown like a tumor for two decades, eating away at

their senses of proportion and decency, devouring their respect for me . . . But how could there ever have been any respect? They had never seen me for what I was. They had only fed on their obsession. I remembered C. P. Snow writing about obsessive love, how people were consumed and destroyed by it, both the lovers and the loved.

I drank some coffee and spread some peanut butter on my toast and ate that. No matter what they had done, I had to force myself to be fair. Why? What did fairness have to do with it? Well, I wasn't sure. But I had to go on living, so I had to be fair. And Mike and Hacker hadn't been part of it, not now, not twenty years later. I had seen the humiliation in them, heard it in their voices, the shame and the guilt and . . . I had to be fair.

I poured more coffee and felt my systems starting to turn on. I didn't want to think about the Belinda Pact anymore. It was like thinking about the Crab Nebula. I didn't understand it and doubted very much if I was going to. So I thought about Harry. What were we going to do about Harry? How were we going to handle him? It was one thing for Mike and Hacker and me to sit around and decide that Harry had killed Peter. It was one thing to sit around and see it clearly and know it was true. But what exactly were we going to do about it? That was the kind of question that you don't sit around and talk about because it's too damn inconvenient. I didn't have any answers at all. If we could only find the gun covered with his fingerprints . . .

My thoughts kept fluttering around the loft like one of those bats over Sally's lake. My attention was splintered by questions needing answers. I was still unsteady from the whole Belinda Pact thing, trying to see the implications it carried deep within it for me, Belinda now. I had to come up with some ideas about dealing with Harry in a way that would make Antonelli and his colleagues pay attention: Harry had killed once and I saw no way of proving it, or even convincing an outsider to take it as a serious accusation.

And I had to get Sally back to civilization. I had to make her see that Harry, not Jack, had killed Venables. Did it matter why? Had he killed him because of me? Or because of Sally and her relationship with him? Or because of both of us, because Peter had come back into Harry's life and was pulling all of it down? Did it matter, really?

Most of all I knew I wanted to be with Sally. I wanted to make sure she was safe.

The phone rang and for some brainless reason I thought it might be Sally.

It was Harry.

"Are you all right, Belinda? You scared me out of my wits last night."

"I'm all right," I said mechanically.

"I want to see you. You understand that, don't you? I have to see you . . . I can understand your reluctance but I'm just about at the breaking point. I've got to see you. You're all my life is about now, Belinda, you're all I want . . . I'm going to have you, I've done something . . ." The words seemed disjointed, unrelated to one another, as if they were random words he was reading on a wall somewhere. He didn't sound like Harry anymore. "I've done something so terrible . . . I can't believe it, you won't believe it. But you've got to give me a chance to explain." He was almost panting. "I'm going to go get Sally, I've got to tell her first, the truth . . . and then I'm coming back, Belinda . . . I'm coming back for you. . . ."

I was about to say something, anything just to make him stop talking, to make the hard, whistling breathing stop, when suddenly the line went dead. I didn't hear a phone slammed, nothing. It just went dead.

I kept calling Sally at the cabin until her line wasn't busy anymore. But then there was no answer. So I kept calling and finally she answered. She sounded calm, remote, but she hadn't killed herself and I was in the mood to be thankful for small favors. I told her I wished she'd come back to the city, come and stay with me for a few days, we'd play at getting things put back together and take surveys of our lives. We could spend some time being pals, like the old days, and see where we were headed. I gave her the works, full nostalgia treatment, but she stayed distant.

"Look, Sal," I said, "there's something else. It's Harry, he's acting very weird. A little crazy . . . he just called me—"

"Oh? Did he really? What did he have to say?"

"He said he'd done something terrible. He didn't sound like Harry anymore. I'm not saying I know what he did, or what he thinks he did, but I am saying he's in pretty spooky shape and he told me he's going up to see you at the cabin. Sal, I don't think you should be there when he arrives . . . I don't think it would do anybody much good. He's pretty shaken up." I sounded like an idiot but I didn't want to let her slip off the hook. I had to convince her.

"Did he say why he was coming all the way up here?" She didn't sound very interested. More like she was making conversation.

"No, he didn't, Sal. But you're a damn fool if you wait around to find out."

"Belinda, Jack killed Venables, not Harry. If that's what's on your mind." She laughed tinnily. "We all know that. Poor Harry's just had some nasty shocks this week. I have been awfully hard on him. I can talk to him. Maybe it'll do him some good."

"You've had some shocks too," I said. "Please, as a favor to me, get in your car and come down here. Just for a night or two. *Please*—"

"Belinda! You really will make me angry if you keep this up! I can deal with Harry. I've dealt with him for quite some time, you know. Now, you just pull yourself together and count to ten! And relax—"

"He's dangerous!" I screamed. "He could kill you, Sal . . . he might do anything! He's off the edge, you've got to realize that! For the love of God, don't be such a fool! You should have heard him, you should have seen him!"

"You saw him?"

"Last night. By accident—he looked god-awful. It's not just me, Sal. Mike and Hacker think so too."

"I don't want to hear this, it's not worthy of you, Belinda. You should be ashamed of yourself. But I understand. It's hard for you, accepting Jack's guilt—"

"Jack didn't do it! You've got to believe me . . ."

But it didn't do any good. She just went on sounding calm and superior, as if she had a direct pipeline to Received Truth and nothing could possibly hurt her. I was sounding like a banshee and she was calm as the grave and she ended the discussion by telling me to get a grip on myself and she'd see me soon. I wasn't supposed to worry. If there was anything in the world she could do, it was handle Harry. She hung up. I felt like breaking everything in the loft.

Maybe she was right. Maybe she *could* handle Harry. Maybe that was the best place for Harry, being handled by Sally. After all, what did she have to fear from him? He had no reason to want to hurt her . . .

No, not much. Only her affair with his fellow Ruffian and the bearing of a secret child and her wanting to leave him and go live in London.

My mind was a garbage dump.

I sat for who knows how long. Then I called Hacker, against my better judgment, but he wasn't home. I sighed like a scenery-chewing tragedienne and called Mike Pierce. His secretary said he hadn't come in and she didn't know when to expect him. I felt almost relieved. I didn't know quite what to say to either of them after last night.

I paced around the loft. Finally my eye came to rest on the sketches for the Central Park piece and I began fiddling with that. My mind shut off and my hands did the work. Therapy. I tried not to think of what Sally had told me she and Harry were doing that day in Central Park.

The telephone didn't ring again until midafternoon.

It was Sally.

No, Harry hadn't been there but she'd been thinking about what I'd said this morning. She'd decided it might be a good idea to come down and stay with me. Old times. We could talk over old times and spin the wheel-of-fortune and see what the future was holding for us.

I practically cried with relief. Finally something was going right.

Chapter Forty-three

It began thundering and then the first big drops of rain splattered on the skylight, slowly, as if the storm were reluctant to let them go. It was dark by early evening. I felt worn out; my psychological stiffness had made me ache in every bone and joint. I dozed on the padded wicker couch, saw the streetlamps come on, heard the rain drumming steadily on the glass. Through the windows onto Prince Street it slanted in sheets. If it hadn't been for the rainstorms that summer the heat would have killed us all. A little breeze flicked occasional drops across the sills. I finally got up and stretched and stood by the window spinning the wheel-of-fortune, wishing Sally would get here. I wondered where Harry was. The thought that he was still out there, looking for Sally, planning on coming back for me, kept that boulder of tightness in my belly.

I stood staring at the sketches of the couple on the bank and the other couple in the rowboat and then I heard her coming up in the elevator. The super had finally done something about the noise and the elevator wasn't quite so obstreperous anymore. I went over and propped the door open to catch the cool breeze that would collect in the elevator shaft now that the storm was bound to drop the temperature a few degrees. Anything for relief.

Sally came in shaking her wet umbrella. She didn't say anything for a moment or two, then shucked out of a faded denim jacket and came over to me. I hugged her and felt her making a little kissing gesture against my cheek.

"I'm so glad you're here," I said. "Was the driving bad? Are you okay?"

She nodded. "No and yes respectively." Her eyes had a glassiness, as if she were watching me through the black irises from behind the window of a control room. I couldn't tell what was going on inside, but then, with Sally that was nothing new. "You're so worried about everything. Why is that, Belinda?"

I had to keep remembering what she'd been through. She didn't sound like herself, but I suppose she wasn't herself, wouldn't be for a while. "Oh, you know . . . things."

"You're not still going on about Harry, I hope."

"I can't help it," I said. "There's no point in my lying about it."

"There's no need to worry about Harry, believe me." She was moving restlessly around the room, looking out the window, staring for a long time at the wheel-of-fortune. I put a record on the stereo, something sinuous by Poulenc. A clarinet, a piano.

"He's out there somewhere with a shotgun," I said softly. "You have to realize that. For your own safety. We've all been through hell in one way or another, but it's got to end soon, we've got to get through it—"

"Harry's not out there with a shotgun," she said. "And it's more or less over. I mean, it must be . . . what more could matter now?"

"But there's no point in taking chances. I think Harry may want to harm you . . . he told me he's done something terrible, Sal."

"Maybe he has, but it doesn't matter. He hasn't killed anyone. I don't want to talk about this anymore, Belinda." She stood listening to the music for a while, silently, swaying slightly to the rhythm, and I finally went to the kitchen and began poking around in the refrigerator. Cheese. Wine. I found some Double Gloucester and Stilton mixed, a chunk of sage Derby, a wedge of pale gold Vermont cheddar, a box of stone-ground crackers, a bottle of white Bordeaux. I got a tray down from the top of the cupboard, a couple of plates, wineglasses, the corkscrew. It would be good, sitting down with Sal, getting her unwound, stay away from unpleasant subjects. It would take some time, but I could start now, tonight. Turn her back into the old Sal. All she had to do was give me the chance. I knew I could do it because she was still Sal, no matter what.

I gathered up the tray and went back into the main room. She was standing at my worktable, scrutinizing something. I set the tray down.

"What's this? Tell me what you've been working on . . . What *is* this?" Her voice had sharpened, as if anger was billowing inside her. She pointed at the sketch of the scene in Central Park and I felt my stomach do one of those little flip-flops. Goddammit! You can't think of everything. I mumbled something hopeless and her eyes were boring into me, black and bottomless in her gaunt face, looking like my terrible dream, the twin barrels of the shotgun pointing at me. "How could you do this? It's Harry and me, isn't it? What do you think you're doing? Drawing little pictures of my life, my pain? I don't understand you, Belinda . . ." She looked back at the sketchpad. "No, I guess I do understand you, but it's taken me such a long time. Better late than never, as they say. Were you spying on us? Is that what was going on? Is that you in the rowboat? You and . . . who? Oh, it doesn't matter. Don't bother to tell me."

I'd been wrong, and it hit me just then. She wasn't Sal anymore. Too much had happened to her. She was in a world of her own. I wasn't so sure I could bring her back, not the way she sounded now. "We weren't spying," I said. "It was an accident. We happened to see you, that's all—"

"And you happened to come home and start drawing pictures of what you saw? That seems a bit much. Not that it matters, it doesn't change anything. You can't help being you, that's the truth of it." She fumbled in the pocket of her gingham check blouse and took out a cigarette, lit it. She stood shaking her head at me.

"What is it? What's the matter?"

She laughed and coughed on the smoke and laughed again. "God, you really are unbelievable. And now you've decided Harry's a murderer. Have any little drawings of him shooting Peter? It could form the basis of your next show. You could think of a clever little name and have a clever little show, using the tragedies of your friends' lives—"

"Stop it, please. This is crazy."

"How true! It is crazy, I'll grant you that." She suddenly smiled disarmingly. "Am I being too hard on you? I'm sorry. We're not ourselves these days, are we? None of us."

The thunder rolled softly, crunching. Rain drummed on the skylight. I felt tense and shaky, and I wished Sally would just relax. She was going somewhere in her mind and I didn't want her to drag me with her. She turned away from the table and the drawing, began pacing. I sat down and pulled my knees up under my chin and hugged myself to stop the trembling. There were only two table lamps lit and she moved out of their reach, stood watching the rain in the street.

She began talking almost as if she were alone, ruminating about how happy we all had once been, how wonderful all our prospects had seemed. I listened quietly, realizing how often I'd done the same thing during the past six months, once I'd accepted the idea that it was all pretty much over.

"Mount Holyoke," she said, as if intoning a magic word. "You were such a golden girl." I cringed at the sound of it but stayed silent. She needed to talk. "So tall and pretty and wholesome and self-possessed. I was so lucky to be your best friend. Remember how we used to tool around in that little red car? My God, that was fun!" She turned to me in the shadow and I imagined her smiling, the wide, thin mouth. "I was the snippy one, the smartass. Something like that. I was livelier, wasn't I? It's been such a long time since I was lively. I guess I was someone else then . . . that's the big secret, isn't it? Everybody changes. How many people are we in our lives? How many masks do we wear?" She didn't expect any answers. I don't think she'd have heard me if I'd spoken. She was there with me but she was alone.

"So what went wrong? Where did the whole thing go off the tracks? Maybe when you threw Harry away in favor of Jack? That was the first nasty thing . . . the first *bad* thing, wasn't it? It wasn't quite so happy after that. It got worse when I let myself fall for Peter—I'd never imagined love and passion like that. I ran the risk of getting pregnant because I loved him and nothing was more important . . . why couldn't I trust what I felt, why couldn't I have married him and led a normal life? I don't suppose I'll ever know now. I mean, time's just about up, isn't it?"

She was leaning against the window frame, half-watching me, somehow looking past me at the shapes of our lives. She was seeing monsters.

"I used to think everything was the fault of the men," she said. "I mean, they're really all the same, aren't they? What they really want is the fucking, isn't that right, Belinda? They all wanted to fuck you . . . they used to celebrate when one of them had fucked you, they'd talk about it, tell each other what it was like to fuck Belinda . . . can you imagine what the stories must have been like?"

I wanted to vomit. Where was this coming from, why was she telling me this? How could she know what I'd only heard of last night? And why was she making it so ugly? They had cared about me, too. I believed them, I had to believe that. They had cared. Started out caring. Venables had been the one, he'd wanted to fuck me . . . nothing more. It was his turn . . . I tried to speak, but nothing came. I was dried out. My stomach was turning.

"They really were all alike." She turned and moved slowly to the window by the wheel-of-fortune. She put her hand out and touched it, the wedding present. Then she gave it a spin and stared into the blur of spokes. "That was the problem. They looked alike, Peter and Harry . . . that's why Peter died that night, in the doorway. The light overhead was burned out and there was only the light from behind—did you know that? With the light out, standing in the doorway, he looked just like Harry. I thought maybe you might have figured that out, you're so smart, so visual. I mean, wouldn't you expect Harry to answer the damn door? It's our house, not Peter's. She kept spinning the wheel, watching it go faster.

"That's the way it was, that last night," she said calmly, explaining everything to someone who was a little slow. "Peter died all because of a burned-out light bulb—I mean, my God, Belinda, you don't think I wanted to kill Peter, do you? I loved him, no matter what. *I loved him.* . . . No, it was Harry I wanted to kill, Harry, it should have been Harry answering the door. But, no, it wasn't . . . when the head sort of flew apart there was still enough left for me to see that it was Peter—I can't tell you what that was like. Pretty bad. So you can see why I wanted to kill myself, can't you? I mean, of course I wanted to kill myself . . . I'd have been crazy if I hadn't wanted to die too. But when the door opened and I was standing there with the shotgun, I was sure it was Harry— Belinda, it was just like when my father taught me to shoot skeet, I just pointed and squeezed and the head wasn't there anymore. Gone, it was all over everything, everywhere. . . .

"It was so easy to get the gun. After that day in the park, when I left Harry sitting on the bank, I went to see Jack, I wanted to talk to him, tell him what Harry had said to me, the terrible things he'd said, and Jack wasn't there and you know how he is with doors. I just went in to wait for him, sat there crying, and through the tears I saw the shotgun in the corner and while I sat there the whole thing formed in my mind and I took the gun away in one of Jack's big Glad trash bags. It all made such perfect sense to me. . . .

"That day in the park I showed Harry the picture of my daughter. I told him I wanted to go away with Peter, and Harry acted like I was crazy, he said I was just as dumb as ever, as dumb as I'd always been. He said that Peter had come back to New York for you, Belinda, not me. He said I should ask Jack if I didn't believe him, he said Peter had told both of them that he wanted you and was going to take you. Well, I couldn't believe a story like that, could I? I was afraid to believe him . . . I couldn't be so wrong, not after what Peter had said to me. But Harry said Peter was just telling me anything so I'd sleep with him. So I went to Jack but he wasn't there and I found the gun. . . . I sat there in Jack's apartment, seeing all those pictures of you on the wall and it was so hot and I was crying and I kept thinking about Harry, how he was always screwing some girl, how he never wanted children, how he married me for my money, and then I saw the shotgun . . . and all I wanted was to stop Harry from telling me the terrible things, how he was in love with another woman and how Peter didn't care about me. . . . After that it was so easy, I was so sure Harry had come home alone, and I'd seen Peter go off with Hacker and Mike . . . but I was wrong,

Harry had gotten home and gone to bed and Peter was home too . . . but there was the man in the doorway . . . and the gun was going off and everything spraying all over and the body going back into the light and I saw I'd killed the wrong man. . . .

"I've been thinking about things, too, Belinda. I went to the cabin and tried to sort it out. You came to see me and I watched you and listened to you and I thought how you've never changed, you're always at the center of things, you're always the one they're after and you didn't give a damn, not ever, you just went from one to another . . . Harry first, then Jack, and now it'll be Hacker . . . and maybe Peter really had come back for you, you'd told me about the pass he made and I had thought you were exaggerating or he was drunk and amorous and it wasn't important, but what if Harry was right? What if I wasn't going to get Peter after all, after I'd told everything to Harry? You know what Harry was saying to me in this picture of yours? He was laughing and telling me Peter wanted you, and he laughed some more and told me I should be used to it by now, hell, he said, he wanted you himself. . . ."

I tried to scream or rush at her, anything to make her stop, but I couldn't move. I felt like a child, too stricken to run away, too disoriented to stand and fight. Her voice came so calmly, so matter-of-factly. She'd thought it all through and she'd figured it out. It was the voice of madness.

"You don't have to worry about Harry," she said from the dim corner where the wheel-of-fortune loomed like an old friend, something to lean on. "He came to the cabin today, just like he told you he would. Yes, he'd done something terrible—he'd realized that I was the killer and he hadn't told anyone, he was letting Jack take the blame.

Jack. A Ruffian. And he came to the cabin to tell me he knew the truth, that he couldn't keep it secret anymore, not with Jack in jail. He said he was going to tell the truth and he told me I was crazy, that I'd never be convicted, that I'd go to a hospital. He wanted to know where the shotgun was. . . . He told me he was going to divorce me because he loved you, he told me he was going to marry you, that he was your first love and he could convince you to love him again once this was over—"

"No," I cried, "no, that's not true!"

"Be quiet, Belinda," she said. "Let me finish. You don't have to worry about Harry. I let him look for the gun, he thought I'd taken it to the cabin, he was looking in the closet, and I took one of the big kitchen knives and I killed him. He won't be marrying you." She laughed distantly. "He deserved to die, he really did. Don't you think so? I think he did. So I killed him. I just stabbed him once and he went down on the floor of the closet and didn't move and I watched the blood spreading across the back of his shirt."

A sob, a scream, something stuck in my throat.

"It's you, Belinda. You're the one, it's always been you, you're the one who made everything go so wrong." She was moving and I managed to stand up. I couldn't see what she was doing. For an instant I thought she'd fainted, and I stepped across to the table to look.

She had bent down and opened the little door on the back of the stand that held the wheel-of-fortune. Where the midget or the child had once controlled the future—I remembered her theory. She pulled the door open and it creaked on its hinge.

When she straightened up she was holding the shotgun.

"Oh, I brought it down here the day after the . . . the day after Peter died. Harry was out, the police were gone, I was alone in the house, I called you and you were out. I didn't care if I did get caught, you see—it really didn't matter. But I didn't want to get caught . . . and I couldn't leave the damn thing under my mattress, in my bedroom. God, it was all so simple. And if you'd been home, well, what difference did it really make? I don't know what I'd have done . . . I guess I'd have left it up to you. Maybe I'd have shot myself with it. . . ."

She came toward me holding the gun level before her. The record was ending, the piano was cascading and the clarinet was making a racket and I heard something, I didn't know what, and she was pointing the gun at me. The two barrels, black and almost inviting, swinging toward me, two bottomless wells of sorrow and hatred and vengeance and pity . . .

"Sal . . ."

"I'm not Sal, not anymore . . . and you're not Belinda, not my Belinda . . . we're other people, you're not even a person, not anymore, Belinda . . . you're just a target."

The other little noise I'd heard was the elevator.

It came up and the door was still propped open and Sally saw something moving, something coming into the room, and I ran, ran backward, trying to get out of the way, and I fell over one of the low wicker chairs, fell backward and saw the flash of the gun and felt the explosion of the lamp beside the chair, felt the base shattering and saw her turning toward the doorway and there was Harry, followed by Hacker, Harry, who wasn't dead, who came into the room with his arms outspread, no color in his face and speckles of blood on his hands and on his shirt, streaks of blood where he must have wiped his hands after somehow bandaging his wound, Harry alive, arms out, coming toward her, calling her name, and there was another deafening roar and Harry spun around, his left shoulder shredded and bloody, the blood spraying across Hacker's face. He sank slowly against Hacker, who caught him, knelt with Harry in his arms. . . .

The shotgun clattered loudly to the floor.

We were all watching Sally.

She moved slowly, someone in a dream. Far beyond my reach.

She reached the wheel-of-fortune, slowly spun it, stood staring into the blur. She might have been watching the old times, the happy times.

Hacker turned to me. He didn't move.

I felt a tear or two on my cheek, but I wasn't crying.

Hacker didn't move, just looked into my eyes.

I think Sally had begun to sob, but all I heard was the pounding of my heart and the steady night rain and a siren far away in the night.

ABOUT THE AUTHOR

DANA CLARINS is a pseudonym for a bestselling novelist who lives and works in New York City. Bantam also published the author's previous novel, *Woman in the Window*.